boundary
COUNTRY

OTHER BOOKS BY TOM WAYMAN

COLLECTIONS OF POEMS:

Waiting for Wayman (1973)
For and Against the Moon (1974)
Money and Rain (1975)
Free Time (1977)
A Planet Mostly Sea (1979)
Living on the Ground (1980)
Introducing Tom Wayman: Selected Poems, 1973–80 (1980)
The Nobel Prize Acceptance Speech (1981)
Counting the Hours (1983)
The Face of Jack Munro (1986)
In a Small House on the Outskirts of Heaven (1989)
Did I Miss Anything? Selected Poems, 1973–1993 (1993)
The Astonishing Weight of the Dead (1994)
I'll Be Right Back: New & Selected Poems, 1980–1996 (1997)
The Colours of the Forest (1999)
My Father's Cup (2002)
High Speed Through Shoaling Water (2007)

NONFICTION:

Inside Job: Essays on the New Work Writing (1983)
A Country Not Considered: Canada, Culture, Work (1993)

ANTHOLOGIES EDITED:

Beaton Abbot's Got the Contract: An Anthology of Working Poems (1974)
A Government Job at Last: An Anthology of Working Poems (1976)
Going for Coffee: Poetry on the Job (1987)
East of Main: An Anthology of Poems from East Vancouver (co-edited with Calvin Wharton, 1989)
Paperwork: Contemporary Poems from the Job (1991)
The Dominion of Love: An Anthology of Contemporary Canadian Love Poems (2001)

boundary COUNTRY

TOM WAYMAN

thistledown press

EASTERN WASHINGTON UNIVERSITY PRESS

Library and Archives Canada Cataloguing in Publication

Wayman, Tom, 1945–
Boundary country / Tom Wayman.

ISBN 978-1-897235-25-6

1. Kootenay Region (B.C.)—Fiction. I. Title.

PS8595.A9B68 2007   C813.54   C2007-901272-8

Cover and book design by Jackie Forrie
Typeset by Thistledown Press
Printed and bound in Canada on acid-free paper
by Marquis Book Printing Inc.

Thistledown Press Ltd.
633 Main Street
Saskatoon, Saskatchewan, S7H 0J8
www.thistledownpress.com

Eastern Washington University Press
Spokane and Cheney, Washington

Thistledown Press gratefully acknowledges the financial assistance of the Canada Council
for the Arts, the Saskatchewan Arts Board, and the Government of Canada through the
Book Publishing Industry Development Program for its publishing program.

ACKNOWLEDGEMENTS

Love and gratitude to Fran Brafman, first and best reader of these tales. My thanks, too, to Gary Katz for his insightful comments on my fiction in its earliest stages and to Verna Relkoff for her sharp editor's eye. I appreciate as well the hospitality shown me by the master of Massey College in the University of Toronto, John Fraser, and all the Massey College community among whom in 1996 I first had the opportunity to concentrate on my prose. As throughout my writing life, Dennis Saleh blazes the trails I try to follow.

The plot of "The Murder" is based upon a family story belonging to David Piasta of Coquitlam, B.C., and is used with permission. Thank you to Haya Fuchs Newman for vetting the Yiddish; any errors are my own.

"The Freelance Demolitionist" is an homage to Stephen Crane.

"Amnesia Cafe" first appeared in *Canadian Fiction Magazine*.
"Boundary Country" first appeared in *The Ontario Review*.
"The Dean of the Distillery" first appeared in *Grain*.
"The Freelance Demolitionist" first appeared in *The Hudson Review*.
"The Murder" first appeared in *Not Quite Mainstream: Canadian Jewish Short Stories* (ed. Norman Ravvin).
"The Photographer" and "Zen Motel" first appeared in *The Windsor Review*.
"The Pleasures of the Shade" first appeared in *The Fiddlehead*.
"The Ring" first appeared in *Descant*.

for Capt. Brian Plummer, CMSG
because he thought I could

Contents

WELCOME TO BOUNDARY COUNTRY

ART CHANGES A THING INTO ANOTHER THING; emotions, ideas, perceptions are transmuted into paint, pottery, fabric, words. The locale or instant or condition where something alters we name a boundary. Thus artists, whose imaginations and hands inhabit border country, have always been fascinated by edges, margins, frontiers.

The stories of this collection reflect my interest in the places and moments we encounter a boundary. My concerns include the line between self and others, between individuals and their community. Fascinating to me is the limit that distinguishes employment from servitude, education from indoctrination, the artificial from the natural. I am intrigued by the location in space and time where love first manifests itself, or crosses into obsession, or dissipates. I consider important where history becomes memory, a goal stiffens into an expectation, desire transforms to belief, and the ghosts of rejected possibilities haunt the choices we have made or that have been imposed upon us.

At times, such a border is accurately surveyed and clearly marked. Other times we drift past as if buoyed on water. In the latter case, we hike a ridgeline in a fog, only aware of a boundary's existence once we have travelled some distance into a different country.

WINTER PASTURE

BOUNDARY COUNTRY

I WAS HEADED HOME THROUGH BOUNDARY COUNTRY when I saw the old fellow standing by the road, thumb out, in the middle of nowhere — I mean, nowhere. I couldn't imagine who would drop off an old guy along a stretch of highway like this in December. Usually, I'm not quick to stop for hitchhikers. I just assumed his car had died, and hit the binders.

This was east of Osoyoos, on Number Three. You know how the highway switchbacks again and again up the practically-vertical valley wall. Pretty dramatic views of the lake below and the distant mountains. Then suddenly you've climbed out of Okanagan mesquite and broom scrub and are into pine forest, and soon after are passing through the usual Interior spruce and hemlock and fir. You're in the Monashees now and the road keeps rising toward Anarchist Mountain summit, whisking you in the direction of Rock Creek. Number Three was built mostly on the wagon track the Royal Engineers constructed in the 1800s to have an all-British route to the East Kootenay goldfields — too many Americans coming up from Idaho or Spokane. The highway hugs the border, though: the US is never more than a few miles south.

At a certain point after Osoyoos the woods open up into rolling plateaus. Patches of evergreens stand along some of the draws and gullies, and cluster at the top of the rises. But there are also these huge expanses of open range. From a ways off, the grasslands look flat — tilted, angled, but smooth. Sometimes the meadows have cows grazing on them, or somebody has plowed under an acre or three, or a tractor across a field is baling hay, although not this time of year. But as the road swings close to some field that you thought as you approached was an even grade like the prairies, you notice its surface actually rolls like the ocean — big swells and depressions all across it.

The old man was standing on the shoulder, back before the land opens up, maybe a quarter-hour from the summit. The highway cuts through the woods at this spot: nothing around but pines, and a few cedars where a creek crosses. My hitchhiker didn't appear agitated or grateful or much of anything when he hauled himself into the van, bringing the smell of cold air with him. No snow yet on this part of the route — okay, a few patches of white were under the trees now and then; obviously it had snowed a few times already.

I picked him up about three-thirty in the afternoon. By the start of December the sun sets pretty early, which means the light was already getting a little dim. The day was cloudy, which might have added to my feeling that an hour later he'd be frozen stiff beside the road in the dark. As I say, it was nippy out — a degree or two above freezing. The poor geezer wasn't particularly dressed for the chill, either: just wearing a thin jacket and a ball cap. Yet the weather didn't seem to bother him, or at least he didn't comment on it when he clambered aboard.

He was short but stocky. His face and hunched body carried that aura of negative intensity some people possess — a thick cloud of knotted rage or gloom or just disappointment. Whatever the energy, it wraps them like a portable environment, so they haul the same mood with them wherever they go. A closed container of a life, although I couldn't read right away what was inside this one.

"Car break down?" I asked after we'd gotten up to speed again.

"Nope."

I waited to see if he'd explain further. From back when I cut hair regular, I'm used to people who don't say much. Regardless of their outlook, some customers prefer to chatter while you're working, some don't. But I was curious, since the old boy had been standing on the shoulder miles and miles from any house, as far as I could tell. I waited a decent interval, then inquired:

"Where you off to, today?"

"Bridesville. You know it?"

I did, as a matter of fact. About twenty miles further. I'd never stopped there, but I'd seen the turn-off sign on the highway about a million times. Not a name you forget. I'd always wondered who would call a burg "Bridesville"? Was there once a "Groomsville" nearby? From the road, the place looks to be a string of houses and maybe a backwoods general store or auto repair shop laid out along a street for a couple of hundred yards parallel to the highway — sort of like a siding next to a railway line.

Or maybe the main road used to go through town. Just to the east is a sign for "Bridesville Cemetery"; perhaps the hamlet was once bigger — a mining town or cattle town, maybe selling across the border. Anyway, it's located on a bench in that open country I was mentioning, before you hit Rock Creek. Occasionally when I'd sped past, I'd idly thought that one day it would be neat to take a few extra minutes and drive through. I don't know why: a tiny adventure. Once in a while I get a notion when I'm driving: what would it be like to live in *that* house — some spiffied-up heritage mansion, maybe — and spend the rest of my life in Midway, say, or on some farm I find particularly appealing out in the boonies, or on an orchard near Keremeos? Not that Bridesville was inviting. Most of the cluster of structures appear tumble-down; obviously nobody has much money for paint or upkeep. At this season, however, I'd see woodsmoke rising from the chimneys so I knew these were somebody's homes.

"What takes you to Bridesville?" I asked.

"Live there."

I switched on the wipers. Some drops were splattering against the windshield — a shower of those large wet plops that are almost snow. "How come you were hitching away out here?"

The cloudburst lasted a minute or so and then dribbled to an end, or we drove out of it.

"Calendar."

I thought I misheard. "Say again?"

"Calendar."

I looked over where he slouched in his seat. From his lap, he lifted a slim envelope and flourished it. "Bill Markin's motel in Osoyoos has calendar. Each year, I like to have."

"Oh yeah?" I didn't quite comprehend.

"I go every December to pick one up before they are gone."

"You hitch all the way for a *calendar*?"

No answer.

"Do you have a car?" I asked him.

"What for? My neighbour gives me ride into Rock Creek if I have to see doctor. Or I hitch. People stop."

We drove back into rain. I glanced across once more. From his accent and Slavic features he seemed Doukhobor. I tried to guess his age, as I used to do when I worked a chair. I still style occasionally if one of my shops is short-handed at a peak time: school break, say, or right before Christmas, or August back-to-school. We make much more from the products, though, than we do styling, these days: conditioners, rinses, tints, lotions, you name it — retail and refill and even bulk.

That's what puts me behind the wheel. We could have the products shipped from the franchise warehouse in Van. And the wife is always after me to agree to that, to not be away on the road so much. But I like to visit each shop in person. Delivering product monthly gives me the excuse. Unload, have a coffee with the manager, nose through the mall or the downtown a little, get a feel for what's happening at the store and in the community. That's how I headed off a problem in Trail a few years ago. Everything on paper appeared fine — sales up, all that. But my manager was never around when I arrived. Shop didn't feel right, somehow. After a couple of coffees over a couple of months with a woman I knew there, Sharleen — used to work for me at the salon in Nelson a while back — I got the picture. I eventually figured the right questions to ask her, and bam, that guy was out of there. You have to draw the line. It's a happier crew now, and my accountant found the guy was skimming me. I always remind the wife of that experience when she needles me about my runs to Van and back. Truth is, I *enjoy* driving around, appreciating the country, connecting with people. I'd go stir-crazy if I just sat at home or in the office. What's the good of finally being my own boss if I can't do what I want to?

So I sized up my hitchhiker and estimated early seventies. With these old boys it's tough to tell. Sometimes a life spent working outdoors wears them down; you guess they're eighty and they're only seventy. Other times the outdoor work leaves them in great shape: you estimate seventy and they turn out to be eighty. This guy had his right hand on the dash and was staring through the rain down the highway. Looked as though his hand had done a lot of hard work: the first finger ended at the first knuckle. Carpenter? Logger? Grey stubble on his cheek, like my Uncle Don after he retired from the Trail smelter and would only shave every few days.

I was about to point-blank my passenger about his age, because the question often gets these fellows yakking, and also gives me a chance to learn how close I've come in my estimate. No big deal, yet I kind of pride myself on my ability to factor everything in and guess right. But something swung into view ahead I'd been curious about for a while. Since my hitchhiker was more or less a local to this stretch of road, I decided to ask what he knew about it.

On the north side of the highway is a crazy jumble of decrepit buildings and fences and badly-daubed homemade signs: "Native Crafts", "Gold Paning" — spelled wrong, "Fresh Keremeos Fruit", "Acers" — spelled wrong — "Of Gemstones." And always a huge "Open". Behind and under and around the forest of signs it's a real Dogpatch. Split-rail fences, board fences, barbed wire, and even snowfencing, all with tilted posts, haphazardly circle a cluster of structures. Three or four weathered sheds have planking you can see daylight between. Most of the window panes in the buildings are smashed. Next to the shacks is an ancient mobile home, with a wooden roof partially completed over it. Lots of house trailers in the Interior have a roof erected over them because mobiles aren't really built to handle a snowload. But the roofing here is half mossy shingles, and the other half only has bare trusses — not even sheathing over them, let alone shingles. Paint is peeling from the exposed top of the mobile, and from its side panels, too. A dilapidated shed nearest a gravel parking area is open-fronted, with rough plank counters that slant downwards, presumably intended to display some product. Clumps of high grass sprout everywhere across the property.

The biggest sign might perpetually say "Open", but I've never noticed any vehicles parked in front. To me this eyesore is more a roadside *dis*traction than any kind of a commercial *at*traction. Yet I'm no longer amazed about what people will spend their money on.

What's visible at this spot accumulated over three or four years. I recall when there was nothing. Then a shed or two. After that the fencing started, and next the house trailer appeared. I knew somebody was at home because lights showed in the mobile's windows and even in the sheds' when I powered by some evenings. I could see smoke from the trailer's chimney, too, on a cold day.

Not that I was paying that much attention, but you know how when you drive a route often enough you kind of mentally note any differences — a new clearcut on a hillside, a road that wasn't there last time punched into a grove of trees by the highway, a barn under construction in what was formerly a field. Outside Cawston is a driveway that for years and years had a sign in bright red letters: "Nels and Sophie Olson." What caught your eye was how tidy the sign was: kept freshly painted, with the background a shade of blue that made the red letters especially stand out. Then one trip I made, the sign just read: "Nels" — and then a big blank space where the words "and Sophie" used to be —"Olson". Some line had been reached, some decision made, and somebody's wife had been painted over. After that, I used to chuckle at the gap in the sign, although I was certain the missing words held a lot of pain for one or other of the couple, or both.

At Dogpatch, the junk stopped accumulating close to a year ago, about the time I noticed there were no more indications of life around the property. At first I thought whoever stayed here simply was away whenever I passed. Then I realized there hadn't been any evidence for months that someone was occupying the trailer. They must have gone under financially and moved, I concluded.

"Bet *you* know the story about what happened at this place," I suggested to my passenger. I glanced towards him, to indicate what I meant with a nod at the approaching site. But he had straightened up rigid in the seat. His eyes were glued in that direction.

His right hand began to shake, drumming on the dash. "You think I lie?" he demanded.

"Say again?" I figured he'd misheard or misunderstood me.

His reply was louder than before. "You think I lie, too?"

"What do you mean?"

"I *saw*." He swung his left hand up to join the vibrating right, which he withdrew. The left hand remained on the dash, trembling, but not as bad. "Parkinson's?" I thought to myself.

"Jail is right place."

"Jail?" I said. "Wait a sec, I — "

"Right place for him."

I was confused. "Hey, listen." I tried to steer the geezer back to my question. "I just assumed you might know, being from around here, something about — "

"How many times *you* see Lucy's face? One black eye, or two black eyes. Or broke teeth."

"Who's Lucy?"

"Stitches to her forehead. They took her by ambulance in March. When she lost the baby. And again, after that."

"Whoa, old-timer," I attempted to break in. "I can't — "

"You heard what he yelled at me in court? 'You're next, Padwinikoff.'"

"Look, slow down. None of this — "

"'I'll be here when you get out, Lindstrom,' is what I tell him. In front of that Grand Forks judge and everybody. You think I did not see?"

"No, just a minute, I — "

"Anybody who says what I testify is wrong, *they* are the liar."

I let the old guy have the last word, since he was obviously worked up about something. The location that prompted his outburst was behind us now. We crested the summit. As we began to descend, the precipitation which had thinned almost to nothing began to fall heavier, landing on the windshield nearly as sleet. I notched the wipers up and concentrated on my driving for a bit.

I can't claim that the disconnected babble from my rider was unfamiliar to me. Lots of people live happily encased in their own world, and then take it for granted you're in there with them. I get this in the chair. "Had a good holiday?" I'll ask a client who's in for a cut after a long weekend. "Oh yeah," they'll reply. "I was over to Bob's, and then him and me we went into town to see Angie." Of course I don't have a clue who Bob or Angie are.

The highway started to drop steeply along a wooded hill; I had to gear down to accommodate four or five pretty abrupt curves. The sleet was sticking to the road in the lee of a couple of cutbanks. Then we coasted out into open country again, and the asphalt was wet and bare. I knew we were near Bridesville, and began keeping a lookout for that. Clouds lowered over the road, but eventually we drove through the patch of storm and I switched off the wipers.

I took the opportunity to reflect on whether there was any connection at all between my original question to my rider and his agitated response. A possibility dawned. I wanted to confirm whether my guess was right, yet I didn't want to send the old boy off on a tangent again.

"Do you mean," I carefully broke the silence, "that the place back there is deserted because the owner was sent to jail?"

"Five years," my passenger replied.

I chewed over that statement for a second, and puzzled out a link between my latest question and his response: "Ah, the man who owned it went to jail for five years." I spoke this as firmly as I could.

"*Deserved* it."

"Okay, okay. I just wondered why the buildings appeared abandoned. Now you've told me. Thank you."

"Mister, I watch her grow up all her life."

I figured I better shut this line of conversation down fast, or I'd be in the middle of another spasm of impassioned, if opaque, pronouncements. "Sure, fine," I said. "But I've never met you before, and I don't know the 'her' you're talking about. I had a simple question and you've answered it. Thanks."

That quieted him for a moment. "If you don't know me," he offered slowly, "why did you say I lie?"

"I didn't say you lied," I emphasized. "I only asked if you knew what happened back there."

"Mrs. Relkoff said to me on the street, 'Alex, before God, you must not bear false witness.'"

The sign for Bridesville was drifting toward us. "I'm going to turn here," I informed my passenger. My comment didn't register.

"She said, 'Whatever the man did, Alex, that is up to God.' I told her: 'Why couldn't I have seen? The judge believed me. I say I hitch by Lindstrom's. If you know something different, you go to court and tell them.'"

I swung onto the access road and pulled over, engine idling. "Do you live in one of these houses? If so, I can run you right to your door."

He stared ahead through the windshield. "She says: 'Oh no, I would never go to court. But God's Word is plain: on this side is right and on that side is wrong. And God sees, Alex.' 'Then He sees what I saw,' I tell her."

I asked him again if this was where he lived.

He faced in my direction, but I'm not sure he was focusing on me. "That lawyer, too, he tells me. 'You've sworn an oath,' he shouts. He says, 'You cannot prove you were on the highway Wednesday.' I say to him: 'You cannot prove I was not.'"

I gave the geezer a choice. "I can let you out now. Or, I'll take you home if you live ahead here. Do you?"

He nodded.

Up close, Bridesville was no different than I expected. The houses are mainly two-storey frame homes, most in poor shape, but a couple better-maintained. There are four or five

23

heritage wooden dwellings, one of which is about the most decrepit of any house along here: a boarded-over window in the upper storey, paint flaking from the siding and trim, a partially caved-in porch, the roof more moss than shingles. The community hall probably was once a church, to judge from a tilted steeple affixed at one end of the roofline. At least three driveways had older logging trucks in them; a gleaming new rig was parked on the street in front of somebody's home.

After a few hundred feet, I asked my passenger: "Which place is yours?"

He gestured forward.

Half the front yards had wrecked cars, or engine blocks, or heaps of used building materials in them; people's piles of heating wood ranged from fastidiously neat to toppled-over. A few old-style large satellite dishes were visible. There's no sidewalk, and only a couple of trees on anyone's lot down the whole line of settlement. Low piles of dirty snow had been left by the plows at intervals along the route. A store advertises itself in unevenly-painted letters as "Store", with "Groceries Organic" smaller underneath. I tried to think who around here would insist on organic food. A faded metal sign on a side wall faintly proclaims the virtues of Orange Crush, with the bottle design I remember from my youth. Suspended from a pole sticking out at a right angle from the building is a modern Coke sign that a city convenience store might display.

Where the street begins to curve back toward the highway is a row of smaller dwellings, single-storied, like motel cabins. I guessed they were once miner's shanties, by the size of them.

My hitchhiker indicated the third on the right. "That's mine."

I eased the van over in front of it. My rider made no effort to climb out, though I kept the motor running.

"That is Mrs. Broughton's." He gestured at the cabin west of his. "I have coffee every day. She was like a mother to Lucy. Lucy stayed whenever her husband hurt her."

"Sounds bad," I murmured. I was forming a hazy sense of what the old boy's story might be.

"I saw what he did to her," he said simply.

"I'm sorry for your troubles." I tried to extricate myself with a small joke; I learned long ago at my job you can't take on other people's difficulties — some boundaries you don't want to cross: "Hey, I better roll, or *I'll* be in trouble with the wife." Streaks of rain drizzled down the windshield. I flicked the wipers on.

My passenger suddenly thrust his maimed right hand toward me, and we shook. He gathered the envelope with his calendar in his left, yet made no move to leave.

"I'm sure you made the right decision," I soothed. "But I should be on my way."

"There are those who think I lie," he responded.

"Yeah, you've mentioned that." I felt he wanted something from me, wished to confess something, maybe. People at times seem compelled to reveal amazingly private details of their lives to stylists — information I don't believe they ought to share. Even in a small town, we're regarded the way I hear bartenders are: as sort of professional strangers a person can blab their secrets to without fear we'll pass them along to anyone they know.

So I asked him what I knew damn well was none of my business. "*Did* you lie?"

He recoiled from me as though I had punched him. His head lifted high over his shoulders, a stance unlike any I'd seen him show since I picked him up — the posture was one of haughtiness, of pride.

He fumbled for the door latch and swung the van door wide into the rain. He waved his fist toward me.

"I speak the *truth*," he yelled, and was gone.

I had to reach across to shut the door. I sat and watched the water pour down onto that burg's sorry roofs. Then I put the vehicle into gear, and a minute later was back on the highway.

THE RING

"I'VE LOST MY RING," COLIN SHOUTED TOWARD Robert over the sound of the river. He turned away from where Robert stood, like him, shin-deep in the current. Colin's left hand was raised in front of his eyes, palm toward his face, displaying the naked four fingers. "My ring's gone," he called, aiming now to attract Jeannette's attention. She was crouched on the further side of the sandbar playing at the edge of the water with William, their three-year-old. The heads of mother and son were almost touching over their earthworks and canals; William had Colin's blonde hair while Jeannette's was brown.

"What?" Jeannette's face lifted toward her husband and Robert, the river purling around the men's legs. "My ring," Colin yelled, shaking the back of his open hand toward her, all his fingers still rigidly outstretched. "It's gone." His other hand gestured downstream. "In the water."

Jeannette climbed to her feet, shading her eyes from the glare of August sun as she gazed across the sand at the two men. Robert could see she didn't quite comprehend yet. Jeannette's bathing suit was modestly cut, but within Robert's chest some organ shifted end-over-end. *She's so beautiful*, he acknowledged to himself. Robert knew moments like this each summer when Colin tore himself free from his Vancouver dentistry practice for a couple of weeks, and he and Jeannette — and now he and Jeannette and William — drove north-east to vacation in the Okanagan Valley, invariably including a visit to Robert in their itinerary. Jeannette had brought Colin to meet him even before she and Colin were married; both Jeannette and Colin talked to Robert every year about how much they wanted to relocate to a rural area as he had. "We're in our thirties," Colin would state. "William is still young. This is the right time."

"The move was easier for me, being a vet," Robert would respond. "There are more animals in the country." His disclaimer, delivered as they dawdled over lunch outside on his deck or at his dining room table over wine at supper, had become almost ceremonial; he didn't mention that his practice here mainly consisted of household pets — cats and dogs — exactly as it had on Kingsway in Vancouver.

"There are plenty of teeth in the country, too," Colin would reply. The three of them always laughed, and Robert never failed to notice delight gleaming in Jeannette's intense eyes at their shared ritual.

She seemed determined to keep the connection between her new life and Robert; he felt grateful for this link. Yet the force of his attraction to her continued to disturb him. A letter from her, when he picked up his mail in the small post office in the village, lay in his hand like a wrapped gift whose contents he both eagerly awaited and dreaded. Was some aspect of him still longing for words that would inform him oh so casually that she and Colin were separating? That was the hope that had raged through him for more than a year after Jeannette's marriage. Bit by bit he had scrunched down that enormous pulsing possibility until it was smaller than a walnut, or an acorn. Or a radish seed. *As it should. As it must,* he told himself, clutching his letters and newspapers as he walked back to the car. He occasionally opened other people's letters first now.

Robert accepted that he had had his chance with Jeannette. Fear had paralyzed him so he could not take the step closer that he now knew was necessary if he was ever to establish a lasting connection with any woman. "Fear of what? What are you afraid of?" probed the counselor who several months ago he had begun driving in to Kelowna to see.

The counselor had been Amy's parting shot. After two years of an affair, Amy had issued the decree Robert was familiar with: "Move in, or move on." The counselor tried to convince Robert that Amy's statement was the culmination of a pattern Robert manipulated his lovers to follow. When Amy declared him a failure at intimacy, she informed him her brother-in-law had been greatly assisted to understand his feelings, or at least to be at ease with them, by a certain Joseph Kostiuk, RSW. She opined Robert needed help more than her brother-in-law ever did. A month after the final argument with Amy, Robert had phoned Kostiuk for an appointment.

Robert scarcely mentioned Jeannette to Kostiuk, though. Was his silence about her because she was ancient history, he wondered? Or because of his shame about how whenever he recognized her handwriting on an unopened letter, a portion of his insides rotated for several seconds?

Robert desired his now-greatly-reduced obsession with Jeannette to disappear entirely. A book Kostiuk had him read, *Apart From Fear: Why He Can't Get Close,* proclaimed that men like Robert were most drawn to women who were unavailable to them — either physically or emotionally. According to the author, people such as Robert felt safe to allow themselves to experience love fully only under these circumstances. Nobody would call their bluff and require them to follow through on their emotions, as Jeannette and Amy had done. Robert concluded the book's rationale made sense, especially when he reviewed Amy's sharply-expressed comments about his emotional deficits.

Another reason Robert wished for an easy friendship with Jeannette, one that would supplant any remnants of his persistent yearning for her, involved Colin. Robert admired Colin. Colin had a vast intelligence of which his dedication to his dentistry practice — including familiarity with the latest advances in orthodontic science and restorative techniques — was only one element. Colin also was slowly acquiring a BFA in sculpture. He had taken a few courses, he told Robert, to help him in motor control and the shaping of fillings. But he had become fascinated by some current issues in the arts. Robert was aware from his infrequent visits to Vancouver that Jeannette's and Colin's house showcased contemporary paintings and sculptures they had bought to support Colin's classmates and instructors at the art college. Colin was unapologetic about the learning he had acquired, yet he never made Robert feel diminished by ignorance. Colin even was cognizant of much about the literary arts. Robert had grown up in a household where literature was treasured. But in many instances, Robert had to admit, Jeanette's husband read with more care than he did. Often Robert was surprised by what Colin had gleaned from his reading of a novel; after a discussion, Robert realized he had missed some fascinating aspect of the writer's achievement. Robert felt enriched by knowing Colin. Jeannette's choice to marry Colin made sense. Compared to him, Robert at times judged himself unworthy, shallow.

Last summer, before the couple's annual visit, Robert had evaluated himself as cured of any lingering attraction to Jeannette. But when she climbed out of the car and stood in front of him, or took possession of the rooms of his house, or toured with him through the new addition to his clinic out on the highway, Robert's conviction about his emotional health wavered. And one sunny morning he had been chatting with Colin at the breakfast table. Jeannette and William were in the bedroom; Colin had left them sleeping after Jeannette had been up several times in the night to soothe their restless child. Jeannette had emerged to join the two men, dressed only in a short and filmy nightgown. She was still misty from sleep, soft and vulnerable to Robert's eyes. *She is absolutely, incredibly lovely,* the almost-silenced voice inside Robert crowed triumphantly. He was awe-struck at this apparition; he tried not to stare as she went through a series of groggy, hesitant motions to pour a cup from the coffeemaker on the counter, add sugar and milk, and seat herself at the table. Robert listened to his voice resume the conversation he was engaged in before she arrived, specifying for Colin an inane list of his favourite jazz musicians. Robert heard Colin begin to question Jeannette about William. But the sight of her undressed this way blocked Robert's comprehension. He knew only he was seated across his kitchen table from an infinitely desirable being. The years of coming to terms with what he felt for her vanished; he remembered the instant he knew he loved her more than he had ever loved any woman.

They were making love for the first time, and he was lost in her beauty: the sweet softness of her skin, shoulders, breasts, nipples, belly. He had entered her for the third time that afternoon, and he was creating a trail of kisses from the front of her neck up her chin, mouth, nose, cheek. Then his lips encountered, and his eyes registered, tears trickling from her eyes. He stopped, horrified. *What's wrong?* he whispered. She shook her head, tears still flowing. *It's nothing,* she whispered back. *I'm just . . . I'm just not used to this. I'm a little sore. It's been a long time. Go ahead. Please. I'm all right.* Robert looked down at her beautiful face staring up at him earnestly, the water in her eyes shining. *She would endure this pain for me,* he thought, and felt a tangle of amazement and joy and reverence for her — almost worship of her — slam into his stomach. He had withdrawn, of course.

Yet this event had not been enough to overcome his anxiety and doubt about settling in with somebody. Three months later Jeannette had delivered her ultimatum: "If you're not willing to be with me, I'm not going to be with you." Robert had been devastated as their paths diverged; he was staggered by the loneliness that permeated his life once the day-to-day connection with Jeannette was severed.

Now at the river beach, Robert observed Jeannette's face tighten. "Your ring?" he heard her call toward her husband. "You lost your ring?"

Colin waved his left hand at the flowing water. "Must have been when we were swimming."

Robert had led their group along a path across a farmer's meadow to a sandbar at the river's edge. The spot, about twenty kilometers south of his house, was a local favourite for picnics, although no one else was around this afternoon. He had shown Colin how you could wade into the river at the upstream end of the beach, lie on your back, and the hefty current would float you rapidly, exhilaratingly, past the thirty-meter length of the sandbar. And the river would whirl you further away, too, if you didn't stand upright just before you reached the far end. The river was never more than waist-deep at this point, clear and cool, fed by snowmelt in the Monashee Mountains that formed the Valley's eastern rim. Standing immersed in the stream, you could feel the power of the water pushing hard against your legs.

Jeannette glanced back at where William contentedly played in the sand. She took two steps toward Colin and Robert. He could see her brows had contracted, her expression fierce.

"You *have* to find the ring, Colin," she decreed, her voice allowing no challenge to her authority. "Those were my grandparents' wedding rings. We're not going to get any others."

"Jeannette, I'm sorry the ring is lost," Colin began with calm reasonableness. "It never slipped off my finger before. But I can't imagine how we're going to find it." He indicated the curling, rippling surface of the water. "The ring could be miles from here by now."

"You have to find it, Colin."

"I wouldn't know where to start. It could be anywhere between here and two miles downstream."

"Gold is heavier than water," Jeannette declared, her voice transmitting a tone of irritation, as though Colin was a willfully disobedient child. "The ring will sink to the bottom where it came off your finger. Go and look."

"The ring is gone, Jeannette," Colin said, anger rising in his words. "I'm sorry about it. But the ring is gone."

"Then it will have to be found, won't it?" Jeannette insisted. Robert had a brief mental image of her stamping her foot on the sand with impatience, but she had not changed position.

Robert was familiar with Jeannette's ability to resolutely stick to any decision of hers once she had arrived at it. He recalled pleading on the telephone to her to reconsider her termination of their intimacy following his failure to satisfactorily increase his commitment to them as a couple. He also had presented his views in a nine-page, single-space letter to her; he phoned her repeatedly. She was unbudgeable. Though he had endured sharp and continuing pain from her decision, Robert envied and marveled at this trait of hers: she could be as dogged in demonstrating love as she could be in breaking off with someone.

Robert noted this concentrated focus in Jeannette's tending of William. If the child asserted his wish for orange juice, she rushed to provide it. And if, after a few sips, William announced he would rather have apple juice, Jeannette poured a glass of apple juice for him often before William had finished his whine.

She applied this ardent involvement to almost everything she did. Each year Robert anticipated with pleasure watching her curry Old Meg, the mare he had acquired in lieu of payment from a local farmer. Robert wasn't much of a rider. But he knew Jeannette loved to ride and so had accepted the elderly horse when it was offered, imagining — accurately, as it turned out — Jeannette's happiness at having an opportunity to care for and ride the animal during her visits. Robert jokingly disparaged Meg as his "eighth-horse," since she was half quarterhorse and half Arab. Jeannette was quick to flare up to Meg's defense, praising her constantly as she combed Meg's coat. This year Robert had purchased a riding helmet for William, but his parents had brought along his bicycle helmet from Vancouver. Jeannette had started showing William how to rub Meg down, although the child quickly lost interest in the repetitive task.

At the river beach, the latest display of Jeannette's single-mindedness, the tension between husband and wife, made Robert nervous. "Let's give it a try, Colin," he urged. Robert very much doubted Jeannette's grasp of science, her prediction of the likely fate of the ring. Mere minutes before, he been carried along by the water's force and was certain the ornament was beyond recovery. But he hoped if Colin and he went through the motions of scouring the river bottom Jeannette would be appeased.

Colin stood rooted, scowling at Jeannette. She folded her arms across her chest and matched her husband's angry glare. Jeannette's small form vibrated with the rightness of her cause.

"Come on, Colin," Robert begged again. He swiveled to wade further into the chill water. The river bed was stony underfoot, the small slippery rocks of varying dimensions difficult — occasionally painful — to traverse in bare feet.

On the present visit, Robert judged he was handling his emotions satisfactorily. The twinge today at the sight of Jeannette in her bathing suit had been the first reappearance of any trace of the old pattern. When Robert had hung up the phone after Jeannette's call to confirm arrival dates for this August, he had retired to his deck and lit a joint in an attempt to ward off any incipient emotional turmoil. He didn't usually indulge by himself. But he had recently augmented his stash in a trade with a counter-culture family for his services when their cat had been hit by a car. In the past, Robert had discovered that being stoned on grass gave him a distance from his ego. A few times he had replayed an awkward or unpleasant interpersonal encounter and learned he could watch himself perform and understand — while he writhed inwardly with embarrassment — why someone had found his behaviour objectionable.

On his porch, Robert experienced the drug's pleasant heaviness waft through his brain. In an effort not to rehearse his ancient, searing loss of Jeanette, he mulled over an observation he had previously ignored: a number of his friends had not especially liked Jeannette. He saw in memory Jeannette interact with these friends at one of his parties, at dinner, on a ski excursion, at a benefit dance for a pro-ecology group. He visualized Jeannette's tilted-up chin as she pronounced on some issue and held her ground. "Why, she's a — " Through his smoky brain a term tried to float upwards to consciousness, only to be yanked under by another part of his mind aghast at the appearance of the word. But the tag bobbed up again. "She's . . . she can be . . . a bit of a . . . a *brat*." Robert had burst out laughing. He registered a flush of guilt, as though he had profaned an ideal, a sacred thing. Yet hilarity continued to surge through him. For a few minutes, he believed he had attained the ultimate perspective on her. When the cloud in his mind dissipated, however, his fear of the crushing vise of his old response to her absence had reasserted itself.

The water swept around Robert's shins and then knees. In a blaze of resentment he felt at her imperious command to Colin, the suppressed descriptor flashed once, twice. The flame was quickly smothered. Robert obediently peered down through the rippled surface at the stones and pebbles that carpeted the river bottom. While he looked, an unfamiliar sensation enveloped him. The world around him thickened unnaturally. A mental calm suffused him, a trance in which he heard a voice: *You might find this ring.*

Robert was startled. But he also was aware of an aura of matter-of-factness that accompanied the revelation. *You might not*, the measured, self-assured voice allowed. *But you might.*

He was thigh-deep in the river now. He heard Colin behind him begin to pace upstream, swinging his legs in short, sideways arcs through water made viscous by its swift passage. "This is ridiculous," Colin muttered, as he overtook Robert and splashed by. "Talk about a needle in a haystack."

"Let's just give it a shot," Robert offered. He kept his eyes scanning back and forth across the muted hues of the stony jumble underfoot. A couple of times he lifted his head to calculate how far offshore he and Colin had floated. "This is pointless!" he heard Colin shout from a distance.

Then, as Robert told his counselor Kostiuk at their regular session the next week, the strange state of mind he was experiencing became audible. A loud buzz reverberated through his head and increased in volume. Robert glimpsed the gold band of a ring angled on the river bottom, propped against a mottled rose-and-black stone. Surprised to experience no shock at the discovery, he bent to retrieve the metal, his chin just touching the water. He lifted the ring out with his right hand and held it above his head, arm dripping. "I've got it," he called over the noise in his mind.

"What?" Colin hadn't heard him.

"I found the ring," Robert shouted. To his amazement, his voice was steady.

"Jeannette!" Colin yelled, waving his arms in her direction as he waded downstream toward Robert. The urgent tone of his cry caused her to lift her head from where it was bent over William's. When the men had initiated their search of the river she had turned her back on them and knelt to resume playing with her son. "Robert found the ring. He found it," Colin shouted.

"Robert found it?" Jeannette's voice sounded incredulous. Robert continued to hold the ring up. "He found it?"

Colin stepped on shore. "You were right," he called. "Robert's got it."

Jeannette was on her feet now, walking toward where Colin stood shedding water on the sandbar. In the midst of the stream, Robert started to move to dry ground, angling toward Colin.

"Do you comprehend what this means?" Kostiuk blurted excitedly as Robert related the events to him. Robert had never seen Kostiuk so animated.

"Uh . . . not really, no."

"You are aware what a river, being in a river, represents in Jungian terms?" Kostiuk demanded.

"Time?" Robert faltered. "The passage of time?" He had not expected Kostiuk to be so intrigued with the story. Robert had thought Kostiuk might be idly amused by the sheer chance of him finding the ring. Had Kostiuk intuited Jeannette's importance to Robert?

"No, no," Kostiuk's left hand impatiently dismissed Robert's suggestion about the significance of the river. "Sex. A flowing river is sex. You were wading, not immersed, in sex. You found the ring of another man in this river and gave it to him. You were once sexually involved with this Jennifer?"

"Jeannette," Robert corrected.

"Yes, okay," Kostiuk's agitated voice indicated that his excitement could not be distracted by details. "Do you know who traditionally hands the groom the ring at a wedding?"

Robert considered for a minute. He had not attended anybody's wedding in years. Jeannette had invited him to her and Colin's wedding, both by a mailed announcement and, more haltingly, on the phone. But Robert had judged himself unable to face the event in person. Who produced the wedding rings? When Robert's friend Kirby was married, Kirby pulled the box containing the ring out of a pocket of his suit. But that had not been a very traditional ceremony; they had all stood in the living room of Kirby's in-laws' home. The image of an overdressed small girl, a ring-bearer, appeared to Robert. Was there an equivalent male figure in a conventional wedding?

"I'm not sure," Robert admitted.

"The best man," Kostiuk burst out triumphantly. "The best man hands the groom the ring to give the bride." He scanned Robert purposefully, but Robert didn't know how to respond.

From what Kostiuk had said, he apparently considered the tableau when Robert had emerged from the water and passed the ring to Colin to be charged with meaning, momentous. But Robert only recollected noticing that the warm sand was infinitely easier under his feet than the uneven, slippery stones of the river. That the vibration in his head faded as he crossed the beach toward Colin, the sound replaced by the ordinary aural background to the day — hiss of the water, the harsh repeated cry of a crow flapping overhead, a truck humming by along the highway on the far side of the valley. He recalled approaching Colin, who waited, his manner expectant. And Robert remembered Jeannette intently watching him, her face otherwise expressionless, as he placed the ring into Colin's open palm.

BODY LOTIONS

IN A LITTLE MORE THAN TWO MONTHS last year, I had three boyfriends, nearly became a Member of Parliament's lady, and found Misty Meadow, my absolutely favourite skin conditioner. Around mid-September, I was supposed to go to this dinner up at Fairview Hall with Arnold, the guy I was dating then. As Arnold explained it, the evening was a combination thank you and pep rally for people working on the NDP's federal election campaign in Nelson. Arnold didn't ordinarily take much notice of politics. But his union had asked for volunteers for the NDP campaign, and one of his buddies from work, Gerry, had talked him into it.

All that Arnold had done to earn an invitation to the dinner was phone a list of names, three nights in a row. He said it was kind of a poll. He wasn't to argue with people, or try to convince them of anything, but just ask whether they supported the federal NDP or not. If he got an earful, he was to hang up quick as possible. If whoever he called was enthusiastic, the idea was to urge them to contribute money, or to put up a lawn sign, or something like that.

I'll give him this: he was mondo conscientious. We were in the pub, Grohman's, when I heard him say to Gerry he'd help with the phoning. I rolled my eyes at Arlene, Gerry's wife. Arlene and I have this thing about what little boys the guys are in some ways, bragging and puffing themselves up about how much they can do and how much they know: *Did you hear me tell off that moron Larry this afternoon? He's supposed to be operating a grader, not a blankety-blank excavator. What he doesn't understand about making a windrow would seal-coat Highway 6 from here to Vernon.* Like they never make a mistake.

If Arnold did refer to politics, he was cussing the provincial government, the ultimate source of money for the company he works for. His firm does surveying. More often, Arnold was upset about some decision of the Highways Ministry. He used to be employed by Highways before a lot of their positions got privatized, including his unit.

He was on a contract for Highways when I met him, the summer Arlene and I were hired as flaggers. We had to take this course, which was pretty interesting, and then we were out in the weather every day. There were a few cute boys on each crew, and also some jerks. Most of the guys were all right. But inevitably we encountered a Grumpy, who believes women should not be hired for jobs that, as far as he's concerned, only a man is suitable for. Arlene, who has quite a mouth on her, would put old Grumpy in his place as soon as he started in at our first lunch break. "You think because I don't have a penis, I'm incapable of directing traffic?" she'd ask, all wide-eyed innocence. Grumpy would drop his sandwich or spill his coffee, turn red, sputter and stutter, and that would be the last mention of that, at least to our faces.

Speaking of reactions, you can't imagine the things that get said to flag ladies by the public. The majority of people in their vehicles are fine, and the women especially seem cheered to see us. We always get a nice wave. But some guys are positively rude, even offensive. I've been called a bleeping bitch, and worse. For no reason. I've had drivers throw apple cores, beer cans, and other unidentified flying objects at me. One immature twit wearing his baseball cap backwards tossed hot coffee in my direction as he drove past, and his pals in the boom-car thought this was a huge joke. I took their plate number, but didn't do anything about it in the end. A drunk tried to run Arlene down once, and she radioed it in to the Mounties. They picked the guy up twenty clicks down the road, and charged him with impaired. She wanted him nailed for attempted murder, but they wouldn't.

The bad part of the job wasn't the people, really. What I hated was how being outdoors the whole day dried my skin. My main moisturizer that summer was English Countryside. It has some of those chemicals every lotion does, although I have no clue why. Who can tell whether Phenoxyethanol or Carbomer 934 or Dimethocone or Butylparaben are good for your skin? But English Countryside has honeysuckle, peony, chamomile and rosemary extract, and smells heavenly. When we were working over in the Okanangan Valley on one job — they put us up in some cheapo motel cabins outside Penticton — I discovered Flaming Apricot, which besides apricot oil has almond oil and kiwi fruit extract. I like Flaming Apricot's aroma even more than English Countryside's. But English Countryside is better as a skin softener.

The Okanagan was where I started going out with Arnold. His crew had successfully bid on a job in the area, despite being based in Nelson, same as us. I blame getting seriously involved with Arnold on a lip gloss I began applying at a rock-scaling site on Highway 97. The country near Penticton is a lot drier than the West Kootenays around Nelson, and my lips felt parched and cracked as the landscape. I tried out this Butterscotch lip gloss, and suddenly Arnold couldn't get enough of me. We'd kissed goodnight before after a couple of dates, but nothing special. All at once he wanted to kiss and kiss, and kept insisting how great my lips tasted. It was rather exciting, and one thing led to another.

I probably shouldn't say "blame" about the impact of Butterscotch lip balm on my love life. But I wasn't too happy with Arnold by the time we got invited to the dinner at Fairview Hall. Arlene snagged Gerry that autumn — she met him through Arnold and me — and has never looked back. She and Gerry were married in the summer, and I was maid of honour. Arlene started pestering me about getting Arnold to propose. Arnold may have his good points, but the thought of being married to him sent ice-cold shivers up my spine. He and I weren't living together, but I was more often over at his place than at my own. He bought a house on Delbruck in Nelson, near the top of Uphill, with a deck that has a view of the mountains and the river to die for. I rent a small bungalow a few blocks above downtown, which means I can walk to work. When we were laid off from flagging, I got a job in the provincial government building on Ward, with the division that processes mining claims.

It's hard to describe why I was dissatisfied with Arnold. Arlene was on my case to explain, and though at the time her nagging definitely bugged me, I can see now that she helped me clarify what I was feeling. If I had to summarize, like this was some kind of report I key in at my job, I'd have to say Arnold is too much into arranging matters precisely as he wants them. Forget how often I was at his house: nobody could ever tell I had set foot in it. Any toothbrush or robe I intended to leave in his bathroom or bedroom closet — I stayed five nights out of seven some weeks — had to be tucked out of sight before we left for work in the morning. He was equally ruthless about his own stuff having a proper place. If we'd been watching TV and snacking in the evening, the living room and kitchen had to be tidied completely with everything put away before we were allowed to go to bed. You couldn't imagine how he'd cope if a kid was living in the house. Bachelors are supposed to be messy, but Arnold was the opposite. Sometimes I felt he considered me a cross between a disruption, a servant, and a pet. I know this explanation is vague, which made it difficult to convey to Arlene my exact misgivings about Arnold. He was tender and loving in bed; I had no complaints in that department. Once we started being a couple, though, our life together seemed very un-spontaneous. Arnold had a correct moment and location for every activity, object and emotion. My task was to intuit the authorized procedure we should be following, and behave accordingly. I felt a bit stifled.

So Arnold's acceptance of Gerry's suggestion to get involved in the campaign was a surprise, because it was way out of the ordinary for Arnold. I attribute his decision to that game the guys play: if you can do something, I have to be able to do it as good, if not better. If you buy a snazzy new pickup with 500 horsepower, I have to buy a new one with 550 horsepower. Or whatever.

I had no inkling where Arnold stood politically, because, as I mentioned, except for him swearing about the g.d. provincial government doing this or not doing that, I never heard him comment one way or another. But he tackled the phone list as though he really cared. I was the tiniest bit impressed, because when Gerry brought the notion up, I was sure that once we were out of the bar Arnold would invent some excuse for not involving himself with a world that usually didn't enter his mind.

I guess if I'm anything politically, I'm NDP. My dad spoke in favour of them around our family dinner table when I was growing up in Trail, although at election time I never saw Dad volunteer for the campaign. We did have NDP lawn signs, the same as most houses in our block. Now I think of it, a whole pocket of NDP supporters like that probably was odd. This area has always been a swing riding, both provincially and federally. If we send an NDPer to Victoria or Ottawa one election, we most often send a Conservative the next time there's a vote. Candidates don't win or lose by much, or at least the two front-runners are close.

As the date for the Fairview Hall dinner approached, articles about it were published in the *Nelson Daily News*. First one, and then two NDP MPs were scheduled to attend. Then, the head of the provincial NDP announced he would appear to help drum up support for our federal candidate. The mayor, who is quite the conservative — he owns a paint store and a lot of real estate — declared he would be present for the benefit of the town. He was most likely hedging his bets on who might win our riding. When Arnold first mentioned the dinner, I thought it would be like a union social. But the more I read about who would be present that evening, I realized I needed to rethink what I would wear. In the mall drugstore, I found Tropic Passion. It's more expensive than I usually buy, but has papaya, passion fruit, jojoba oil, as well as shea butter. Also sea kelp, though I don't understand how seaweed is particularly tropical.

Mid-September, here in the mountains, the days are quite hot and then the temperature plummets as soon as the sun drops behind a ridge. On the other hand, Fairview Hall's air-conditioning system is no match for a large crowd. The space can become mondo overheated even in winter. The hall has a retractable centre partition, so Arlene and Gerry's wedding reception only used half of it, while the city's Centennial Dance in February '97 filled the whole room. But both functions were steamers. For the political dinner, I chose the sundress I consider my most becoming, the lilac and green one. It's short, but not a mini. I took along my good black cardigan, just in case.

Our seats were at the union table that included the various survey guys Gerry had talked into helping. It's the same union I'm in, but another component, naturally. I knew a few others at our table besides Arlene and the survey crew, including a couple of women from the outer office on our floor at work. Of course I ran into scads of other friends, and people I recognized, like my doctor. Seems like the dinner was *the* place to be in Nelson that evening. Some of my former teachers from good old Lakeside Senior Secondary were even present. I did grades 11 and 12 at LSS after my parents sent me off to live with an aunt in Nelson when they decided I was enjoying school in Trail way too much.

In Fairview Hall, people were excited, noisy and feeling important, and you had to wait in line at the bar. The meal was buffet, by table number, so there was tons of kidding about that: table nine insisting it was table six, and jeers and boos when the emcee missed one table in the sequence. Dinner was nothing to write home about: creamed chicken or fish, served out of cafeteria-style steam trays. The desserts were much fancier than the main course, with chocolate drizzled over the plates and pastries.

Our table had barely tucked into the delectable desserts when the speeches began. I tried to look interested, even though I wasn't. Arlene leaned across and started whispering some gossip she'd picked up in the Ladies about one of the hunky LSS teachers whose class we'd been in, but Arnold frowned at us so I cut it short. Then it was the candidate's turn to address the crowd.

I'd like to claim it was love at first sight, but actually my first impression was that when he smiled, he had the saddest expression. My heart kind of flopped over. I wanted to put my arms around him and make everything okay. His name is Riley LaFontaine, and the LaFontaines are a long-established family hereabouts; different ones have hardware stores in Nelson, Kaslo and Trail, and one of them is the city clerk in Castlegar, and another is a Nelson building inspector. Riley and a cousin operate a plant nursery and garden supply store a few kilometers from Nelson up the North Shore of the Lake. Riley's face is boyish, all earnest and sincere. I guessed he was a convincing speaker, because at the dinner people were laughing and hooting and applauding like mad. I simply watched him, not registering a word he was saying. I'd seen pictures of him before, in connection with the campaign, and if I thought anything, I figured he was sort of geeky. His straw hair is a mop on top, thinning at the sides although he's only five years older than me. But up at the microphone at Fairview Hall, with the crowd cheering and laughing, he seemed very much in control, in charge, the boss. Nothing like a geek. When the applause went on and on after some phrase he said, he'd smile. Then you could see the sadness in him.

Arlene must have noticed me staring at him with That Look, because she leaned forward and whispered, "Stop drooling." I jumped, and was racking my brains to think of a bright comeback, when she added: "Have to admit:

he could leave his shoes under my bed anytime." I glanced nervously at Arnold to check if my behaviour was obvious, but he had his back to me, gazing toward Riley, too. Probably listening so he and Gerry could discuss the speech later, and pronounce whether it was satisfactory or not. Just so we girls were properly informed.

I didn't observe any women on the platform, except for one of the Castlegar city councillors, and I was dying to ask Arlene if she knew whether Riley was married. I couldn't imagine anybody running for office if they didn't have a spouse and two-point-four kids. But maybe not anymore. Some Members of Parliament are even gay these days.

Suddenly everybody leaped to their feet, and gave Riley a standing ovation. I stood, too. After a while the clapping faded and a loud wave of talk swelled in the room, along with a huge rustling sound as everybody sat down. Then the evening began to resemble a night in the pub, at least at our table. The guys, sure enough, were providing each other and the world with their opinions of Riley's speech. The rest of us were left to converse about other topics, most immediately a comparison of recipes for pastry dough, inspired by the dessert selection.

Except that Riley, accompanied by an entourage of three or four, was working the room. Out of the corner of my eye, I saw him shaking hands and chatting to guests at table after table. Occasionally a woman or man would envelop him in a bear hug. A couple of tables from us he sat and drank a beer at the insistence of a white-haired gent who was unmistakably half tanked.

Then, after the guys at our table were on to weighing the Canucks' chances on the ice this coming season, and Arlene was holding forth about dreading a Thanksgiving weekend visit by her in-laws, Riley and his group reached us. Gerry sprang up and shook Riley's hand, then played host, acting as if we had been descended upon by the Queen. Everybody was introduced by Gerry, one after another, while Riley made eye contact and nodded, as if he could ever possibly remember who was who. As the focus of Gerry's presentations swept up my side of the table, a blush started heating my face. I knew what was coming, due to my nickname.

Gerry's hand pointed at me. "And this is Buzz Cutter." He grinned. "Short for 'buzzard' I think."

"Buzzard?" Riley's sad smile was washing over me.

My voice was squeakier than normal. "In high school, I showed up one day with most of my hair chopped off. So I got stuck with 'Buzz'. Because of my last name." The story sounded juvenile to me. Why did I still let my friends call me by a gag tag from school?

"Your last name is Cutter?"

I was amazed Riley had retained that information, after having been introduced to about a hundred people at nine other tables, and with a dozen more tables ahead of him.

"Yeah," I blurted. Then, feeling I should display more class: "Uh, yes. It is. Cutter. That's me," I babbled. 'Sophisticated' is this girl's middle name, I didn't say.

"You wouldn't be related to Pat Cutter, in Trail? Works in the zinc plant at the smelter?"

I felt my mouth sag open. "Pat's my father. How did you — ?"

Riley's eyes sparkled, and his laugh sounded genuine. "I worked with your dad for about eight months. When I got out of school and was kicking around. He took me under his wing, though he probably wouldn't remember me. This was years ago. He's a great guy. How is he doing?"

"Fine. He's fine," I managed.

"He didn't say anything about having a daughter."

"Two daughters. I have an older sister. She's married, in Trail." Like he really wants to know about my family, I thought. "Dad was pretty protective of us, while we were growing up. He thought the plant was full of rough customers, and that we shouldn't go out with any smelter rats."

Riley laughed again. "Will you remember me to him? It'll be, gee, fourteen years ago now." He was staring right at me, and I felt all flustered and awkward.

"Sure. Yeah. Yes. Yes, I will."

He gave me the sad smile again. "I'd appreciate it. Wonderful human being, your dad."

Gerry broke in impatiently with Denise and Bob's names, who were seated to my left, and that was that. In a moment, Riley's party had moved on to the next table. When I caught Arlene's eye, she winked. I took a slug of my rye and seven. As I put my glass down, Arnold was gawking at me like I was royalty myself. Before he could utter a word, I asked him if the evening had inspired him to undertake more on behalf of the campaign. That got him pontificating, and all I had to do was nod and "yeah, uh-huh" in the correct places, which gave me time to calm my jangly nerves.

Then somebody was at the microphone again. Behind it, the city dance band had assembled themselves. The conductor was my old music teacher from LSS, who also played sax. A minute later the cleared space in front of the platform was filled with waltzing couples. One of those '70s disco balls had been rigged up, radiating spangles of light across the dancers. Though I knew the request was hopeless, I put my hand on Arnold's arm, leaned in, and asked if he wanted to. His usual behaviour, when we were at a place with music, was to put off dancing with me until the very end of the evening. By then he'd drunk enough to not be concerned that he isn't so skilled a dancer, though the alcohol makes his stumbling and lack of any sense of rhythm even worse. But we were a twosome, and I felt guilty at how much the interaction with Riley, even if brief, had revved up some very pleasant sensations inside me. Arnold said he wasn't into dancing right now, maybe later, which was his standard response.

I was anticipating pumping Arlene, hopefully in the privacy of the Ladies, for what she knew about Riley's status. Not that I had any hope to connect with him, of course, but I was curious in the same way you like to know whether your favourite TV star or movie actor is happily married or unhappily married or on the loose. But Gerry whisked Arlene to the dance floor. Since about half our table was there as well, I was just staring across the room at my fellow Nelsonites as they kicked up their heels and enjoyed the evening. The band played a polka, and frequent shrieks sounded as the dancers cavorted and skipped, trying to keep up with the beat. Arnold was hunched away from me, drawing on a paper napkin, and a few other guys were crowded around contributing their thoughts on whatever was being sketched: a hockey play, a little-known spot to find firewood or hunt elk, some problem from their job they were reconsidering. The music was too loud to hear the subject they were analyzing or arguing about. The polka finished, and the band's version of the Beatles' "Lady Madonna" began.

"Care to dance, Ms. Cutter?" I spun in my chair; Riley's serious face loomed above me. I was so startled, I flinched back, and came within a hair's breadth of tipping my rye and seven all over the table. Real cool, girl, I was thinking. But my feet automatically hoisted me up. Mere seconds afterwards, I

was doing the rock-and-roll shuffle in the midst of a crowd —
but in very near proximity to Mr. Riley LaFontaine.

As soon as we started dancing, I noticed him grinning
at me. I didn't know what *that* meant, except he appeared to
be having a good time. My insides were in a tumult, since I
was flattered he'd asked me to dance, while an inner voice
cautioned me not to read more into this than a politician
encouraging the troops. Or maybe he was tickled to be
dancing with Pat Cutter's daughter. My dad evidently had
meant something to Riley as a young millworker. I wanted
to ask him how he got from the Cominco smelter in Trail
to being co-owner of a nursery on the North Shore. But the
band was cooking and conversation beyond a few shouted
monosyllables was impossible. Anyway, higher on my agenda
was to ask him whether he was married. "Too bad your wife
couldn't make it tonight," was the sentence I was rehearsing.
The words registered with me as a tad transparent. So I said
nothing, but swayed and shifted my weight from foot to foot
along with the tune.

Riley had more rhythm in him than Arnold, though that
isn't saying much. When the number finished, we clapped
with the others. I thought that was it for me dancing with
the candidate. The musicians launched immediately into a
waltz. Half the dancers returned to their tables, a different set
of people streamed onto the floor, and Riley stepped forward
and wrapped me in his arms.

I couldn't believe how natural and safe and welcomed
I felt with him holding me, me holding him, and our feet
gliding perfectly through their steps by themselves. I inhaled
his scent: tangy and spicy, like a pleasantly smoky incense.
I heard him murmur into the top of my hair, and realized I

had been resting my head against him. I tilted back. "What? I mean, pardon?"

He had that sweet sad smile. "I was saying how delightful your hair smells." He sniffed. "Mmmm. Good enough to eat."

I nestled against him again. Good old Waterfall shampoo, I thought: banana, coconut, guava and ginger. Since he responded to Waterfall, I speculated for an instant about how much more he might savor a direct exposure to Tropic Passion. Then I tried to change the mental subject, reminding myself that he almost certainly was spoken for.

But he didn't let go of my hand in the pause between songs, even though everybody around us was clapping. We both pretended to ignore this fact, and just looked at each other or at the crowd around us.

"One more?" he asked.

The next tune was rock-and-roll again, so we had to release each other. And a few minutes into the number, a man was standing speaking into Riley's ear. He stopped dancing and so did I. The man continued to mutter at Riley.

He nodded, stepped toward me, and with his hand at the small of my back escorted me away from the dance floor.

"Duty calls, Buzz, I'm sorry to say," he told me when we'd proceeded far enough from the musicians that we could talk more easily. His hand abandoned my back, but he kept eye contact with me. "I have to go and be obliging to some folks. I really enjoyed dancing with you. We'll do it again soon, okay?" Then that heart-twisting smile again, and I was walking alone back to my table, trying to decide whether his parting words meant anything.

Arnold hadn't even twigged that I had been off dancing, as far as I could judge. Arlene raised and lowered her eyebrows about five times in a row, to communicate to me that she had been scoping us and was bursting with questions. In the Ladies, she didn't have any information about Riley, but promised that she'd discretely dispatch Gerry to gather hard data over the next few days. I insisted she swear to be tactful in her request to Gerry, since he and Arnold were buds and I didn't want a big deal made from what was obviously nothing.

Back at our table, I sat wrapped in a rose-hued fog. Luckily, with the noise level in the room, I wasn't the only one staring blankly into the ozone, sipping on a drink. Arnold, with his uncanny sense of timing, eventually stirred himself to ask me to dance, one number before the home waltz. I hadn't seen Riley in the meantime, but he was out on the floor for this song, too, squiring a grey-haired overweight old cow in a tacky black gown.

I didn't run into Riley again until six days after the dinner. Arlene discovered through Gerry that Riley was separated from his wife. They had split up in the spring when he announced he would seek the NDP candidacy. For PR reasons, the state of his marriage was downplayed while he fought to be selected as the NDP flag-bearer. And of course the party didn't want it an issue during the campaign itself. For some reason, the media to date had ignored his marital status, too. Arlene said he was nominally living at his business partner's, since his wife kept possession of their house. But because our federal riding extends from the southern Okanagan to the east shore of Kootenay Lake, and from Boundary Country to as far north as Revelstoke, Riley was living in hotels mainly, as he toured the region canvassing votes.

I lectured myself without pause that my encounter with Riley was just one more whistle stop for him, the equivalent of chucking a toddler under the chin, or kissing a baby. I couldn't help wondering what his kisses *were* like, though. I was certain I'd never dance with him again. But during the following three days I applied Butterscotch lip gloss several times, even though the weather had turned rainy. And after work on Thursday, I cruised through the Body Shop outlet in the mall and then the big Pharmasave downtown on Baker Street. From the latter's skin care display, I chose Sultry Herbs, which combines lemon grass, sage, safflower and cucumber extract. I also bought a Mandarin Orange lip balm. I don't know why.

Arnold and I weren't together much during that week after the dinner. I was irritated with him almost continually. Even those quirks of his I had once found endearing, such as his constant critical commentary on the driving habits of other motorists, I was now impatient with. I agreed to go for supper with him Wednesday. When he began to rage about the driver of a small car in front of us who had failed to speed through a yellow light, I blurted out: "Who appointed you driving instructor?" He was silent the rest of the route to the restaurant, and throughout most of the meal. Which was okay with me. After supper, I complained of a headache and went home by myself.

On Friday, about five o'clock I was driving back from Safeway when I sighted Riley on Front Street. As I approached, I slowed to observe him, ignoring a chain of cars piling up behind. Riley was electioneering door to door, with a clump of pamphlets in his hand. As I rolled past, he knocked at one house and, when there evidently was no answer, returned up the walk and along the street to the next place. In the rear mirror, I caught a glimpse of him speaking to a man in the doorway.

Riley looked so forlorn, campaigning by himself as if nobody else in the world could be bothered to assist him. I'd always believed when a politician went door-to-door, two or three other people accompanied him to provide support and to show that he was the choice of an organized group and not just some flake out annoying householders. I pulled over and parked.

After a minute summoning my courage, I climbed out and sauntered nonchalantly down the sidewalk. I paused at the curb while he finished at one address. When he approached where I waited, his eyes lit up.

"Uh, Riley, I'm Buzz Cutter. We met on Saturday at — "

He cut me off. "I know who you are. My marvelous dancing partner." His smile appeared less melancholy for an instant, or maybe I was only hoping that was true.

I asked if he wanted help or at least company. I had promised to stop by Arnold's later, but I was confident I could deal with that, depending on Riley's answer. He seemed pathetically grateful for my offer. I told him I'd dash home and change, and meet him in a few minutes.

Gunning back to my place, I was frantically considering what to wear. The temperature would drop if we were out very late, but maybe we'd go for a drink afterwards and I wanted to dazzle him when I removed my coat. At the house, I flung the groceries into the fridge and shelves, and slipped into my laciest bra. I have a dressy blouse, with frills and pearl buttons and cut low in front, and I look rather hot in it, in my opinion. I agonized over whether to wear my best jeans or a skirt, but decided that, after all, this was Nelson. Nobody, on a fall night, would expect even campaigners to be wearing a skirt. Besides, I like the snug fit of those jeans; I feel sensational in them, and ready for action. I applied some

Butterscotch balm, put the jar in my coat pocket for refills, and had one hand on the door latch heading outside when I remembered Arnold.

My arm hung suspended over the phone while I debated what to say. I knew he was at work till six, so I'd be inter-acting with his answering machine. Should I lie, and claim I was sick? Or should I calmly inform him I was off to solicit votes at the doorstep, and would see him tomorrow? Honesty being the best policy, I determined I'd tell him I was out campaigning, without exactly stating who with.

I caught up to Riley a few blocks down Front Street from where I had left him. Listening to him canvass people was a treat: he was unfailingly courteous, even if a resident was rude. Yet he could hold his own if someone truly wished to engage the issues. He was passionate about the ideas he intended to bring to Ottawa, about the beneficial force he believed he could be for our riding, even as an opposition MP. I admired him, too, for how he never lost his sense of humor even if we were hit with four or five negative responses in a row.

By about eight o'clock, I was horribly hungry, and so cold my teeth were threatening to chatter. Riley called it quits a few minutes after the hour and offered to buy me a meal from campaign funds. Once I thawed out in the café, I was flooded with a sort of goofy happiness at having every kilowatt of Riley's intelligence and passion about politics focused in my direction. I invited him back to my house for coffee.

I arranged matters so we had coffee side by side on the couch, and began that slow escalation of contact: first touching each other for emphasis as we talked, then his arm along the back of the couch behind me, then a kiss, followed up with hugs and *mega* kissing. He got to explore my high-end bra, and more, before we retired to the bedroom. I'd never previously started a relationship with one guy while still seeing another. For the sake of being next to Riley, I apparently was willing to compromise a few principles.

I'm convinced of the need to keep a clean back yard, however, so I broke up with Arnold less than twenty-four hours later. Riley was away to the south Okanagan for a couple of days, but he promised to phone me and did. We planned to meet Monday night when he returned to Nelson.

Arnold was miffed, I think, rather than hurt by my announcement that I didn't want to continue our connection. He went rapidly through the Boyfriend's Seven Stages of Breaking Up: shock, anger, bargaining, pleading, weeping, being vulnerable for the first time in the entire g.d. relationship, and, finally, acceptance. I didn't mention Riley. I debriefed with Arlene immediately after leaving Arnold's place. We vowed to continue being best buds even though we recognized we were in for some awkwardness, given that Arnold and Gerry were friends. "You go, girl," she wished me well with Riley.

My house became Riley's Nelson headquarters so fast, I scarcely had the opportunity to blink. I didn't mind, though: I was awed and grateful that such an amazing guy would be so interested in me. First he took to crashing at my place when he was in town, instead of making the drive out the North Shore to his cousin's. Then, because communication is the heartbeat of a campaign, as everybody on his team assured me, he began to receive messages on my phone. Soon there were strategy conferences in my living room, lawn signs and posters and pamphlets stacked in the dining nook, Riley's suits and jeans in my closets, and the phone rang continually: "Riley around?" I loved it; other kinds of conversations and negotiations occurred on the couch and in the bedroom, all delightful. He never failed to be attuned to what I was feeling and thinking. Regardless of being beat after a long day campaigning, he had that extra energy to discover how I was, how *my* day had been, whether he could do something to please me. Or my body. I tried varying between Butterscotch and Mandarin Orange lip gloss without any noticeable effect. But I didn't change shampoos, since Riley had praised Waterfall's scent. I switched back to Tropic Passion as my skin lotion, though, since I'd worn it the night we'd met and it had brought me luck.

When I accompanied Riley to public events, at first I was part of his group, hanging back among the advisors and gophers. Bit by bit he wanted me more visible than that: for instance, there's that famous news photo of him kissing me right after he stepped down amid deafening cheers from the podium of the big rally at the Trail Arena. My parents were on the phone about two seconds after the *Trail Times* hit their porch, since Riley and I were spread across the front page. I had advised my folks I'd broken up with Arnold, and they knew I was seeing someone else. But I'd hedged the details. Since the picture was published in the *NDN*, too, next day at work the girls had it clipped and up on the bulletin board. I was mondo embarrassed and mondo pleased.

Riley's handlers weren't that overjoyed, since they had worked hard to keep the collapse of his marriage out of the public eye. He received quite a blast at a special How To Deal With Buzz Cutter emergency damage control session, he told me. For two nights I had to attend special training on how to conduct myself during a campaign. The handouts were titled Spousal Briefing Material at the top, which caused my heart to pound and my stomach to flutter with astonishingly-coloured and delicate butterflies each time I read the words. I found it difficult to concentrate on what I was being lectured about, which miffed the self-important, power-suited, so-called media expert who was supposed to instruct me on proper deportment, attire, greeting the public, and all that. She was younger than me, from Victoria, on loan from the BC party because the brass felt Riley needed an extra edge of slick election tactics to win the seat. Personally, I think she was jealous of me. How could any woman work on Riley's campaign and not fall a little in love with him?

Riley remained slightly ahead in the polls, which meant nobody could complain too loudly about my presence. His closest competitor was the incumbent, who I learned had dozed through the past six years on the back benches in Ottawa. One Friday night, Riley took me to Creston where he was touring the brewery and a fruit orchard and then conducting a rally at a community hall. At the close of his speech, which was super as always, everybody was being wildly enthusiastic and yelling and whistling and clapping while Riley recited his customary list of thank yous. Then he said a bunch about me and held out his hand toward where I was sitting in the front row, beckoning me onto the platform. I went absolutely numb the first instant my name boomed over the PA, and what happened after that is a blank. Except I've seen the photos, so apparently I climbed up beside him without falling on my big fat behind and there we are, hand in hand, with our other hands raised to salute the standing ovation the crowd is providing. I look entirely poised beside him, as though I did this every day. A real pro. The candidate's, uh, um, girlfriend.

Once or twice a future for us after the election was mentioned, but mostly the days were a blur of my job, linking up with the campaign where I could, hearing about the election's twists and turns, and loving Riley. I seldom had the chance to contact Arlene, so she started phoning me at work for updates on my "fab-glam" life, as she began to call it. A week before the vote, a poll showed Riley had increased his lead from two per cent to three per cent. Lots of the commentators said the race was still too close to call, and I agreed. But Riley at supper seemed ecstatic at the news, claiming that once a trend starts this late in a campaign it's the decisive shift.

"So, Buzz, have you thought about where you might want us to live in Ottawa?" he asked me. "The Market Area? Hull, across the river? The Gatineau Hills?" We were in Brisco's, the small café off the alley between Hall Street and Josephine Street. Riley had inquired where I'd like to eat to celebrate. I've always thought that Brisco's, though expensive, is quite elegant. But I got a kind of red roaring in my ears at his words. I choked for a moment on the fancy endive and cilantro salad I was forking into my mouth.

"Are you asking me to go with you out East if you win?" I point-blanked him, after a hurried sip of wine.

"*When* I win, you mean." He grinned at me. His smile had never entirely lost that underlay of sadness, but I kept telling myself less of it was present the longer we were together.

"Okay, when you win." I let the silence hang to ensure he didn't joke his way off the hook.

"Don't you want to?"

"You haven't asked me," I observed.

"We're practically living together now," he countered.

I didn't say anything. My fencing with him was fun, but I wanted to nudge him to actually ask me the question, since this was no small matter, at least to me. I knew I was so much in love with Riley I could hardly stand it. But when I looked at a calendar, I was amazed to realize we'd only been together a bit more than three weeks. Our connection felt like what I've read about wartime romances — lovers swept up in turbulent times. Start with the excitement of important, life-and-death activity in the outside world. Add the intensity of any new love affair. No wonder the fireworks are spectacular, dazzling. And time expands when your emotions are throbbing at peak capacity. An hour seems a day, a day a month, a week a year.

Yet was I ready to quit my job, leave Nelson, and relocate to Ottawa as a brand-new Member of Parliament's . . . girlfriend? Partner? Common-law wife? Though we had spoken a little about Riley's ex, the context was invariably him describing where his marriage had gone sour for him. I awarded Riley full marks for being willing to reveal his intimate life to me. But of course we hadn't been able to discuss this fully: our days and nights were crammed. He assured me he simply had not had the opportunity to proceed beyond the separation stage in dissolving his marriage. First he had been attempting to snag the NDP nomination, and then almost immediately the election race was on. I was convinced he loved me, but did I really understand enough of who he was to commit to moving away with him?

Some supporter stopped at our table in the restaurant, and interrupted our conversation about Ottawa. Snuggling up to Riley in the car driving home, I put the issue on hold by thanking him for raising the notion of me accompanying him East. I was exhilarated by the idea, though the soberer side of me insisted I better mull this over with Arlene to be sure any decision I arrived at would be right for me.

Riley also brought up the Ottawa possibility in an offhand comment when he accepted my parents' invitation for dinner. My mom had been bugging me to bring him home as soon as her shock at that picture of us in the *Times* subsided. As Riley's schedule worked out, he had a few hours for a supper break in Trail the evening before election day.

I wasn't worried about how my folks and Riley might relate. He seemed eager to meet Dad again, and was so perfectly charming to both my parents that it took my breath away. My parents, too, were on their best behaviour: they acted as though Prince William or Prince Andrew was engaged to their daughter. When we pulled up in front of their house, my dad had no less than seven Riley LaFontaine signs crowded onto the lawn. My mother had cooked her holiday honey-and-pineapple roast chicken, along with her incredible saskatoon berry pie.

Riley had my parents laughing three minutes after we were in the door. He listened, apparently rapt, to Dad's tales from the smelter potlines, and the lost fight to keep the Mine-Mill union in and Steel out during the Red-baiting days, even though Riley had probably already heard these yarns when he was a kid on Dad's crew. Then, joking with my mother, he promised her an audience with the Governor-General when she and my dad visited us in Ottawa. You could hear a pin drop following that remark. I plunged in to remind everybody that a move to the nation's capital was not a done deal on my part. Nor on Riley's, since the election still had to be won. The rest of supper I could sense the wheels spinning around behind Mom's eyes: has he asked her to marry him, or not? And why haven't I been told? She tried to corner me in the kitchen a couple of times as I helped clear away Granny Martha's best china. Luckily, we had to race off after dessert to Riley's next appearance. And I knew I was safe from her inquiries for at least a day, since I was taking tomorrow off from work as a mental health day, while we waited for the ballots to be cast. Once the votes were tallied, the issue of Ottawa might be moot.

All that final week, Riley had exuded supreme confidence that he would win. I was nervous as could be. To bolster myself, forty-eight hours before the election I had blitzed through the standard outlets looking for something special to wear.

Nothing caught my attention until, out of desperation, I browsed a bed-and-bath store, Sweet Sheets, that had opened on the main drag. I had stuck my nose in previously, but none of their stock appealed. The merchandise was overpriced and tacky: snobby emphasis on stitches-per-inch in their bedding sets, garish towel colours with matching floor mats, retro Betty Boop night lights.

But they also carry Misty Meadow. Scanning their lotion shelves without much conviction, I picked up a bottle of M-and-M, as I refer to it now. A cursory sniff, and I was a devotee. Misty Meadow offers extracts of rosemary, horsetail, calendula, plus wild rose — an exquisitely fragrant blend. But M-and-M also boasts an ingredient called Dimethicone Copolyol Meadow Foamate, which I regard as M-and-M's secret punch. I have no idea what a "foamate" is, but I love the vision of a field of wildflowers all foamed together and spread over my skin. Tasty and smooth and sexy. I've basically used only M-and-M since I first tried it on the big day.

Riley and I showed up at Nelson's NDP election central at eight p.m. when the polls closed. The plan was to await results in the Hume Hotel's largest banquet room. A couple of hundred supporters were milling around the tables, and banks of TVs and computers were lined up along one wall, opposite a cash bar.

A big cheer echoed as Riley and I entered, and somebody at a microphone announced "the Right Honourable Riley LaFontaine, the next Member of Parliament for West Kootenay-Boundary-Revelstoke." The first poll results reported a slight lead for Riley, and he was whipped away by riding officials to meet with this person and that. I picked up a rye and seven from the bar, and settled down at a table to watch the universe unfold. I was wishing I'd thought to invite Arlene. But I hadn't wanted her to imagine I was dragging her out to witness my glory as the sidekick, or whatever, of the area's new MP. I also figured Gerry would be along for sure, as a loyal NDP supporter, and he's usually accompanied by Arlene. But Gerry didn't appear, maybe out of loyalty to poor old Arnold.

Feeling sort of lonely proved to be the least of my worries. By eight-thirty, the news filtered in from Osoyoos and Grand Forks and Creston that the incumbent had organized labor contractors across the southern part of the riding to bring busloads of migrant fieldworkers to the polls to vote for him. The lumber industry is the basis for jobs in the northern two-thirds of the riding. On the other hand, agriculture is the mainstay for employment around Creston, in Boundary Country, and in the south Okanagan. Riley's biggest strength was in the northern districts of the riding and among the smelter workers in Trail, though he'd put plenty of effort into the communities where he was less well known. But the lumber towns and villages, and Trail, are where most of the voters live, or so everybody had figured.

The apple harvest was on in the orchards. Young people, mainly from Quebec, drift into the growing areas to pick, some of them sticking around from cherries in the spring to apples in the fall. Also East Indian harvesters are trucked up from the Fraser Valley as the fruit ripens. None of these folks know much more about the BC Interior than the pickers' camps where they're housed. But apparently their bosses snowed them that the incumbent had promised to improve their situation; then the contractors did the patriotic deed of transporting the pickers to the nearest voting stations. Some of them cast ballots for Riley, naturally. But enough of the field hands either were eager to please the contractor, or regarded the excursion to the polls as a holiday and why not dance with the one that brung ya? By two in the morning, Riley had lost by one hundred and fifty-four votes. Pending a recount, which two days later officially narrowed the gap by fourteen, Riley had to admit defeat.

Election evening was such a cliffhanger that everyone was emotionally fried, baked, crisped by the time Riley, through gritted teeth, placed his congratulatory phone call to the victor. Then he delivered the we-did-our-best-but-the-people-have-spoken speech to an absolutely silent room. I noticed his hand that held the paper with his notes was shaking. He looked close to tears.

By the time he finished talking, I was already bawling, along with quite a few others. As poll after poll had reported, and the vote went down to the wire, Riley's handlers wouldn't allow me near him. I could see across the room where group after group of suits huddled with him. The televisions were displaying results that were bad. But when I temporarily left my spot a few times to try to connect with Riley, I wasn't permitted in to comfort him. Or he, me. So as Riley lost, I did my crying on the shoulder of somebody else.

About the middle of the long, long evening, a guy had appeared at my table with his laptop and a sheaf of papers, searching for a clear space to crunch some numbers. The room had become increasingly crowded as the hours ticked past, and there were fewer places at the tables to perch. The newcomer introduced himself as Brian, asked if he could sit down opposite me, and said he was just a boring statistician who had been requested to provide some analysis of the Revelstoke polls based on votes that had been tallied so far.

His eyes were the most gorgeous I'd ever seen in my life. Despite his introduction, he didn't seem boring in the slightest. Nobody else at my table had spoken to me; in fact, the reason Brian could sit where he did was that empty chairs surrounded me, as though I had the plague or AIDS. I recognized lots of folks in the room, and had chatted briefly with a few as they circulated among the tables. But nobody would plunk down and talk with me. At first I thought it was kind of funny: like I had the curse of celebrity, me being the candidate's whoever. As the hours crawled past, though, I began to feel sorry for myself.

So when this creature with eyes so sweet and deep you could joyfully swim around in them forever seated himself across from me, I was awfully glad. I knew he wanted to work; his fingers inched repeatedly toward his keyboard. But I unleashed a string of questions. After some initial reluctance on his side, we were soon chattering away. He's my age exactly — I'm two months younger than him, to be precise. I learned he works for Forestry as a project financial manager — an accountant, really — and only moved to Nelson in February. He had helped out in the last provincial election in Vancouver, where he lived before he transferred to the Kootenay Lake District office. His decision to volunteer for

Riley was partly, he confessed, to meet people outside his job.

After a half hour, I let him tackle his computer chores. But he asked me to keep my eye on his laptop when he went off to report the results, and he returned with a beer for himself and a rye and seven for me. I couldn't remember informing him of my choice of beverage. He must have slipped the question into our conversation. That's how sneakily thoughtful Brian can be.

I was feeling soft toward him by the end of the night. Not that I even thought about cheating on Riley, since I remained crazy about him. But it's reassuring to know that more guys are around who are worth your time than the one you're with, given the dismal track record of most of my buds' boyfriends and husbands.

When we rose to our feet and pressed to the front of the room to listen to Riley's farewell, Brian was beside me in the crowd. He put his arms awkwardly around me while I sobbed. I wasn't so upset I didn't notice, and snuffled my thanks before we disentangled. I composed myself enough to push through the people around Riley, and wrapped him tight as I could, as though I would never let him go. He kissed me absently when at last I released him, but he held my hand as he soothed one by one each of the four hundred people encircling us.

We finally extricated ourselves and walked into the chill black night. Riley asked me to drive his car. His complexion was perfectly grey when we got home. I bundled him into bed and he slept until the next afternoon.

I had enough smarts not to start in with the "what now for Riley LaFontaine?" questions, figuring his plans would take shape in their own good time. But it was as if, after having put out immense amounts of energy and optimism for week upon week, first in contesting the nomination and then in fighting the election itself, he was drained dry. When I left for work he'd be in bed, and when I returned he evidently had spent the day on the couch watching TV. The floor beside the couch was littered with empty cookie packages and chip bags and coke cans and beer cans. He didn't seem to have the wherewithal left even to pick up after himself.

In bed, too, there was nothing there. His sex drive had shrunk to zero. "He's mourning, probably," Arlene told me. "He had a ton at stake on winning the election. He likely also needs to mourn his marriage."

"How long does this go on?" I wanted to know.

"What am I, a psychologist?" Arlene said. "Ask Riley."

After a solid week of Riley moping around, I convinced him to visit his business partner to touch base about his former job. He was sulkier than ever following that excursion. He didn't talk much, as though the plot of an episode of *Star Trek: The Next Generation* was more important than his future, our future. Finally, during a commercial, he admitted that after the issues and activities of the campaign he wasn't sure he could go back to recommending this fertilizer rather than that to a home gardener, or outlining to customers which varieties of geraniums or clematis were in stock. "You've got to do something," I pointed out. His cheeks were gaunt these days, and his mouth downcast, nothing but sad.

A few evenings later, as I tried to pry Riley's attention from the season premiere of *Xena the Warrior Princess*, a bit of anger surfaced in him. He explained with some heat that if you've been elected an MP you establish enough contacts that even if you're subsequently defeated, you can scuffle up some challenging and rewarding position. But a failed first-time candidate is a one hundred per cent nobody.

"You're not nobody," I insisted. "You're a wonderful guy. You've had some blows, no question. But you've got to pick yourself up and get on with life."

He sneered. "Put on a happy face, is that what you're telling me."

"No," I said. "That's not what I'm telling you." I took a breath. "A couple of weeks ago you were talking about us going to Ottawa to live together. Now you hardly speak to me. I know I'm no prize like being elected an MP. But wasn't hooking up with me a positive result of the campaign?"

He grunted that he guessed so, but his eyes were already flicking back to the tube. Try as I might, I couldn't get him to alter his mood, to really talk to me.

After another week of him brooding in my living room, being surly when we tried to have a conversation while we ate the dinner I cooked, and his non-performance in bed, I decided I wasn't doing Mr. Riley LaFontaine any favours by mothering him. I told him I loved him, and hated to see him like this, but the present arrangement wasn't good for either of us and he had to leave.

I had some hope that being on his own would snap him back into the awesome, loveable Riley I first knew. In the immediate aftermath of my ultimatum, as I helped him pack up his gear strewn all around my house, he did begin to make more sense than he had recently.

"Maybe I jammed into your life too soon," he suggested. "Too soon after we met. And too soon after my marriage broke up."

"You could be right," I acknowledged. "But we've got time. Maybe things will work out between us in the end."

After a week of not hearing from him, I phoned the nursery and learned he had worn out his welcome at his cousin's, too. He had asked to be bought out of his half of the operation, which his relative couldn't afford to do, so Riley had disappeared down to the coast. Nobody could say for how long. "I know he cares for you, Buzz," the cousin told me. "He's just pretty low right now. Going through a bad patch."

I was mad, though, that he'd take off without a word to me, after what I supposedly meant to him. I tried scouring the stores to distract myself, but I couldn't find anything that inspired me to replace Misty Meadow. I was blue for several days about Riley and me; I jumped every time the phone rang. One evening Arlene called him a sore loser, which for some reason struck me as humorous. Once we finished a giggling fit, she offered to fix me up with Arnold again. I knew I couldn't stomach that.

So I bided my time. The next week I had a phone call from Brian, the computer guy. He said he'd heard that Riley had left town and I was still around, and would I perhaps be interested in taking in the movie with him on Friday? Nelson only has one movie theatre, and I was aware a comedy was the current feature. I told Brian I didn't feel like dating, but it was very nice of him to ask. After we talked a while longer, I decided I *would* go with him, in case the show cheered me up. We sprinted through the rain to the Glacier Café for coffee after the film let out. By the time we said goodnight when he dropped me off at home, I was regretting I hadn't brought along my Butterscotch lip balm.

The Pleasures of the Shade

DAVID'S CHEV CRESTED A SLOPE AND BEGAN to descend. The two-lane highway was carved into a dark forest that edged near to the shoulder on both sides — mainly cedar and hemlock and fir. As the valley widened ahead, the intense fire of the July sun lifted over wooded hills. On the ridges, the uniform blur of coniferous trees was interrupted by stands of luminous yellow-green alder and birch.

He had gotten away in plenty of time. An hour or so to Arlene's house, David calculated. Breakfast there. Then load her and the children, and head south. Unless the kids aren't packed or something, we should make central Oregon by suppertime. Say, another nine hours. And late tomorrow, Disneyland. Maybe ten or eleven more hours. With Arlene to spell me off driving, this should be an easy trip. Or as easy as a drive can be with an eight- and a ten-year-old in the back. Arlene insists George and Ray can't wait to make the trip with their granddad. Of course, she's probably the one happy to have me tag along. Up to last Monday, the plan had been for her boyfriend Ted to accompany them. But he turned out unreliable as ever. Wish she'd dump him; she's worth far better. At least I know enough not to bring up that subject. Her sister made me promise, and I think she's right.

David took another sip of the coffee he had picked up at Rooster's Donuts on his route out of town. He felt the hot fluid slip down his throat and reach his chest. A sense of contentedness mixed with his excitement at being on the road. There had been a lineup as always at Rooster's, even at six on a Saturday morning. He remembered the start-of-the-day coffees with the other Hydro crews at Rooster's after seven. The place jammed and noisy with morning energy. On an ordinary shift, the Hydro guys picked up their assignments at the Wandage Road shops, signed out their vehicles, and then rendezvoused at Rooster's for the caffeine buzz that got them through to the first break at nine-thirty. He and Henry arguing across the table about hockey. Still a mystery how anybody born and raised in the West like Henry could be a Canadiens fan. Nobody else at their table could understand it, either. Henry certainly enjoyed an argument. He and Henry squared off about baseball, about public sector privatization, about immigrants.

The bulk of a chip truck loomed ahead — a tractor pulling two enormous, boxy semitrailers. The lumberyard smell of fresh-cut, wet wood streamed behind the rig. The chips were being hauled to the Castlegar pulp mill, David guessed; the weight of the load slowed the truck even on the slight grade the highway now climbed. He checked that the centre line was flashing a broken yellow stripe, glanced in his left outside mirror, and flung a double-check look over his left shoulder. Then he slipped his signal wand down and pulled out into the other lane.

The old Chev sure had plenty of power, David exulted, as he sped smoothly along the dim wall of the chip truck. The car broke into sunshine as he accelerated past the tractor and steered into the right lane again. The road rushed forward, empty in the clean morning light. What a difference between the Chev and that pig of a Hydro truck he had driven the past eight years. Ford F-700 with Lift-all boom and bucket. Henry didn't seem to mind it, but when David was at the controls he felt like he was steering a balky house. Not like the Internationals they had used before. The Ford was reluctant to react to the wheel and was unresponsive to the brakes in a manner that sometimes scared him. On this trip, Arlene had wanted them to take her clunky old station wagon. "Dad, I'm the one who promised the boys Disneyland. There's no reason for you to put the miles on your Chevy." But his car had more room and was in better shape. Obviously best for a long road trip like this. "Bigger engine means more safety," he informed Arlene, just as he'd insisted to her mother each time they went shopping for a new car. Yeah, you paid more. But you stayed alive. What was the point of me being active with the safety committee, he always told Sandra, bugging the company for improved contract language for health and safety, if I don't follow through in my home life?

He knew Arlene worried about him since Sandra died. And even more since he accepted the early retirement package in January. "Listen, I'm supposed to worry about you," he tried to straighten her out when she was over at the house last month. "You're the single mom left with two kids." And a worthless boyfriend, although David hadn't said that. "Dad," Arlene shot back, "I've got a good job at the equipment dealer's. There aren't many females selling ATVs and Ski-Doos, and everybody at work tells me I'm going to go far. I've got a nice place to live — at least I kept the house when Brian walked out. But it's less than two years since you lost Mom, and you married her when you were both kids yourselves. Plus you took the buyout from the company. What do you do with yourself all day? Which of your old crew stop by? Who of your and Mom's friends ever invite you for supper? That's why I worry. I won't even mention your health."

With Sandra gone, and the kids moved away, what was the point of staying on at Hydro? He had a good pension, which was one of the reasons for sticking with the company so long. Really, Hydro was the only job he'd had since the air force, except the one time he quit when Sandra's brother Luther talked him into being part of that construction crew. A bad move, as he quickly discovered. But Hydro had taken him back. So when they offered the buyout, he accepted. At 65, when the Canada Pension kicked in, he would be making almost as much take-home as he did dragging himself to work each day. Why work? He'd keep busy: fish in the summers, curl in the winters. He'd been on four fishing trips already this year, not counting the times he put the boat in for a few hours off Balfour. Two trips to the coast; one a fly-in to Dean Channel up by Bella Coola. Somebody was usually around who was anxious to put a line in the water — his cousin Mike, or that friend of Henry's. And Glen at the Legion was forever trying to convince him to be more serious about his golf. Wanted him to take part in the tournament at Spokane this September with the American Legion guys. Well, maybe by next summer his game would be good enough — now he had days on the course that were okay, and days that were plain embarrassing. Glen also had asked him to curl with his rink this winter. But he planned to check with Ian, the dispatcher who retired year before last, to see if *he* needed anybody. Ian knew more about curling than Glen ever would.

Arlene was just a worrier. Which was new, since the divorce. Arlene at sixteen or seventeen was fearless, bombing through the woods near Hall Siding on his snowmobile. Even a collision with a tree and a broken wrist failed to slow her down. What did she mean about his health? She's probably still dwelling on that thing in November. A fluke. Kidney stones, though everybody had been convinced at the time it was a heart attack. He had to admit the pain had been something. Sharp stabs in his gut like he'd never experienced before, sick to his stomach. His youngest, Janice, white as a sheet, on the phone for the ambulance. Janice just happened to be home from Kelowna. But he actually knew one of the ambulance guys, Bruce, who had worked for Hydro for a while two or three winters ago. Young guy, quiet and competent. He and Bruce had cracked jokes all the way into Nelson. Janice was pretty upset; the three of them crammed into the back of the ambulance. Finally she got mad while he was telling a dirty joke to Bruce. "Don't you realize how serious this is, Dad? You could *die*." So he shut up. Tears on her face. He thought he was helping by being funny through the pain. He hadn't meant to scare her. Of the two girls, Janice always had been the more emotional.

But the hospital was months behind him now. There was the diet he was supposed to follow. And he did, most of the time. He was sixty-two: young, really. Wait until he was eighty-two. Everyone said he couldn't possibly have retired, since he looked so fit. "C'mon, you won the lottery, right?" was Gwen's comment when he was introduced to her at the Legion. He liked Gwen. She was not Sandra — more outgoing, but not as deep. He asked her to the Fish & Game dance, and out for dinner a couple of times. He enjoyed talking to Gwen. Her husband had passed on. Cancer. "When you lose a spouse, you join a club you didn't know existed," she said once. Was that ever true. Sandra's absence made it hard to socialize with Larry and Eva, or any of the other couples he and Sandra had been close to. Larry and Eva were all right. But when they had him over to their place for dinner once, he caught Eva looking at him strangely — pity? He didn't need pity. He missed Sandra. But Sandra knew life went on. They had even spoken about it. He wouldn't have wanted her to dry up and stop living if he'd gone first.

A laden minivan chugged in front, canoe on the roof, three bicycles precariously tied to the rear. David went through his checks, swung out around the van, and back into his lane. As he passed, he automatically peered in: Dad at the wheel, Mom beside him kneeling with her back to the windshield to tend one of the kids in the rear seat. That family must have gotten an early start; David looked at the clock on his instrument panel: 6:45. He and Arlene and the kids would be rolling soon themselves. Anybody who passes *us* in an hour will see another family travelling somewhere.

He wasn't certain if he was serious about Gwen. "There's no rush; just let things develop, or not." That was Arlene's advice, and he agreed. Not that he asked his girls for tips on dating. But he had let them know the second time he and Gwen went out. No secrets from the girls was his policy after Sandra died. They were a much smaller family without her. Less room to hide anything. No reason to — not that there had been before. Or did he need the girls more now? Gwen was sure he did.

Arlene seemed less excited than Janice at the idea of him seeing Gwen. But then Arlene had more on her own plate. Janice wasn't very settled — a new boyfriend every time he phoned, and unable to decide whether to stay in Kelowna or move to the coast to take some course at the university. Janice nagged him about the house whenever she visited. "The place is getting run-down, Dad. Junk everywhere. Dirty dishes. The toilet and sink and tub need scrubbing. I'm not going to do it for you. These things can't wait until I get back every six months. If you don't want to keep the place tidy yourself, for God's sake hire a cleaning lady. The floors haven't been waxed or the rug vacuumed. Keeping the house in shape is important if you're going to date. Women notice these things."

He'd get to it. Yet there wasn't any urgency; nobody except family dropped by and he didn't intend to invite Gwen over anytime soon. A couple of days after he was back from Disneyland, he and his cousin were headed to the Shuswap for some fishing. They planned to take Mike's RV as well as the Chev; he'd stop in and visit Janice en route home. He probably wouldn't even see Gwen for three weeks or more, though he had promised to bring her something from Disneyland.

The highway flashed along the base of a steep ridge, squeezed between a forested slope and a creek of boulders and white water. The road here lay in deep shadow, yet David could see the sun striking the tops of evergreens at the summit of the hill that rose from the creek's other side. Then as the asphalt turned southeast, following a bend in the narrow valley, the sun blasted through a gap in the mountains directly into the windshield and David's eyes.

He clawed down the visor. He tried to remember where his sunglasses were: the glove compartment? The kitchen table at home, most likely. He could pick up a pair at the drugstore in the mall near Arlene's, if the mall was open this early. Bugs and streaks were everyplace on the windshield. He hit the washer button, and the wiper smeared a mess across his vision. By the third sweep, the windscreen was a little better. He'd do a proper job when he next filled up.

David lifted his coffee and swallowed another mouthful. He felt lightheaded. Of course, he hadn't slept much last night in anticipation of the trip. Or maybe the sensation was due to a combination of the sun hammering into his eyes and that high-octane coffee Rooster's served. He wasn't dizzy exactly: a bit logy with a slight headache. The feeling should disappear in a few moments.

He noticed the sun at its present angle coated the road in such brightness the asphalt was almost silver. Except for the centre line. The highway markings had been recently repainted after their winter punishment by snowplow blades. The stripes were a rich orange-yellow. Occasionally the precision of the lines was marred by tread marks where a tire had crossed still-wet paint.

The road ran straight into the sun. David took another sip of coffee, but put the Styrofoam down quickly as he felt a bubble of heartburn rise in his chest. Henry always said Rooster's coffee was bad for you: too strong. Yet it got you going in the morning. David decided he would be glad when the highway curved out of the brightness; he'd feel more comfortable. Hurtling into the glare was hard on his eyes without sunglasses; probably that was the cause of the burst of agony above his eyebrows — that plus his sinuses. And his head still wasn't clear. But the road showed no sign of altering direction. He couldn't fathom any impediment to vehicles passing on this long straight stretch, yet the highway markings displayed a continuous double line. Then as if the paint had been applied too thinly, the stripes became smeared, merging eventually into a misshapen linear blob rushing down the centre of the asphalt. Somebody should have caught hell for a paint job this poor.

David accelerated slightly; his physical distress did not diminish. He wondered if he should pull the Chev over to the shoulder to take a break for a minute from the sunlight battering at his eyes. He acknowledged he felt queasy — perhaps a touch of flu? In a minute the road is bound to turn, and once I'm not headed into the sun I'll be fine. He jammed his foot a half-inch further down on the accelerator. The Chev did not respond as promptly as usual. Odd. Or was it his imagination? He lifted his foot again, yet the car was sluggish about resuming its previous pace. A chill prickled the back of David's neck. Had the accelerator linkage become sticky? Was there a problem with an emission sensor? Or was his condition causing him to misjudge how the vehicle was behaving? He recalled that soon after Sandra died he became convinced the drivetrain in the bucket truck was vibrating more than it should. He could sense the increased oscillation through his boot. The mechanics claimed they couldn't find anything wrong. Eventually they told him they had serviced something in the universals, probably just to appease him.

If the Chev crapped out that would serve him right for bragging to Arlene about how reliable his car was. He imagined having to phone her and the kids to say the trip was off — or at least would have to be postponed. She's sure to suggest we drive her beater as an alternative. But I don't want to risk it. Too far. A jolt of anger pulsed through him. Why would the damn car choose to screw up *now*? He was aware how pleased he had been when Arlene had asked him to accompany her, had needed him to, when Ted bailed on this trip.

Adrenaline flooded his body, followed by an urgent caution to himself: *Stay calm.* His foot nudged the pedal again. This time the Chev reacted as it was supposed to. But when he lifted his shoe, the car did not reduce speed. As in a dream. Or was he on a downhill grade, the descent masked by the angle of the slope the highway cut through here? Whatever the situation, it wasn't right.

A stitch of severe pain at the top of his stomach caused David to gasp. He struggled momentarily to catch a breath. The road thrummed under his tires. He exhaled with caution around the agony in his gut, then inhaled even more tentatively, as if lungs and diaphragm might detonate at any instant.

He clutched at the wheel as much for support as to guide the vehicle. In the speeding car, he felt a surge of dread, exactly as he had experienced in the whitecaps on Slocan Lake last September. He had been canoeing by himself, aiming north toward the beach at Evans Creek when a storm arose. Despite strenuous efforts with his paddle, the canoe was shoved more than ninety degrees from where he had been pointed. He tried three times to bring the bow around, digging as deeply and furiously into the chop as he could. On each attempt the flat hands of wind and water heaved him southwestward toward the rocky shore instead. He felt helpless in the grip of forces that regarded him as less than insignificant, that in fact did not consider him at all.

David stared desperately through the windshield. Ahead, he saw the route vanished into black. At last a rock bluff, or hillside above the asphalt, provided an escape from the pounding sunshine. Whatever the cause, an edge of darkness crossed the highway in the rapidly-decreasing distance: fierce brilliance on this side of the line, a tunnel of shade on the other.

Hope sparked in David. The wall blocking the light was very close. Perhaps the car's malfunctioning and the searing pressure below his ribs and behind his forehead were indeed a result of the sun smashing into his eyes. The hood of the vehicle entered the dark that cascaded over David like a wave of well-being, relief. He waited to feel his pains ease. The car glided effortlessly in the shadow. His hand shook as he raised his cup to his lips and drank.

Ducks in a Row

WHO COULD HAVE THOUGHT I WOULD CHAIR a meeting initiated, and attended, by Paul McCartney — *Sir* Paul McCartney — formerly of the Beatles? Nelson, BC, where I live, ordinarily is far under the radar of the monied and famed, though the town's setting on Kootenay Lake deep in the Selkirk Mountains is duly spectacular. Perhaps because of the area's scenic remoteness, our settlement of nine thousand souls *has* attracted more than its share of artistic types to reside hereabouts. One American travel guide even termed the place "Canada's best little arts town."

The awarding of such a label was much to the delight of the Nelson and District Arts Council, who trumpeted the news in any ear they could, and was much to the annoyance of the Baker Street Boys, that informal coalition of main street store owners and real estate tycoons who consider themselves the civic kingmakers or breakers and policy yea- or nay-sayers. Baker Street regards the arts as a lower life form than the lamprey eel, albeit they adjudge artists as sharing the identical level of parasitism.

The Chamber of Commerce isn't united around Baker Street's views, though. A significant bunch of Nelson's merchants depend on tourism for their livelihood, and no travel promo can be all bad. A dollar from an artistically-inclined bank account remarkably resembles that from a golfer's or from a back-country ski nut's or from somebody's with a yearning to fish Kokanee salmon out of Kootenay Lake.

Baker Street wrestles with the same dilemma around *eco*-tourism. The main street mafia are mostly old money, convinced that municipal and personal wealth originates from cutting down and milling every stick of standing timber, damming any river capable of yielding a megawatt, and digging deep into each ridge that promises to surrender a bucket of ore — ore wrested either from veins or from tailing piles by technology unavailable during the mining boom-and-bust of the 1890s that brought white folks to this region of southeastern BC in the first place. Once you've got bucks flowing in from resources, then you can offer hotels, hot water tanks, haircuts or whatever else the practitioners of industry demand.

Hard to argue with the economics of that. Of course, as the twentieth century clanged and groaned to a stop and the twenty-first uneasily lurched into gear, primary resources were looking a mite pasty. The logging companies were hauling pecker-poles to the mills, since any trees of size had long since become two-by-fours. The dams were generating money, but once the construction booms finished, precious few electrodollars were sticking around the valleys where they were born. And despite the newest extraction and smelting processes, the pursuit of lead and zinc and silver no longer netted anything near the impressive sums of a century ago.

Instead, along came geeks who wished to gawk at peaks, or to kayak in the parks, or to tramp through the ever-dwindling forest cover. This sort of visitor was opposed to anybody who shot bears, stocked the alpine lakes with sporty trout or developed jumbo ski resorts. But such misinformed and misguided urbanites scattered behind them — down Baker Street, as well as throughout its environs — a trail of coin of the Realm, US Jacksons, Deutsche euros, and yen.

All you could do if you were one of the Baker Street Boys — and Girls, I better add — was suck wind and accept the moolah whatever its origin. But you didn't have to say anything positive about the experience. Unless your business catered to such weenies. Sound like a town divided? Absolutely. Why would Paul McCartney — Sir Paul — want to have any truck with such a place?

"He's coming *here*? You've got to be joking," was how I phrased my incredulity to the president of the arts council when she phoned me. Madam President, Gail Emerson, is somebody I admire, if you can imagine me admiring anyone. She's a single mom, early forties, a veritable whirlwind of energy. She and her former husband moved here in the mid-eighties to open a B&B. When the marriage imploded, she and some girlfriends started a craft gallery, the Golden Osprey, on — wait for it — Baker Street. The G.O. Gallery was successful until the landlord — my dentist, as it turns out — thought he could scoop some of their hard-won lucre by boosting the rent. That pushed the G.O. under. Quite the scandal, since by this time Gail was a mover and shaker in the Chamber of Commerce and Rotary, and quoted in the local paper about every third day as spokesperson for some civic commission or other. But Gail never missed a beat: within six months she launched a coffee bar, Bean There, that caught the cappuccino tsunami when it finally swept this far into the Interior.

Through all her personal downs and ups, she was steadfast in her support of the city's potters, painters, weavers, fine woodworkers, authors, sculptors, metalworkers. And jewellers, jewellers, how could I forget? My wife Mary is a representative of the latter species; in fact, I met her at the kick-off of a show of hers at the G.O. Dreadful stuff, as I pointed out to Mary that night: her bracelets, necklaces and broaches looked as if they were crafted by somebody from the Bauhaus on acid. She forgave my aesthetics, I forgave her design sense, and we've gotten on like a house on fire ever since. But that long-ago opening, and how Gail uses even the Bean There to promote the region's artistes, are among the reasons I have a soft spot for Madam President.

When Gail asked me to sit on the arts council, I accepted after the usual demurrers. "You'll be there to represent the faculty at the art school," she said, once we completed the oh-I-couldn't, yes-you-could dance. "And by extension, you'll speak for art education generally."

"I don't represent anything but myself," I told her. "Never have, never will. I get into less trouble that way."

"You're the president of the faculty and staff union, Bill, for God's sake," Gail said.

"I'll tell you what I tell them," I countered. "I'm elected to carry out their wishes. Once they've discussed an issue and voted, I do what they tell me. Now, I've got opinions, same as everybody else — "

"You're kidding," Gail interjected. "You?"

"I'll ignore your feeble effort at sarcasm, in light of previous good behaviour. My point is I don't speak on the union's behalf unless our members have had a chance to determine what their 'behalf' is. I won't act any different on your arts council."

"Done," Gail said.

She's the ideal chairperson for the group, since she has a foot in both the business world — or rather, worlds — and the artistic whirl — or whirls. For the so-called arts community isn't any more together than their avowed arch-opponents, the only-in-it-for-a-buck crowd.

I don't refer just to our artistes' personal jealousies, rivalries, backstabbing, gossip and hate. Psychology assures us the less a person has to lose, the larger the smallest matter looms. No, I mean our creative types were unable to unite to prevent the disappearance in the 1980s of a summer festival of the arts that had operated for decades. They let one very competent woman burn herself out putting the festival together year after year after year, and when she fried to a crisp and moved on all they could do was whimper and whine. Also, they've still never even managed to win public support for a decent civic art gallery.

The problem is, as I tell my Professional Practices class — much to my students' annoyance and dismay — most artists are losers with a capital "L". Artists declare that, because they're not good at things most people are competent at and value, the arts have a unique perspective: a different and hence, perhaps, maybe, dare one say it? *superior* vision. But even if we grant that unlikely scenario, does possession of an enhanced vision automatically exempt artists from having to earn a living?

What an artist creates certainly may have worth immeasurable in mere dollars. It may not, too, but that's another story. Let's say a painting or pot *is* a pearl beyond price. That still begs the question of who pays for the creator's food, shelter, and duds. Church, state and the wealthy in various eras have been conned into agreeing they ought to shell out. But all three have been notoriously fickle providers in the long haul, as well as inconsistent judges of who best to reward.

That leaves the artist face to face eventually with that soulless monster, the market. Most artistes flee screaming at the sight. Others try half-heartedly to reach an accommodation with the beast. A pitiful few have a great relationship with Wallet World. Most artists, though, are failures as business people. They have a product they want their fellow citizens to purchase and treasure, but the population is unswayed. You'd think, as a result, artists would decide that successful business people might have something to teach them, just as artists are unshakably convinced they have a lot to teach business people — along with the rest of the human race.

My pitch is that the artistic milieu isn't as remote from the grubby world of buying and selling as artists like to imagine. I don't know if it works the other way. But argue with me long enough, and I may grudgingly concede that art offers a bigger and more rewarding experience of being alive than mere getting and spending does. Could all sides have more reasons for respecting each other than they think? You can see why my students' not-so-secret nickname for me is "Dollar Bill".

I've been on Gail's arts council three years now, and since my attitude aligns closer to hers than most members', I'm never surprised when she is on the phone with a scheme she wants to bounce off me, or she needs to vent about the latest machination of some faction either of the commercialistas or our resident artistes. But Paul McCartney?

"The mayor just phoned me," Gail said. "McCartney's office contacted him."

"I'm amazed they've heard of Nelson."

"Me, too. But you know McCartney's doing this continent-wide series of feedback sessions. Apparently, we're on the list."

"Unbelievable." I'd heard on CBC radio and read in the paper about Paul's plan to solicit public opinion on a musical project. His idea was to record a CD of a selection of Beatles songs with himself playing and singing all the parts. He claimed he had Ringo's okay, John and George of course were out of it, but Paul was sensitive to the abiding devotion Beatles fans have to the original tunes. His aim was to set up a series of public meetings in England and across North America to elicit input on the rerecording concept from "ordinary people," as the news items had it.

Critics were quick to slam the notion of seeking feedback as simply advance PR for the album, or McCartney attempting to augment his personal popularity — or obtain an ego boost — at the expense of the artistic achievement of the Fab Four. Paul countered by saying the meetings would be low-key and minimally publicized, because he really wished to know what fans and even non-Beatles-aficionados thought. If majority opinion was against the rerecording, he insisted, he'd shelve the idea.

Television's and the tabloids' attention span concerning the project expired in a few days, when the latest marriage, infidelity or divorce of somebody called Jen or Julia or Brad became the newest achievement of the human race. A week afterwards, one of my Professional Practices students brought up McCartney's announcement. I'd been in the midst of my classroom shtick about the need for artists to understand as much as they can about marketing, even if they have contempt for it. My example was how when long-playing records — thirty-three-and-a-thirds — were invented, record company executives were positive the major use for LPs would be for classical music: you could get an entire symphony on one disc instead of three or four. That consideration led us to pop music and pop culture, and art's interactive relationship with these. I'd eloquently stressed that while pop culture is scorned in some quarters, there are certainly as many bad *fine* artists as bad *recording* artists.

In reply to the student's query about Sir Paul, I said I applauded his idea but wasn't advocating poll-driven art — no pun intended. I paused to let them figure that out, and a few gratifyingly groaned.

If an artist means to engage the public with his or her cultural product, I continued, it can't hurt to discover what ordinary folks' initial reaction is likely to be. As I recall, I praised McCartney's decision not to announce in advance which cities he'd be visiting, so he could field-test opinion removed from the glare of the media. The thought he'd choose Nelson didn't enter my mind.

"You sure this isn't a hoax?" I questioned Gail. "Mayor Hadley isn't known for a sense of humor. But some of his cronies may have put him up to yanking your chain."

Gail sighed. "I admit it sounds far-fetched. But he gave me the phone number of McCartney's North American tour organizer. The arts council is supposed to come up with somebody to chair the meeting."

"Shouldn't that be the mayor? Welcome Paul to our fair city, and all that?"

"McCartney's people are requesting a lower level of civic involvement. Less hype the better, or something. They want to work through cultural commissions or community arts organizations. Mayor Hadley tossed the ball to us."

"Maybe His Honour has never heard of the Beatles?"

"Don't be snarky, Bill. My guess is that whoever spoke to Mayor Hadley radiated corporate smoothness. I can't imagine McCartney's organization being anything other than slick. You know how the mayor responds to that sort of approach."

Our esteemed civic chief executive is proprietor of Hadley's Paint and Flooring. He also owns — besides a low-end apartment building tenanted in part by suspiciously artistic types — a couple of downtown buildings rented by avid members of his Business Coalition for a Better Community. The BCBC was an ad hoc municipal political organization that supported his bid for election on a platform of making the streets safe for strip malls. Douglas R. Hadley's first term was marked by a number of the usual municipal scandals — a secret deal to sell a portion of Lakeside Park to provide additional parking for Nelson's big-box discount store, and awarding the contract to reno city hall to one of the mayor's major financial backers. His Honour and the slate of councillors elected with him courted every fast food franchise not already promoting the acquisition of arterio-sclerosis by the local citizenry, and traveled a certain distance down a slippery incline toward public monetary assistance for a swanky resort and conference centre to be constructed just across the bridge out of town. Even the mayor's Baker Street buddies were not amused by the last, since it would draw business away from downtown, and they quickly put paid to that scam.

I confess I *have* heard Mayor Hadley say the word "art". He was interviewed by CBC at a meeting of Interior mayors not long after Nelson got named the "best little arts town." The motherhood question he and the other mayors were answering was, "Why would anyone want to live in your great city?" The mayor produced the customary, Chamber of Commerce-approved list: abundant-natural-resources-quality-of-life-open-to-investment-tourism-huntin'-and-fishin'. Then he added, "There's also, uh, art." Yet, in spite of all the artistic folks domiciled hereabouts, His Honour Hadley got reelected two years ago by a forty per cent margin. *Somebody* voted for him. .

"I can't believe Hadley is passing up the chance to schmooze Paul," I said. "How often do you get to convene a meeting in the presence of a person more important than Jesus?"

"I think John said the Beatles as a *group* were better-known than Jesus," Gail corrected me. "Anyway, Paul has rejected the mayor. That leaves us."

"You nervous about chairing?" I asked. "It's quite an honour. I hope I'm allowed to attend. What a gas to see one of the Beatles up close."

"I'm not the right person to chair, Bill," Gail said. She paused, and the pause continued several seconds too long.

"Forget it," I stated. "Absolutely not. No way." The thought of being in the spotlight, as it were, in the very presence of Paul McCartney terrified me.

"You're better than I am at public meetings," Gail replied. "I'm okay in committee-sized groups. But the mayor says they want a hundred or more people present. That's not my style."

"You're the chair of the arts council. It's your job."

"My job is to improve the climate for the arts in Nelson and district. That means figuring out what's best for the arts community. Having you chair the meeting, on behalf of area artists, is putting our best foot forward. I know you're excellent at chairing the union meetings at the art school. Everybody tells me so."

"Say, that could be a line from a song."

"Don't try to change the subject, Bill."

"Don't try to butter me up. Nobody could do an adequate job chairing a union meeting attended mainly by artists."

"That's not what I hear. Also, I've seen how you handle the crowd at the art auction fundraisers the past couple of years. You have them eating out of your palm."

"Liar. Martin is the auctioneer, and he's the one who keeps them happy. I just call the ragtag and bobtail to order, and wrap up when Martin has hauled in the loot."

"You intervene constantly to keep things moving and everybody laughing."

"People are already in a good mood at the auctions. Who knows what the meeting with McCartney is going to be like?"

"Exactly. I'm too stilted a chair." Gail's comment surprised me. Her approach is a tad formal for my taste, but she can keep an agenda from becoming sidetracked or stalled. "We need somebody who can roll with the punches," Gail went on. "Here's where you earn the big bucks you get for serving on the arts council."

"Big bucks? We're volunteers. We're not paid a dime."

"Nor should you be. City hall realizes that money can't buy you love."

"Gail — "

"Bill," her tone was earnest, "you're the right person. We both know the kooks come out of the woodwork at any public meeting. At this one, with an opportunity to rub shoulders with a world-class superstar, the Kootenay eccentrics will be out in force." Her voice took on the sharpness of command, her full-blown Madam President authority. "You're better with a crowd than I am. I'm not budging on this."

I chewed Gail's request over for a few lengthy moments and concluded: *What the hell. Everybody needs a little adventure in life.* "Okay, "I told her. "I cave. Despite my innumerable misgivings. But you owe me, big. What precisely are the arrangements for this deal? When is it supposed to happen? I need a lot more info."

"I have the number for McCartney's organization in New York, courtesy of the mayor. I'm sure they'll fill you in. And thanks, Bill, really. You'll do a terrific job. Don't worry. Remember: all you need is love."

Throughout the next week I became increasingly anxious, as my brain registered what I had agreed to. McCartney's people and I played telephone tag for a couple of days. Meanwhile, I tripped out repeatedly on the image: Paul McCartney and me in the very same room. Not only occupying the same room, but me shaking hands with him, talking to him one-on-one. Then introducing him: "And now, right here in Nelson, the man who requires no introduction, a living icon, a genius of words and music, the embodied spirit of a generation, I give you, on behalf of the Nelson and District Arts Council, with great pride, Sir Paul McCartney." Wild sustained cheers and applause. And the extro: "Paul has left the building. Thank you, and good night." No, wait; that's been done.

A few times at the dinner table, or in bed supposedly reading before lights out, I came to and found my wife staring at me quizzically. "Hel-*lo*. Anybody home? Are you all right, Bill? You seem a little . . . absent."

"Just having a brush with celebrity, dear."

Mary undertook a big show of checking all around the room. "Who? Where? I don't see anybody." Her eyes narrowed. "You might just be losing it."

"Common folk like yourself probably aren't capable of understanding the mental environment of we jet-setters," I sighed.

Mary snorted. "No question you're the embodiment of the elite. You teach design, technical drawing, and professional practices at a second-rate art school in the middle of nowhere. And you haven't been on a jet since we flew to Toronto to visit my family two summers ago."

"Besides enduring the paparazzi, our sort are used to petty quibbles from the unwashed masses," I informed her. "However, if you display toward me the groveling respect to which I am entitled, I will let you afterwards touch the very hand that shook the hand of Paul McCartney."

"Fat chance. I think you should act your age," was all she could muster as a response.

But in fact, the promise of a close encounter with a Beatle had reawakened memories of my participation in Beatlemania during my youth. I was raised on the Coast in Vancouver, a nine hour drive west from Nelson. Yet the first occasion I heard those immortal lyrics *Yeah, yeah, yeah,* they were pouring out of a café jukebox in Squamish up Howe Sound, north of the city. The Scout troop I belonged to was driving back from a weekend camping trip in the Rubble Creek area below the Black Tusk alpine meadows. An older boy in our troop explained to me who the Beatles were. At that point, the mop-tops were just another new rock and roll band.

By the time they were first booked to play Vancouver, however, they had become a phenomenon. My high school friends and I weren't able to buy tickets — either because the concert was sold out or we lacked the money; I can no longer recall. But we resonated in our own way to the excitement that gripped the city at the presence of the Liverpudlian quartet. One of my pals was working that summer at the airport, and he wrangled permission for us to visit the control tower so we could witness from this vantage point the Beatles' departure by chartered aircraft. What we saw was identical to any other small passenger jet trundling down the runway. No other takeoff, though, would induce a group of young men to concoct elaborate arrangements just to stare at such an apparently mundane occurrence.

I was always a Beatles fan, rather than preferring the Stones — as many in the youthful Vancouver art scene did. Contemporaries of mine found the Stones edgier, weirder, more in-your-face. But the Beatles were musicians for all seasons, every state of being; they had plenty of rebellious lyrics, but also tunes that matched or augmented the shifting moods of restlessness, attraction, bliss, and heartbreak that are love's spectrum.

I was living in a co-op house in the city's East End when *Sgt. Pepper* was released. Bubble gum music in the years before and since may have grossed more dollars, yet never previously or afterwards have I encountered an album that gripped an entire demographic as a cultural experience to the extent that *Sgt. Pepper* did. People I knew talked of nothing but that music week after week. The house I shared was rented by a mix of my friends, some from the Vancouver College of Art working summer jobs and others with no particular artistic bent who had already entered the city's work force. All were heads. And the whole household was awakened that August at six-thirty each morning when Murray, who was employed on a night shift of a Fraser River tugboat, returned home, toked up, and put the album on, loud. People remonstrated with him about his insistence on rousing the house's inhabitants in this manner, day after day after day. Dawn arrived awfully early for the rest of us at the co-op, following the smoky, music-filled nights. But Murray, who was larger than two or three of us art school wimps put together, would just give anyone who stumbled out of bed to complain a stoner's beneficent grin. He would suck down another blast of sweet herb, and lean his head even closer to the living room's giant speakers. His actions implied that, as far as he was concerned, he was fixing a hole where the rain got in and stopped his mind from wandering. And that it didn't really matter if he was wrong or right.

Ah, youth. Soon it'll be *twice* twenty years ago today since that time.

Paul's people were all business and no nostalgia, however. "Who's this, then?" was barked at me when a secretary finally transferred me through to the guy on the tour team I was supposed to confer with. The voice sounded as young as we were in 1967, but in rampant possession of, besides a low-class English accent, an MBA, if not an MBE. And of considerable attitude. I had to enumerate my credentials as prospective chair of the Nelson session, and the voice balked at my mention of the union presidency. "This can't be sponsored by a bleeding *union*," he said, his vocal tones curling into a sneer I could visualize all the way from New York. "It isn't," I told him. "You asked me who I was, and why the arts council put my name forward. Since I obviously don't meet your lofty qualifications, I'm out of here. Great talking to you."

"Now, now, mate. Don't be 'asty," he soothed. "We arf to check these things out, don't we? Paul wants everything smooth, you dig?"

We interacted a little better after that. He outlined the parameters of the meeting. A hundred and fifty people max. A hundred tickets for the general public, in response to a single ad that would be placed in the local paper. Word of mouth would carry the message further. The arts council could invite up to fifty of their own choosing. We were urged to remember the purpose of the assembly, and to invite accordingly. A mix of ages was essential. "And Paul wants real people. No music pedants, aldermen's wives, or fooking cultural theorists." Attendees could ask questions, but no speeches. Order had to be maintained by the chair, or Paul and company were gone. Assuming things went tickety-boo, once I as chair deemed comments from the floor had run out of juice, the meeting would take a show-of-hands vote. The session would be videotaped. Paul would be the last into the room, first to leave. No press interviews. Paul donates $1,000 US to the sponsoring body, in this case the arts council.

I had drawn up a list of procedural and logistical questions: who rents the hall? Sound system? Who handles security? Where does Sir Paul sit, relative to the podium? The more details I nailed down, the friendlier the guy I was talking to sounded. "You do seem on tawp of it, mate," he said. "That's what our Paulie likes, he does. Everything smooth." Then I insisted that three pieces of paper be duplicated and available to the audience the moment they walked in: an agenda, the ground rules for the meeting spelled out, and an unequivocal statement of the question McCartney wanted people to respond to.

The guy hemmed and hawed at providing paper. One of Paul's staff would present the issue verbally. I maintained that the paper I requested was non-negotiable. My experience was that such paper was a means to ensure the Nelson gathering ran without a hitch. "Isn't that what you tell me Sir Paul wants?"

I have no idea if anybody else has discovered an initial distribution of printed information is a requirement for an effective meeting these days. People are less and less print-oriented. Probably TV is the cause; from what I've read, the one-eyed stupefier has decidedly reduced concentration abilities. My students suffer from the syndrome a little more each semester. One consequence is a superstitious respect for handouts.

No one will actually read them, but handouts function as talismans among the functionally illiterate. Existing within a chaotic world of jump-cuts and unprocessed bits of disconnected information, televictims appear to find reassurance in clutching a sheet of paper that displays writing they are told encapsulates their immediate situation. Sort of a *TV Guide* for reality. Their damaged intellects will continue to skip and hop as if from clip to sound bite while they fade in and out of paying attention. But their possession of a few pages of orderly words suggests to them that somebody has organized the surrounding swirl of impressions with the intent to entertain them, amuse them, even benefit them.

That's why whether I conduct a class, or chair a union meeting, I like to have all my ducks in a row beforehand. People who attend are going to be provided with a veritable stack of dead trees, which — to mix a few metaphors — serve as islands of solid ground on which the recipients' minds can stand amid the soggy, quicksand-filled swamp that constitutes the world as perceived by most of them. As I've said, the handouts won't be *read* by those who pick them up: folks enrolled in the class or who show up at the meeting might scan the sheets of paper or surf them for as long as they are capable of focusing on a topic — mere microseconds, in most cases. But the relief in the room once the handouts are distributed is tangible. I've observed there is much less tendency for attendees to act out or wander off track, and we can go forward with fewer distractions, irrelevancies, or displays of mental meltdown.

Our union meetings at the art school involve faculty whose disconnect from consistent thought processes can be traced to their artistic proclivity, as much as to behavioural telemodification. Whatever the cause, I make certain that when a member of our local enters the designated room, they walk past a table offering piles of the agenda, minutes of the previous meeting, copies of correspondence, reports, and draft motions. So when the member sits, grasping all this paper, what's left of their brain has begun to direct their erratic mental activity to a tiny extent toward the task at hand.

I don't mean to exaggerate the benefits of advance preparation. Colleagues of mine remain complete wackos. We'll be in the middle of hot and heavy debate regarding some concern, when one of our potters, Wilbur Carson, will blurt out an utterance like "I move we Wednesday." I've learned over time that there *is* a convoluted logic behind Wilbur's staggeringly nonsensical suggestions. If you can induce him to follow the bouncing ball back through the maze of short-circuiting connections inside his malformed cerebral lobes, his pronouncements are not one hundred per cent off the wall. Perhaps, for example, he has been thinking of some activity the administration, or his department, or even he himself does every Wednesday — or did one Wednesday — and his motion was intended to propose that the bargaining unit do the same.

So I'll stress again that having my ducks in a row before a union meeting doesn't guarantee the absence of confusion, disorder and folly. As crazed as our gatherings can become, however, before I began to chair them they used to be as scattered and out of control as the perceptions ricocheting within the protuberances atop some of my union brothers' and sisters' necks. We continually repeat to our students that creativity lies in thinking outside the box. In order to model such belief, some of my colleagues have removed their thoughts from the vicinity of the box to such a distance that, not only is the box no longer discernible, the faculty member is unable any longer to recollect where the box originally was or how it appeared.

Given what I endure as chair of our bargaining unit, I was determined to be as ready as I could for the public's proximity to Paul McCartney. I've been a resident of Nelson for nearly twenty years. My nightmare was that the most loosey-goosey union meeting would seem, in comparison to the feedback event, a performance by a military precision drill squad.

When the small ad appeared in the *Nelson Daily News* inviting people to secure a ticket from city hall, rumors about what Paul's visit would or wouldn't involve flared, mutated and blazed again through the populace. McCartney's advance team, though, when they appeared, were consummate professionals. The assembly was scheduled for a Thursday evening, in a large second storey space they selected above a row of Baker Street stores. The place, now vacant, had been used most recently as a fitness studio. Paul's crew conferred with the Nelson cops for security, and even hired a few off-duty Mounties. The arts council arranged the sound system. All of us in the official party had around-the-neck picture ID, as at a convention. A rehearsal was held on the Tuesday night so the team and I were crystal clear about procedures. Sound and lighting checks assured us the audio and video technology was functional. Once attendees were checked off the list by security at the door, they would be invited to pick up a copy of the agenda, ground rules, and description of the question Paul wanted addressed, as I had asked. Paul's people had reproduced this material on different colours of paper, which I thought was a nice touch.

I didn't sleep much Wednesday night. But I lie awake before our union meetings, too, reviewing the agenda we've devised and speculating what can possibly go wrong. I acknowledged that I was more keyed up about the McCartney session than I had been since the earliest days of our local: the original certification vote, for example.

On Thursday, I was at the appointed spot a good three-quarters of an hour early for a last-minute check, and to stand by the door to joke around with people I knew as they entered. One of the most useful insights I discovered as union president is that a meeting begins the moment somebody walks in the door, not the moment the opening gavel descends. Thirty minutes spent schmoozing with early-comers before the start time is worth any amount of desperate pleas for order once the entire venture jumps the rails.

Nearly every seat was taken by five minutes to eight, an unusual occurrence in these parts. Nelson is known for running on "Kootenay time", meaning that people are habitually late to everything. I've heard the town described as "Mexican, but without the climate." I couldn't tell whether people's promptness boded good or ill.

Sharp at eight I strode up to the podium, accompanied by a few good-natured catcalls from friends. I did the welcome and reviewed the agenda and the guidelines for how the session would unfold. One of Paul's bunch summarized the sheet everybody had been given concerning the desired focus of the evening. The audience was bristling with expectation, as is customary at the very start of a meeting.

McCartney not yet having shown, I drew the room's attention to the presence of Gail, who had arrived with the mayor, and then of His Honour himself. Some young folks toward the back started to jeer the latter.

"Buskers rule," one shouted. The town's youth had been particularly incensed by a recent city council decision to ban street musicians. These musicians included — or the bylaw may have been aimed directly at — groups of kids who had taken to hanging around the amenity benches on Baker Street pounding for hours on drums, to the annoyance of the majority of merchants within range. At the McCartney gathering, three or four youngsters suddenly initiated a ragged chant: "Buskers rule. Buskers rule." I could sense the tension in the room escalate by the increasing rustle of people's bodies shifting to stare, plus urgent whisperings.

Perfect, I thought. *Sir Paul is going to walk smack dab into the midst of Nelson airing its dirty intergenerational laundry.* I put my mouth close to the microphone. "You know," I said as slowly and distinctly as I could, the PA overriding the chant. "I wonder what the buskers' rule *is*? I mean, I know the golden rule, but what's the buskers' rule?" That got a big laugh, as anything uttered to loosen a sticky public moment will. A joke, no matter how lame, will carry the day at these junctures; people mostly don't want trouble. I could see the mayor scowling at me. But the chanting died away; would His Honour have preferred I let the kids keep scourging him? I spoke into the mic again, attempting to keep my voice as yo-ho-ho hearty as I could. "I've always thought the buskers' rule was to relax, entertain people, and . . . let's all have a good time." That got a swell of noisy applause and laughter; I could see shoulders loosen and faces light up. At that instant, Sir Paul and a half-dozen outriders walked into the room.

My first impression was identical to the comment everybody blurts: "He's a lot smaller in person than I expected." Then he was beside me up at the podium, and I was being introduced to him by one of his entourage. Our hands clasped: I was shaking hands with Paul McCartney.

I stepped deferentially back, and Sir Paul said a few words of thanks to the crowd. The room was noiseless with awe. I *think* it was awe; maybe in the secret recesses of people's brains they didn't really believe Paul McCartney would appear in a second-storey former fitness centre in downtown Nelson, BC. That hypothesis would account for the pervasive silence in the room as originating from a state of shock.

Sir Paul seated himself in the front row to my left, two chairs in from the aisle for a quick getaway if needed. His was one of a cluster of seats marked "Reserved" at that end of the first and second rows. A few beefy types in his employ sat to his left and right, and behind him. He was thus surrounded on three sides by his people, just in case. I invited members of the audience who wished to speak to approach the floor mics — we had two, one in the centre aisle and one in the aisle to my right. A small lineup formed behind each mic, I pointed to the centre aisle's, and we were off.

For about forty minutes I was proud of everybody. The responders were unanimously supportive of Sir Paul's project. They lauded the Beatles' achievements and offered amusing anecdotes, often hilarious, about how individual songs had had vast significance in their loves and lives. The consensus was that Sir Paul's CD would not undercut or diminish all the Fab Four had accomplished, but would be a recasting and thus a renewal, a freshening of the power of the group's magical lyrics and music. Only one person asked a question whose answer was provided on a handout — the intended release date for the CD, should McCartney decide to proceed. Several folks seated by the mic called out the information before the guy finished his dumb inquiry. He retired in confusion, chased by some amiable ribbing.

A few latecomers had slipped in, mostly younger types, but they weren't disruptive about locating the few vacant chairs and settling down. One hugely-bearded fellow, a guitarist who sometimes plays in the lounge at the Hume Hotel, asked something horribly technical about the anticipated recording procedures. He sounded sincere, though. Like everyone else, I've frequently heard a question at a public occasion that translates as: "You and I know more than the rubes here, don't we, famous person?" Yet our Beardy seemed genuinely curious. I doubted if this technical a subject was within the realm of requested audience response, but I looked over at the McCartney cluster to see if they had any visual clues regarding how they wanted me to deflect this. To my surprise, Sir Paul rose and, after asking my permission — asking *my* permission — took over the podium for two or three minutes and had a little chat with the dude at the mic on these abstruse details. Sir Paul was extremely gracious about the exchange, always careful to explain to the crowd in layman's terms what he and Beardy were on about. A great hand of applause escorted Sir Paul back to his seat.

The energy in the room altered after that, regrettably. For a minute or so nobody was up at the mics. Then the loon parade began. I've noticed this shift during our union meetings, too. At best, people can hold it more or less together for forty or forty-five minutes. Agenda items are dealt with briskly, good suggestions and contributions arise from many sources, including some unexpected ones. Then the bubble of rationality pops, the air leaks out of the sanity balloon. Troublesome folks awaken. Keeping the meeting thereafter to the point under consideration becomes a tough slog. It's *weirdo* time.

A young woman with stringy hair, dressed in baggy skateboard attire, reached up to try to adjust the mic. The sound system had excellent omnidirectional pickups and nobody to date had needed to fool with them — the audio carried fine. During my explanation of this to her, her efforts to yank the mic here and there produced grating bangs and whines and crackles over the PA. Even as I was attempting to induce her to desist, I realized I'd seen her before in the art school's hallowed halls. One of ours.

"Wow, like, there are such cool vibes here, aren't there?" she began, her voice strident. "Having Paul McCartney in Nelson, I mean, wow, way cool." The crowd laughed uneasily at her enthusiasm. "I've been, like, sitting here? I just *had* to write a poem about how all this is, like . . . just, *wow.*" She raised a vibrating piece of paper — the back of one of my handouts, of course.

"All of us came
Through the mountain dark night
To this place,
To be with the trees
and bears and
the water, to speak
together, to be one
in the presence of one
who came to us, here

in the mountain dark night
to — "

"Excuse me," I broke in. "We appreciate your, uh, poem. But this meeting was called for a specific purpose, so we have to limit discussion to —"

"I'm almost done.
In the mountain night
a great spirit, Paul,
came to our spirit, our — "

"No, no," I cut her off. "I was very clear at the start of the meeting: no statements."

"Huh?"

"You were told that discussion is confined to only the topic at hand. I'm going to ask you to sit down."

"I'm just, like, sharing what I feel."

"I'm sure you are," I stated. "But that's not the purpose of this meeting. Didn't you hear what was said at the beginning?"

"I came in late."

"Please sit down, and let somebody speak to the matter we're here to consider."

She flipped me the bird. "*Fuck* you."

A red burst of rage detonated in my head. I try to anticipate every eventuality I can; I strive to ensure that a meeting is free of glitches, that it functions responsibly, professionally. Then an inflated ego like this feels entitled to drift in, me-me-me all over the place, and screw things up. Part of me yearned to abandon the podium, race down the aisle, grip my hands around her startled neck and choke the life out of her. Another part of me urged me not to think badly of the afflicted, to stay calm, don't respond in kind, take the high ground.

A buzz of agitated talk lifted over the assembly as Ms. Poet flounced back to her chair. Before lowering herself to her seat, she announced something in harsh tones to those around her I couldn't catch. A tall, thin young man with dreadlocks floated toward the mic.

He turned his head to where Ms. Poet was sulking. "Hey, Raven Girl, that poem was awesome. Thank you for sharing."

Then he addressed all of us. "Hey, I don't even *know* what we're supposed to be doing here; I came in late, too." He giggled briefly. "I just want to say to Paul: you're awesome. This is so cosmic, having you here. It's like a kind of — "

I could see where this was going, or more exactly, not going. "No off-topic statements, remember? All of us are delighted, I'm sure, that Mr. McCartney chose Nelson as a place to sample public opinion. But I'm going to ask you either to speak to the point, or move away from the microphone."

"Huh? What?"

"Do you have a comment about Mr. McCartney's proposal? Otherwise, please sit down so that others who wish to — "

Mr. Cosmic scowled at me. "I don't know what trip you're on, man. You should run for fucking *mayor*."

A few yells of agreement rose from the seats around Ms. Poet. One of Nelson's street artists, currently calling himself Wicca, replaced my dreadlocked one-man nominating committee. Wicca is a Sixties relic whose head sports a two foot sphere of shaggy hair and a three foot spray of beard, both grey.

"Paul," he began, "you probably don't know it, man, but there's a *reason* you came to Nelson. See, this area may appear to be nothing but mountains, but actually — "

"Again, please keep to the topic," I cautioned.

"In a moment, in a moment. Paul, you don't know it, but you're on a *coastline*, man. The Kootenays are where the coast of California travelled north and joined up with the North American land mass. I'm talking geologic time, man. But we're standing on a ghost beach. Our mountains are the result of the big collision, see, and there are spiritual spin-offs. This place is a spiritual vortex; the Indians — "

"No, Wicca," I said. "You're aware of the purpose of the meeting. No off-topic statements. Please sit down."

"This *is* relevant. It's no *accident* Paul is here. This place is an edge, it's where one world joined another. That's why it's a centre of spiritual consciousness, man, why it's — "

"The meeting's guidelines were specific, Wicca. You're out of order. Sit down."

"I only — "

"Sit down, please."

A couple of emphatic endorsements of my request were audible from divergent locations in the audience. Wicca shook his hairy head and shambled away from the mic.

I figured three loons was enough, so before the meeting degenerated any further I asked if people were ready to vote. Paul's idea was approved without a dissenting hand raised. The instant the verdict was delivered, he and his immediate entourage were on their feet, down the aisle and out the door. As planned, to allow Paul time to escape I recited a list of thank-yous. Then I declared the session adjourned.

The tension in my body eased as the assembly dissolved into loud chatter. The crowd stood, collected up coats, and slowly flowed toward the exit. My stomach surged unpleasantly. The feeling was familiar from every union meeting I chair, probably the consequence of an adrenaline overdose. But accompanying this vaguely nauseous sensation is a bleakness, a regret: if only I hadn't been so harsh with X; I shouldn't have said Y; how did I not think of mentioning Z? I feel I haven't been as astute, as effectual, as brilliant as the situation warranted, as I would have liked to have been. In this instance, I also winced when I thought of Paul hearing the moronic inappropriateness of the last responders. I was embarrassed to be associated, albeit only geographically, with such damaged goods. I could imagine he and his advisors later mocking our spaced-out Hicksville-in-the-mountains.

Those of Paul's staff still present were energetically stacking chairs and dismantling the audio system, darting between remnants of the audience that had formed into small clumps of happily gabbing friends. Four or five people I know wandered up to the front to convene a post-mortem — ostensibly with me. I felt drained and didn't contribute much. The consensus was that the gathering had been a success, though the antics of the reality-challenged had left a bad taste in more people's minds than mine. Mary, who had driven her car to the meeting after I'd gone ahead, stood beside me as the talk in our little circle swelled and dwindled and grew animated once more.

Then a young guy was at my elbow. I could see he was wearing the ID that labelled him one of McCartney's team. He drew me aside.

"Paul said to tell you he appreciates the job you did. He thinks you handled the nutters jolly well."

"Thanks," I said. I remembered Robert Altman's movie *Nashville*, where musicians are forever saying positive things when they encounter each other while slagging them behind their backs.

"No, truly," Paul's messenger insisted, catching the skepticism in my tone. "You should have been in Minneapolis.

One imbecile at the mic after another. And the chairman bloody hopeless. Total breakdown. You were super."

I looked closely at him for the first time, trying to detect some Nashvillian insincerity. He was either an accomplished fake, which might have been why Sir Paul hired him in the first place, or he meant the compliment. I couldn't be certain.

"I'm sorry about the bozos at the end," I said. "This area attracts more than our share. It's about us being so far from cities, although many of these types — "

"You did fine, chum," he patted me on the arm. "Naught to apologize for. No meeting is flawless. Paul is grateful to you for how you managed the chin-wag."

The thought leaped into my head that I should ask if this guy could obtain Paul's autograph for me, say on a copy of tonight's agenda. I remembered how much I would have cherished the autograph of any of the Beatles years before. Wasn't I still a kid at heart? I flashed on hoary black-and-white newsreels of young girls shrieking with joy at one of the nattily-suited Fab Four signing their bared arm, or the cast of a broken leg, or an album cover brought to the concert. Then I recalled racks of merchandise that bore facsimiles of John's, George's, Ringo's and Paul's signatures. Paul's name on a piece of paper, despite being scrawled in person, at this late date would appear no more authentic than a reproduction of his autograph on an antique Beatles lunch kit or lampshade or school binder.

My gang at the front wanted to decamp to the lounge at the Hume to continue their analysis of the event. Mary said she didn't care to, but that I should go ahead. I begged off, pleading chair burnout.

At home, I poured Mary and me a couple of scotches, and placed my old Abbey Road album on the turntable. We settled side-by-side on the couch amid the music, and dissected the evening. I confessed I had been amazed by the extent of my anger at the first of the loons, the art student. "I *knew* something like this would happen, no matter how painstakingly the meeting was organized. Why was I *so* upset? I wanted to kill her." I told Mary what Sir Paul's sidekick had said about my skills as chair, and rambled on with praise for the main man himself. "Paul was so cool. Did you see how he finessed that technical question? *Paul* should have been chair. He would have done a better job than me. If that guy afterwards wasn't lying, Paul wasn't fazed a bit by the ozone-dwellers."

Mary waved away a refill. "Maybe Paul is more accepting than you of people as they are. Could be that's why he's kept writing his wonderful silly love songs. I don't know him, but I do know you. You become enraged at — "

"You can't take anyone at face value, Mary," I started to set her straight. "They — "

"Bill, let me finish. People disappoint you because they don't live up to your standards. I'm not saying you shouldn't work to convince the world to behave the way you imagine it ought to. But — "

"Not likely I'd accept — "

"Stop interrupting. I was impressed by Paul, also, and how he interacted with the crowd. Yet you've had an opportunity that he, because of his fame and fortune at such an early age, could never have. You've gotten to live in an actual community, a little town perched on a mountainside by a lake. You've been able to contribute to that community, possibly change it for the better. Or the worse." She leaned over to give me a kiss. "If you were as much a cynic about people as you often sound, you wouldn't bother trying. Even the ugliest side to a community is part of what it is. As I think you know. That's just human nature, at least for your and my lifetime."

She was wrong, of course, but the scotch all at once had made me incredibly tired. I promised her I would demolish her arguments in the morning. I shut off the stereo. And while Mary was finishing in the bathroom, I sat and stared again at the album's photo of four young men filing across a street, Paul out of step, and barefoot.

Winter Pasture

A COLD AUTUMN LIGHT EASED THROUGH THE pines. *Sweater weather again*, Stephen had thought when he dressed that morning. He noticed, as he drove up the Lake toward Dan and Tammy's a couple of hours later, that the roadside ferns were sere and brown. Yellow-gold larches speckled the forested valley walls amid the fir, spruce and cedar. Now Stephen felt the chill on face and hands as he followed Tammy across the lawn toward the corral.

The log-rail enclosure in the trees held only one horse that loomed larger and larger as Stephen and Tammy approached. To Stephen, horses viewed from the highway in a field looked almost toy-like. "Expensive pets," he'd heard them described. But up close they seemed much different, threatening. Stephen hung back while Tammy raised the wire that secured the corral gate and strode up to the giant animal. Its dark-brown fur was thick, shaggy. The horse watched the woman draw near. An acrid, earthy smell of manure hung in the air.

"Hand me some grass, will you, Stephen?" Tammy requested, not removing her gaze from the creature. She began murmuring endearments toward the wary round

114

eye that regarded her. Stephen bent to tear off a clump of greenery. As he entered the corral, he made certain he kept Tammy between himself and the horse.

"This grass okay?"

"Yeah. Hold it out for her."

"Uh, I think you should do it." The beast towered over both of them.

"Go on, she won't hurt you." Tammy's voice hummed with a note of delight at Stephen's fear.

"I'd still rather you did it," he declared. "My only experience around horses was when I was eight, at summer camp. I was terrified. The counselors eventually gave up on me. When everybody else went riding, I had to clean stables. Which I preferred to do."

The animal lowered its enormous head toward the woman's left hand and accepted the grass. Tammy stroked the side of its neck as it chewed. "Come and pat her," she said. "She's friendly, aren't you, girl?" Tammy kissed the mare below the eye. "She did eat that visitor last year. But you didn't mean to, did you, sweetheart?" Tammy flashed a grin at Stephen.

He stepped forward and tentatively put a hand out to stroke along the hard ridge that ran between the ears and nostrils. He gave the fur there a few pats, then jerked back his hand as the head lifted momentarily, powerfully. The creature's jaws continued to rotate sideways as it ate.

"I don't like anything this big that doesn't have a reverse gear," he tried to joke.

"Oh, Mandy will go backwards for you, won't you, darling?" Tammy crooned. "Mandy's a good old horse." The mare had finished devouring the grass and its neck was rising again when Tammy abruptly flung the halter she had been holding in her right hand over its head. "C'mon, now," Tammy said reassuringly as she fumbled to tighten straps around the animal's face. Then, in a sterner tone: "Settle down, Mandy," as the horse tossed neck and head to protest the harnessing.

Stephen stumbled back in alarm as the beast suddenly paced sideways toward him, trying to pull away from where Tammy, directly in front of it, struggled to fasten a strap. He thought maybe he should call Dan for help, and pivoted to look behind him. Up at the house, Dan had connected the horse-trailer behind his pickup and was bent over the hitch, fiddling with the safety chain. Stephen felt confident Dan could handle any problem with the creature. "Good girl, yeah," Stephen heard Tammy utter more calmly. He turned toward her. Some crisis in the procedure had been weathered. The mare's unpredictable motions ceased, and Tammy was stroking the haltered nose. "That's my good Mandy. That wasn't so bad, was it, darling?" Tammy leaned to kiss its cheek again. Then, gripping the halter, she guided the horse toward a corral post where a rope was coiled. Stephen sensed the immense weight of the animal as its legs thudded one by one into the dust. The woman grabbed the coiled rope, and Stephen saw the line ended in a metal clasp which she snapped onto a ring on the side of the halter.

She led the mare through the corral gate and stopped just beyond. "Here," she said to Stephen, who had trailed after, careful to keep out of range of the rear hooves.

"What?"

Tammy offered the rope. "Hang onto her for a few minutes. I'll see if Dan has the trailer ready."

"You mean, keep it here?"

"Yeah. Just for a couple of minutes. Then we'll load her."

Anxiety coursed through Stephen. "I don't know if I can," he managed to blurt, reluctant to decline a task that to Tammy clearly represented no more than holding the leash of a dog.

"C'mon. Mandy won't go anywhere. Just for a minute."

The rope was suddenly heavy in Stephen's fingers. Tammy was hurrying across the clearing toward her husband, who fussed over a latch at the rear door of the trailer.

Stephen heard the wind high in the pines around the corral. Cold clear air surged and fell. He and the horse waited.

Ellen, he thought. *For fifteen minutes, I haven't remembered Ellen*. His nervousness around the animal had served like a fifty-minute class of his grade eights. The attention required to try to interest adolescents in Canadian geography was all-absorbing. And he was glad for any break from his mind's relentless, compulsive replaying of his months with Ellen. He recently had reread the chapter on obsession in *Burning Issues: The Crucible of Your Feelings*, a book that, ironically enough, Ellen had given him when they began dating. Obsession was a way of punishing oneself, the book's author proclaimed. Stephen could agree that his present focus on Ellen had more to do with his own emotional needs than with the person who preoccupied him.

The beast's massive head and neck descended and its teeth began to crop at the grass around its hooves. Ellen was a single mother of two; Stephen had met her at a Parent Advisory Council social. She was exactly his age, thirty-eight. She had been the first woman he had been involved with since his divorce from Anne, two years ago. Slowly, cautiously, he and Ellen had become important to each other; they spent hours talking about their first marriages, and what they had discovered about patterns of behaviour, their parents' influences on their lives, their own parenting styles. On one of their first dates, Ellen had taken him to hear a talk in town by a visiting relationship expert, Charles Fawcett. Ellen knew Fawcett from having participated in several workshops conducted by him over the past five years, beginning when she was still married. "He's got his own issues," Ellen pronounced breezily when she and Stephen went for a drink after Fawcett's lecture. She detailed Fawcett's strengths and flaws. "He tends to take the man's side, inevitably, in any situation. Although you can call him on that."

Her response to the speaker amazed Stephen. He had been consciously trying to stay open to whatever the expert said, to not be judgmental, which Anne had insisted was one of his biggest faults.

Subsequent to Fawcett's talk, Stephen had found in the self-help section of the bookstore in town a volume on merged families. He had read it, and discussed the writer's insights with Ellen. This activity had impressed her; her son was in third grade and her daughter in sixth. Stephen's little guy, Brian, was around every other weekend, so their children had gotten to know each other. Brian was the same age as Ellen's son, Jason, although the boys were in different classes at the school. The boys usually played well together, or as well as eight-year-olds could.

But in the end Ellen had announced she did not want to continue their relationship. "You're too jittery, too twitchy," she told Stephen. "Living with you would drive me insane."

"I'm nervous because I really love you and want things to work out between you and me," Stephen had stormed. "I wouldn't be so damn jumpy if I heard more from you that this relationship is something you value. That you care for me as much as I do for you."

"There's an aura of tension around you every time we're together," Ellen retorted. "I can't stand it. I need somebody who's more relaxed. I'm tense enough myself."

"Roger is pretty damn laid back," Stephen pressed, referring to her ex-husband. "You told me you hated his attitude."

"Maybe I'm looking for more of a balance, a middle ground. I don't know. Maybe I'm just confused," Ellen said. "Whatever the reason, I don't think it's good for me to keep seeing you."

Their final argument had occurred at his place. Stephen remembered the silent twenty-minute drive down the valley to her acreage. His truck had rolled past the school where they had met and past the community hall where on an early date they attended a harvest dance, an evening that had led to them first spending the night together. These familiar twenty-five kilometers of back road seemed to Stephen like an unwinding film of their seven-month courtship. He and Ellen were polite with each other when they parted; she had even phoned a few days later to check on how he was coping.

Ellen, he thought now, clutching a rope at Dan and Tammy's corral. Mandy shifted a half-step away from him in search of better grass. Stephen carefully payed out another short length of tether.

Nothing in Stephen's experience of parting with his ex-wife Anne had prepared him for the successive waves of shock, of loss, that swamped him and dragged him under after his failure with Ellen. He had been ready to leave Anne for more than a year. Once he got past the initial strangeness of being on his own after nearly a decade, the actual separation had left him cheerful about the future. Losing Ellen, however, meant a kind of terror: what would happen to him? Who was he? Who cared whether he lived or didn't?

For a week after he and Ellen broke up, he awoke each morning into a sensation of free-falling. All day — except when distracted by classroom duties — his body felt rigid, braced in anticipation of a painful landing. The calves of his legs throbbed continually with the strain.

Even after the vertiginous quality to his days started to fade, *Ellen, Ellen, Ellen* continued to hammer through his mind like a pulse. Hour after hour, month upon month, he reexamined the razor-edged shards of Ellen's and his time together. Alone, concentrating solely on her, on his loss of her, he would discover himself close to tears in a mist of self-pity. Accompanying this mood was a weightiness of spirit that had a physical manifestation: on weekday evenings, exhaustion drained him by nine; on weekends he needed frequent afternoon naps.

In his head, a labyrinthine dialogue with Ellen repeated. He would invent a speech to convince her to resume their relationship. Then he could hear her pick flaws in his argument. Even in an imaginary discussion between them, he heard a coolness, a distance in her tone that he felt disparaged by.

Yet she was an incessant presence. *Ellen would enjoy seeing this* was his first thought as he observed a flowering clump of forget-me-nots growing near his compost pile. *That blouse would look great on Ellen* was his reaction to viewing an item of clothing as he leafed through a sportswear catalog that arrived in his mail.

Ellen's solicitous post-breakup phone call — and during the next week, a second one — had pained and discomfited him more than it aided him. The wound gaped again. He was not sure what to tell Brian when the child asked whether he could visit Jason to play together. Stephen could not bring himself to phone Ellen to arrange for the boys to meet. He was certain she would welcome the idea, but he decided the toll on his own feelings was too great. Nor was Anne adverse to twisting the knife when he picked Brian up. "I hear you and your girlfriend are having some problems," she casually mentioned when he dropped by for the first time after Ellen's withdrawal. "I hope it's something you two can solve."

Anger pervaded Stephen at Anne's calculatedly offhand comment. But he choked down any response. This valley was too small; a change in any aspect of a valley relationship was public knowledge for fifty kilometers in both directions within hours of the event. Stephen liked the pace and texture of rural living. But the moment trouble overtook a valley resident, he or she became a character in a widely discussed soap opera.

In Stephen's efforts to adjust to Ellen's absence, he felt carried along against his will into a vortex of emotions as indifferent to his welfare as some implacable scientific law or natural process — lightning and thunder that overtook him while he hiked across an alpine meadow. Or a snowstorm that struck while he was driving home from town some evening, the plows not yet called out, forcing him to inch forward through the drifting, treacherous white. Even this morning on the highway to Dan and Tammy's place, his nerves leaped when a car passed him with a license plate that read *ELN* followed by three numerals. *Got to quit reacting like this*, he chastised himself. *This is so stupid.* Yet moments later he had overtaken a car whose identifying letters were *EMT*. His face flushed and his heart raced. *Ellen Margaret Turner*, a merciless part of his mind had gut-punched him.

Mandy pulled hard on the rope. The animal had shuffled an additional couple of steps distant, to an area of uncropped tufts. A few seconds later, it yanked at the line again.

Sweat immediately coated each centimeter of Stephen's skin. In the creature's pulls, he comprehended he was linked to a being magnitudes stronger than himself. He stared down the now-taut rope at the neck, a glacier of muscle and hair. His grip tightened; his eyes shifted rapidly around the clearing. If the animal was determined to escape, he recognized he would be powerless to stop it.

After a minute, he released the damp fingers of his left hand from the rope and wiped them on his jeans. He curled his fingers into his palm and straightened them several times. Repositioning his left hand on the rope, he repeated the unkinking procedure with his other hand. The beast continued to chew.

Stephen altered his stance, to brace against any renewed lunge toward freedom by the force he was supposed to contain. He was conscious of the futility of this gesture. Should he try to loop the rope around a corral post to secure the mare? He felt his existence had become a race against time. He fervently wished for Tammy's speedy return, and for the animal to stay calm until she did show up.

As if in response to Stephen's unspoken prayer, the creature heaved itself a further meter distant. Stephen was tugged partially off balance. Panic flooded through him; he could taste copper on his tongue. He regained his footing as the mare paused. Resentment quickly replaced terror — resentment at being left in a situation beyond his ability to cope. He raged inside at the uncooperative animal, at Tammy, at his indecisiveness about whether to attempt to fasten the beast to a tree or other anchor sturdier than he could ever be.

Why had he lacked the courage to inform Tammy he could not handle tending her horse?

The animal had resumed eating. Stephen swiveled his head to search for his hosts. Dan was disappearing in the front door of the house, and Tammy was using a broom to sweep a ramp leading to the rear of the trailer. For a second Stephen had a wild notion to call for relief from his predicament. He could imagine Tammy's and Dan's incredulous faces peering down toward the corral. What would they see? The mare grazing and himself idly holding the rope that secured it. They would think he had lost his mind.

Maybe his obsession with Ellen *had* driven him mad. A burst of anger surfaced. *Why can't I stop this endless thinking about her?* He could scarcely remember what it felt like not to be at the mercy of his mind's fixation on her.

The wind poured through the branches above Stephen, then died away. "I see Mandy hasn't run off with you," Tammy said, startling him. An ache he was suddenly aware of in his shoulders began to dissipate as he handed her the rope.

Stephen had met Dan Freydahl and his wife Tammy a year before, when Dan and he had been part of an advisory committee to a regional land-use planning commission. Most of the staff at Stephen's school were determinedly pro-ecology, and he had been chosen by his colleagues to attend a pre-commission hearing as their representative. He had spoken a couple of times at that gathering — he said nothing memorable, at least to his own ears. But he found himself nominated from that meeting to serve on the advisory committee. He did not decline the nomination; in his post-Anne, pre-Ellen days, his time off was free of obligations, except for custodial weekends with Brian.

From the first session of the committee he had been impressed by Dan's laconic manner and common sense. Dan, who was about Stephen's age, represented the hunting sector. Dan frequently worked as a horse guide in the East Kootenays and as far north as the Yukon. In addition, he had a Christmas-tree-growing operation south of Nelson near Salmo.

"No watersheds are left into the Rockies that don't have trails or roads up them," Dan had announced in the opening round of statements that inaugurated the committee's work. "I can take a hunting party three days up the back of beyond and we'll be having breakfast when a helicopter flies overhead. If there's a tree left standing, or a grizzly left walking, it's because we choose to let this happen. That choice is quite a responsibility and I don't think we know how to deal with it. The only true wilderness that remains is within ourselves."

Stephen had joined the half-circle of people standing talking to Dan in the coffee break. Over several meetings Dan and he had become solid acquaintances, if not friends. Stephen and Ellen enjoyed Dan and Tammy's company during a couple of potluck suppers at committee members' houses in Nelson before the group had fulfilled its mandate. The Freydahls had repeatedly urged Stephen and Ellen to visit their home, but they never did.

The previous Monday, some query in the staff room concerning the committee had sparked Stephen's recollection of the Freydahls' invitation. Anxious for ways to distract himself, he had phoned Dan that same evening. Dan was enthusiastic about Stephen's proposal to motor up on Saturday. "We'll be hauling the last of the horses to winter pasture," Dan had said. "Won't take long. When that's done, we'll sit around and drink a few beers and tell a few lies. Tammy and I look forward to seeing you."

Now the small procession climbed from the corral toward the house. Stephen observed that the rear of the horse-trailer, once lowered, formed an incline to allow animals to enter. With the mare in tow, Tammy walked directly up the ramp. The creature placed one hoof on it, and then a second; Stephen was astonished by the loudness of the echoing boom as each hoof struck the wood planks. The horse, too, appeared shaken by the noise and balked, half-on and half-off the ramp.

"C'mon, girl," Tammy urged. "Up you come." The mare pulled back, neck stretched between its rearward motion and where Tammy grasped the rope.

"Mandy!" Dan abruptly shouted from behind the animal. "Go!" At the sound of his words, the creature shunted its body sideways, without relaxing its stance of retreat. Its eye nearest to Stephen widened and the pupil jerked in every direction.

"Mandy, you've been in this thing a hundred times," Dan said, exasperation in his voice.

"She doesn't like the trailer?" Stephen asked.

"I don't think she remembers," Dan said. "Anyway, horses are conservative. Except when it's time to eat, whatever they're doing is what they want to keep doing. The trailer represents some kind of change."

"I'll try another way," Tammy suggested. She descended the ramp, allowing the mare to take a series of ungainly steps backwards onto the lawn. The woman stood talking sooth-ingly to the animal for a few moments, then began to lead it in a circle across the grass behind the trailer. Three times the pair made a wide circuit, with Tammy near the mare's head speaking reassuringly as they paced. As they completed the fourth round, the horse without protest stomped up the ramp alongside Tammy and into the trailer.

Tammy was squeezed between the mare and the vehicle's sides, but managed to tie the rope to a board provided for that purpose at the front. She wormed past the animal and strode down the ramp. She and Dan lifted and fastened it upright to form the back of the trailer, then tightened a chain across the now-vertical wooden panel. Stephen admired how even in the small tasks of closing the rear of the conveyance Tammy and Dan appeared to function perfectly as a team; each respected the other's abilities, but was ready to assist if either encountered any difficulty. *Ellen and I never had time to develop such closeness,* he thought. *Even Anne and I lacked the easy give-and-take of Tammy and Dan.* He remembered disagreements between Anne and himself about child-rearing that had arisen almost as soon as Brian was born. *Of course, Tammy and Dan have no kids. And maybe they fight like mad when nobody is around.* But there was no sign of friction between the couple.

Jammed into the pickup's seat between Tammy and the door, Stephen declared how impressed he was at her technique for convincing the mare to enter the trailer. "Tammy's great with horses," Dan agreed, as he steered down the bumpy drive. Where the gravel eventually met asphalt, he braked, waited for a loaded logging truck to pass by, then turned onto the highway. "But even if Mandy hadn't gone along with what Tammy tried, we'd have gotten her aboard. We never force a critter to enter. People will hit at them from behind, all that, but it doesn't work."

"Next step is to offer them oats," Tammy said.

"I've even climbed into the trailer and just leaned back on the rope and waited," Dan said. "I'll stay like that fifteen or twenty minutes. Eventually the horse gets tired of the strain on its neck and quits being ornery."

"It's still impressive," Stephen said. "A horse is so big and you guys get it to do whatever you want."

Dan tapped his head. "Brain beats brawn," he stated.

"Patience," Tammy said. "It's also having the patience to try this and try that and not freak when one method doesn't work."

"When you've been around critters a lot, you have a better idea how they behave," Dan added. "You're ready for what they're going to try."

"Well, you're *usually* ready," Tammy laughed. "Anyhow, Mandy is a sweetheart. She's my favourite. But could we have some heat?" Dan adjusted the controls.

There was silence in the cab; then their talk considered the fall weather. The highway rounded curve after curve as it followed the wooded lakeshore north. With decreasing frequency they passed houses and fields, or driveways that disappeared into the forest above the road. Enveloped by the warmth in the cab, and the end of the tension he had experienced at the corral, Stephen became drowsy. Ellen flickered in and out of his mind.

Dan slowed, and swung off the pavement onto a dirt road that led up a steeply treed ridge to their left. They continued to climb for several minutes. The autumn forest here crowded both shoulders of the route, interspersed occasionally with a meadow on which a house or trailer was sited.

Dan geared down. "There's Andy's place." A small two-storey house with metal roof was approaching on the right.

Stephen roused himself. "Where we're leaving the horse?"

"Yeah. We took the other two up last weekend."

"Can your friend make a living out here?" Stephen inquired. The fields on either side of this house looked extensive.

"It's a hobby farm, really," Tammy said. "Andy owns seventy acres, but works for Highways out of Nelson."

Fifty meters or so past the driveway to the house, the pickup stopped. A gate into the field was marked by a tall pole topped with fluttering fluorescent tape. "Want me to open it?" Stephen offered.

Dan nodded. "You can leave it open, too. We're coming back this way. The pasture is up higher, and has its own gate."

Stepping down from the heated cocoon of the cab was a shock to Stephen. The icy air had more bite to it than at Dan and Tammy's; the wind much fiercer. As Stephen fumbled with the gate latch, he saw the tall, dried-out grasses of the field bow and ripple away in waves. Two rutted tracks led across the meadow. He scrambled back into the front seat.

The pickup jounced and lurched along the parallel grooves of bare earth winding through the field. Dan braked at a second gate, and shut down the engine.

Now they stood in a lake of grass, ringed by forest, and further off by sharply angled mountain peaks. Many of the summits glistened white with new snow. Stephen zipped his jacket against the wind, whose chill seemed to be brought directly from the visible glaciers. He stuck freezing hands into his jacket pockets. Tammy and Dan were unlatching the trailer ramp; Stephen asked Tammy if there was anything he could do to help.

"Why don't you roll open the gate," she suggested. "We'll be finished this in a sec."

The gate here was a section of barbed wire, stiffened somewhat by four vertical poles woven between the strands. A loop of other wire linked the last pole to a fence post. Stephen freed the gate and tugged it ajar, careful not to cut his hands or snag any of his clothing on a barb. By the time he had hauled the gate aside, Dan was backing the horse down the ramp.

"Get ready to close the fence," Dan said as he guided the mare past Stephen and through the opening. Stephen gingerly retrieved the end pole of the gate and stood by to pull the jumble of barbed wire to its original position. He watched as Dan slipped the halter off. "Hi-YAH!" Dan yelled, waving his arms in large semicircles. In his right hand, the removed halter and rope coil flapped weirdly.

The mare, startled, trotted a few paces forward into the meadow and stopped. Dan scampered back through the opening in the fence. Then Tammy was beside Stephen, wearing thick work gloves she had brought from the truck, helping him heave the gate closed. Dan positioned the loop of wire that fastened the gate. The three humans stood together, staring at the horse, which looked at them over its shoulder. It appeared unsure what to do.

Stephen saw the wind lift the hairs on the animal's back. "The horse will stay out all winter?"

"There's plenty to eat," Dan confirmed. "The second hay wasn't taken off. They can paw for grass through the snow. And there's water." He pointed to a pipe and trough arrangement Stephen had not noticed, flowing from a creek that cut through the pasture a few meters from where they watched.

The mare began to pace down the field away from them.

"Where are your other horses?" Stephen asked.

Dan shrugged. "Probably down in a draw out of the wind. Or else they're over on the other side, where we can't see them."

The animal they had just released was a considerable distance across the pasture by now, plodding ahead. To Stephen the horse looked incredibly small and frail, alone under the mountains. He felt a pressure of sadness explode in his chest and rise into his throat. Tears pooled his eyes, though he was not certain if they were caused by the buffeting wind or by this unexpected surge of emotion.

"I'm glad it's her and not me out there," he heard Tammy say. Dan put his arm around Tammy and she put hers around him. The three listened to the wind for a minute or so. Stephen began shivering.

"Hey, let's head home and grab some chow," Dan announced. He and Tammy returned to the trailer and began to lift the ramp. Stephen, though he shook with cold, remained gazing after the mare. It was not much larger than a dot.

Grief subsumed Stephen. He felt sorry for the horse, sorry for himself. All at once the tendril of another sorrow started to unfurl: he felt sorry for Ellen. An immensely powerful thing that had been his and Ellen's had been cut loose as if into a field, and abandoned.

"Goodbye, Mandy," he whispered. He imagined the mare enduring the vicissitudes of the weather, the icy days ahead. Despite Dan's comments about the presence of the other horses, Stephen pictured her isolated, without companions in a frozen landscape. Yet he recalled how Dan and Tammy regarded this undertaking. The loss, the agony here had a limit, a season.

The horn of the pickup blasted. He started, and swung around. The motor revved, and through the truck window, Tammy beckoned him. Stiff with cold he crossed toward the vehicle. He opened the door and clambered gratefully into the heat of the cab.

THE PLACE NO ONE
BUT MYSELF REMEMBERS

The Freelance Demolitionist

"I'LL EXPLAIN WHAT I CAN, CAPTAIN. BUT there's not much more to say than is written in my report.

"From the beginning, Sir? After Shiloh, my unit was ordered to this area, where we helped establish the emplacements around Morrisburg. We were told these would block any advance of Confederate cavalry up Deer Creek valley. When that threat diminished, I was detailed to take a sergeant and ten mounted men of my choosing and proceed toward Box Crossing. Our orders were to deny the enemy any possible future use of the rail line, which cuts through the mountains in that country in roughly a northwest-southeast direction.

"We left the encampment here on Wednesday. Sir? No, last Wednesday, June twenty-fourth, Captain. We requisitioned two wagons with powder, provisions, tents, mess gear. I believe we rode through our lines about nine-thirty in the forenoon and set out toward . . .

"The colonel, Colonel Whitney, was the source of my orders, Captain. The orders were conveyed to me by the major. Sir? Yes, I . . . No, that's right. He's Artillery, but we've been functioning more or less as an engineering unit. Should I continue, sir?

"We headed approximately south along the Morrisburg road and intersected the railway by about two p.m. The country there is thickly wooded and hilly. Beech and maple in the bottoms, and juniper and piney toward the ridges. We encountered no sign of enemy troop movements, and indeed saw nobody. We came upon one or two stump ranches, but these were deserted. We found no livestock. Probably the inhabitants fled in May, when we know the 4th Tennessee Volunteers made a sweep through this region. Yes, sir. Possibly a recon, or a feint. But they burned down the court-house at Box Crossing, and took the first hay which had been stored by farmers thereabouts, as well as their cows and pigs and all of their chickens they could get. Some barns were burned, too, I believe. The colonel told us at that time that the 4th Tennessee was part of the brigade under General Crittenden, operating from a bivouac downriver, just over the state border.

"Once we reached the rail line we used the horses and hand tools to remove rails and ties for a considerable distance. We then began to work our way southeast. During the balance of Wednesday and on Thursday we destroyed four bridges using the powder we had brought with us. Three others we left standing, including the largest one over Still Woman Creek near the Lexington Pike. These we intended to wreck on our return journey. The bridges we left intact were all some distance from the road; that is, we would have to bring the wagons across them if we returned down the rail bed rather than along the road. I didn't want to cut off a possible alternate route for us if we were forced to withdraw for any reason. My expectation, as I mentioned, was fully to render these bridges unusable on our way back to the camp at Morrisburg.

"Early Friday morning, however, we encountered an unexpected opportunity. The detachment was advancing along the rail line, when the woods suddenly opened up into a forested canyon. The extent of the canyon was not accurately indicated on the maps we carried: the canyon floor is seventy or eighty feet below the rail bed we were standing on. And the route of the railway follows a wide curve across the mouth of a tributary canyon of perhaps three-fourths that depth. Two very large wooden trestles, each curved, bridged the opening. The longest trestle had a span of three hundred and fifty feet, give or take a few feet, while the lesser was fully two hundred feet. The cribbing rising from the canyon floor in both cases was, of course, substantial. To take out these trestles would render the rail line impassable for a few months, at least, in my best judgment. Destruction of these structures would represent a far more decisive action against the enemy than the damage we had been able to inflict up to this moment. To be frank, what we had accomplished to that point could be repaired by determined crews within several days. But these impressive trestles — if we could remove or burn a large enough portion of them — could not be rebuilt without the deployment of considerable engineering skills, men, and timber. Such an undertaking naturally would also consume much time.

"The sergeant and I looked at each other, and I could see he instantly grasped our good fortune as well. Sir? Sergeant Mitchell. Yes, sir, Ethan Mitchell.

"We brought the troop to a halt, and the sergeant and I dismounted and walked a little distance out onto the nearest trestle, discussing how we might inflict the maximum damage.

We knew roughly our inventory of remaining powder, and were inspecting the structure's construction while debating the best manner to utilize that matériel. Our goal was not only to topple the cribbing into the canyon but also to render as much of the timber as we could unsuitable for employment in any attempt to reconstruct the trestles.

"These were erected of tarred wood, each beam about the height and width of a railway tie, although many of the struts were longer in span. The beams were spiked or bolted in place, depending on the stresses they were designed to bear.

"The sergeant and I were standing perhaps two dozen yards or more out on the trestle, talking. The troop was at ease close to where the trestles joined the rail bed; the men were dismounted, a few smoking their pipes, a couple more sprawled out taking some rest. Since, as I mention, we had seen no sign of human presence, let alone evidence of the enemy, I had not seen fit to post any sort of picket. The day was sunny with a few clouds; thrush and robin were singing in the woods around us. The gentlest of breezes was wafting up the canyon, shimmering the leaves in the woods all about.

"Suddenly an explosion erupted on a cliff face behind the troop, a face past which the rail line travelled and below which we had just ridden. The sound and smoke and force of the explosion was as if a ball from one of the heaviest cannons had landed. Or maybe twice that effect. So it appeared to me, since the scene about us displayed such utter tranquility just moments before. The war had seemed that summer morning very, very far away.

"In seconds, however, my men had responded with as much alacrity as any commander could wish. The horses were calmed and led under cover of the trees, the wagons spurred as well to a place of safety in the woods, the men were deployed by their corporal along the track under what protection they could find, carbines and Springfields had been loaded and were pointing back the direction we had come. A scout was dispatched to circle through the forest and ascend the rear of the cliff to observe what he could.

"As the sergeant and I ran back atop the trestle toward the men, I was braced for the crash of a second shell announcing a cannonade. I was in counter-battery fire at Shiloh, sir. The carnage in our lines there deeply terrified me; I confess it affects me still. That was the first place I saw a man dismembered, Captain. Literally dis-membered. The arm and part of a shoulder was lying on the ground by itself. My friend from upstate, whom I had known since we both enlisted, had half of his face torn away and died on the ground after a while. There was screaming and shouting and the cannon fire kept landing without a trace of God's mercy. Sir? Yes, sir.

"My mouth was completely dry as I raced towards my troop; I had trouble swallowing. But I was also turning over and over in my thoughts a question as I watched my feet land on every second tie along the trestle. How could a battery of such heavy artillery be sited so as to have us in range, when we had no indication a Rebel force of any size was in the vicinity? No one but a madman would send heavy guns forward as the point of an advance.

"I flung myself down behind some boulders at trackside where the corporal was lying. The smoke and dust at the foot of the cliff had begun to dissipate, and I observed that a very large heap of shattered rock lay across the rails. From my vantage point, the pile of rubble appeared to effectively block our ability to take the wagons back up the rail right-of-way. Any tactical maneuver from here would mean either abandoning our wagons, or attempting to drive them across the trestles. Intentionally or not, the cannon shot had blocked any retreat with our equipment. And taking a wagon across a trestle under fire would be out of the question. We were finished, I felt, as a demolition detachment. The task ahead was to elude any Confederate patrols originating from a force that had to be at least the size of a division, to be accompanied by such heavy cannons. I was evaluating in my mind possible routes we could use to slip back to Morrisburg with news of the Rebel advance.

"By now the echoes of the cannon shot were dying away, and the birds again were audible from the branches of the trees about us. The last sounds of tumbling stones ceased, and I observed a fresh, clean aspect to the rock on the upper portion of the cliff. The cannonball obviously had dislocated and pulverized a sizeable slab of granite. Then I heard a yell from someplace on the far side of the pile of shattered rock, where a plume of dust still hovered: 'Union men. Union men. Do not shoot. I am your friend.'

"The voice was male, with a sing-song sort of intonation. There was also the trace of an accent. Sir? No, not Southern. European. Scandahoovian, as it turned out. But at the time it was the sing-song nature of the shout that seemed so odd. 'Union men. Do not shoot. I am your friend.'

"A white handkerchief lofted on a stick was raised behind the pile of stones. The corporal whispered at me: 'I sent McKay up through the woods, sir. Once he reaches the cliff-edge he'll have the drop on whoever is behind those rocks.' The sergeant rolled across open ground toward me from a sort of ditch where he had positioned himself. 'Think it's a ruse, Lieutenant?' he inquired. 'I wonder if there's more of 'em. Maybe they followed us down the line from where we blew the last bridge.'

"'I detailed McKay to scout the situation,' the corporal informed the sergeant, pointing toward the cliff. Mitchell snorted. 'McKay. He was in Albany when they handed out the brains. No telling whether he'll open fire single-handed on a regiment of Rebs, or turn tail and run from an old woman driving a cow in to be milked.'

"'Who *should* I have sent, then, Sergeant?' the corporal asked irritably. 'Do you want me to dispatch somebody else to help McKay?'

"'Likely as not, whoever came climbing up behind McKay would be shot dead sure,' Mitchell said. 'McKay don't think. Anyhow, damage is done. We'll have to work with what we got.'

"The corporal started to protest, but I hissed at them for quiet. I could hear the voice shouting something further from under the white handkerchief beyond the rocks.

"'Dis my verk,' the voice called. 'I explode dis, ya? I can help you wit' dese bridges here.' And after a pause, the voice repeated: 'Union men. I am your friend.'

"We three crouching behind the boulder stared at one another. 'Could it be true?' I whispered. 'That it wasn't cannon fire?' The sergeant raised his eyebrows and shrugged. I made a decision.

"'Show yourself,' I shouted. 'Hands up and come into the open.'

"Almost simultaneously a cry erupted from the top of the cliff. 'I've got him in my sights, Lieutenant,' McKay screeched excitedly, as if he were just off the farm and not already a veteran of nine months of war. Then, again from McKay above: 'Hands up, Reb. You heard the lieutenant.'

"'Take cover, McKay, you fool. There may be more of 'em,' the corporal bellowed. The sergeant shook his head resignedly. The white flag wavered, and around the rocks stepped a figure wearing a brown wide-brimmed hat, and a long brown canvas coat. His arms were raised, and one of his hands lifted the branch with the white rag fluttering from it.

"The man paced confidently toward us a few yards and stopped.

"'I don't *see* nobody else, Corporal,' McKay called down plaintively. He had followed orders, though, and was once more hidden from view. "What now, Lieutenant?" the sergeant asked me.

I was cogitating as fast as I could, attempting to give weight to every factor in our predicament. Was this man a diversion, to catch us off guard while an enemy patrol encircled us? His lack of uniform meant nothing, of course; you know how Johnny Reb has never been too particular about such matters. As if reading my thoughts, the man holding the white flag yelled again. 'Dere's yoost me. I am a friend. I homestead over by da Rutland Lake. Dere's no Confeds be around.' Then after a moment of silence from us, he uttered his strange boast once more. 'Dis vas my verk. I can help you blow dose bridges.'

"I assessed our circumstances for another full minute. No other shots had landed since the initial explosion. The man before me claimed to be responsible for the blast, as unlikely as that sounded. I gave my orders. Two troopers were detailed to mount up and retrace our route a mile or so in search of the enemy. McKay was withdrawn from the heights and another man was posted aloft with my binoculars.

"I should interject that I had selected McKay out of my company for our present duty because I had witnessed him scrappy in a fight with the Rebs on the road to Corinth in

April. But experience has led me to trust Sergeant Mitchell's judgment. If he regarded McKay as exhibiting crucial defects of character — I was not previously aware of this — I would accord his evaluation much weight.

"I directed that the horses be brought to trackside, although the wagons were left where they had been shifted. I established a picket in the woods to the east of us. To the west the canyon fell away; we could easily observe from out on the nearest trestle any enemy activity from that quarter. I had some logs felled and dragged a distance onto the trestle to create an observation post that offered its user some protection. Once these chores were completed, I commanded that the newcomer, whom I had placed under guard, should be brought over and seated on the ground before me for interrogation.

"From a closer vantage I could see he was larger than average in height, with straw-coloured hair and eyes of an unusually deep blue. His face was clean-shaven, except for a full mustache. His clothing was rough but serviceable. He said his name was Olaf Jorgenson, and that he had emigrated as a child from Sweden with his family, who had settled in the Wabash Valley in Illinois. He had struck out on his own to try his luck farming some miles northwest of our present location, travelling infrequently to Morrisburg or westerly to New Brighton, the county seat, to sell any surplus crops and purchase supplies. He said he felt no compunction to enlist, since 'dere seem to be plenty soldier-boys,' and until the previous month the war had seemed remote. For the third time he repeated his offer to assist in the demolition ahead of us. 'Ven I saw smoke from your verk de last couple days,' he announced, 'I got on my hoss and rode over to help you, ya? I figured you vould vant to blow dese tings . . . ' He gestured out at the trestles. 'I haf someting dat can make your job yoost like back dere . . . ' He indicated the cliff. I asked how precisely he could aid us in our task.

"See dere, see dere?" he animatedly pointed up the rail line where the pile of rock lay. 'I can do dat to dese.' His hand now indicated the structures spanning the canyon.

"I was starting to wonder if the man might not have become crazed by loneliness, striving by himself to subsist on some break-heart farm in such sparsely settled country. But there was the nagging matter of the explosion that had heralded his presence. Had he really set off that blast?

"No trace of powder was evident on his hands. I commanded a search of his person, and he willingly turned out his pockets, revealing only a pocket knife, a length of string, tobacco, pipe, a few lucifers, an apple, pencil stub, handkerchief. Under the insole of one of his boots were a few coins, the discovery of which caused some excitement among the troopers inspecting the footwear. One private ventured the opinion that no farmer he'd ever known or heard of would carry cash money with him when about his ordinary occupations. The coins were taken as evidence that this was Judas himself in front of us, still in possession of his thirty pieces of silver. In this instance the thirty pence were payment for service as a Confederate spy rather than for the betrayal of Our Lord.

"Jorgenson exhibited the utmost calm during the soldier's outburst. Either his command of English was insufficient to understand the mortal threat implied by the private's words, or Jorgenson considered himself completely protected by his innocence. Or by his insanity, I was inclined to think. And yet there was that shattered rockface. If not his doing, whose?

"The sergeant beckoned me aside as I was mulling over these propositions. Mitchell had formed the opinion that the man was a Berry Picker who had been hiding out nearby. Fearing that our detachment would eventually discover his abode, he had concocted a tale that ... Captain? Berry Picker, sir. The men of this corps apply that term to deserters. Yes, sir, gone to pick berries. But also, I believe, a play upon 'to desert' and a 'dessert' that one eats, if you take my meaning. Yes, sir.

"I asked the sergeant how he could account for the demolished cliff side, if Jorgenson's story was false. Happenstance, was the sergeant's view. But that still left the mystery of who had fired a shot of such weight in our direction, and from where?

"I put the question directly to the prisoner, and he reiterated doggedly that the explosion was of his devising. 'Where is your gunpowder?' I demanded of him, and he began to recount a history of his family in Sweden, which further bolstered my inclination to regard him as lunatic. He had not spoken more than two or three sentences on this topic, though, when our scouts rode back into camp.

"The troopers had acquired two extra horses — one saddled and the other a pack animal fully laden, the load covered with a tarpaulin lashed in place. At the sight of these animals, Jorgenson became quite agitated. But I sternly bid him to remain seated and cautioned the trooper guarding him to keep him where he was. I walked over to hear from the scouting party, with some trepidation concerning what they might have discovered about the origin of the bombardment. I was already considering how best to deal with a madman if we had to speedily withdraw towards Morrisburg, especially since Jorgenson had the potential to betray us if the enemy were not aware of our exact position.

"However, my men had encountered nothing in the area that would indicate the presence of the Rebels. The troopers had pushed through the woods along a stream bed out to the road, and conducted a reconnaissance in both directions from that point. All was peaceful. On the outward leg of their excursion they had located the horses they had returned with. The horses had been tethered in a clearing a little distance from the rail line, not far up the track. As my men passed, their mounts had sensed the others, and the subsequent nickering back and forth had alerted the troopers to what was evidently Jorgenson's equipage.

"A quick check of the madman's saddlebags produced a content not so innocent as that of his pockets. A Colt long-barreled revolver plus a surprising quantity of cartridges were found within, along with a tobacco pouch containing what appeared to be percussion caps for a type of musket or rifle I was unfamiliar with. In addition, the saddlebags contained a well-creased map of the area with notations on it in a language I couldn't read, presumably Swedish. If he was a spy, was he a spy for the Swedish army? I had read in the Cincinnati newspapers — which are delivered to the Morrisburg encampment from time to time, although why all the way from Cincinnati I have no idea — that the British and French navies are aiding the Confederacy in eluding our blockade. Were the Swedes now enlisted in the Rebel cause?

"Jorgenson began to shout something about the need for caution and care as we removed the canvas from his pack horse. Two heavy wooden boxes measuring about two feet in each dimension, with secured lids, served as panniers. The animal also carried tools and ropes of various sorts wrapped in a tent, and some foodstuffs and cooking implements.

"All the men not assigned to duty gathered around as Jorgenson's possessions were unloaded from the pack mare. After an unsuccessful attempt to use a bayonet to pry open a padlock securing the first of the wooden boxes, we backed away and one of the troopers, McKay, lifted his carbine to shoot the lock. At this Jorgenson shrieked something unintelligible — or perhaps Swedish — and leaped suddenly to his feet. He pushed the surprised private guarding him to the ground, and began to run in our direction, still hollering, with both arms windmilling rapidly. His guard came charging in pursuit several paces behind.

"McKay, who had been taking aim at the padlock, brought his rifle smartly up to shoot the onrushing lunatic. Not wishing to have the Swede summarily executed in this manner, I slammed my shoulder into McKay as he was about to fire. The weapon discharged and the bullet whistled past Jorgenson scant inches above and to the left of his head. Flocks of birds rose from the forest at the report, and wheeled in confusion a few moments before settling again into the trees. I pulled my revolver from its holster.

"Jorgenson crumpled to his knees at the sound of the rifle, put his hands over his face, and fell forward. For a second I thought he had been hit, but in a moment his guard and the other troopers pounced upon him. They quickly secured his hands behind him with a rope and hauled him erect. They shoved and kicked at him to encourage him to move in my direction. I had them seat him on one of the boxes we had taken from his horse; I sat on the other, my revolver still in my hand.

"While I was composing myself to resolve this situation, Jorgenson began to speak rapidly. He led me to understand that the boxes contained explosive matériel, and that he had used this substance to bring down a good portion of the cliff face. He proposed to employ the contents of the boxes to assist me in the demolition of the trestles.

"I was dubious about the truth of his statements, given that the boxes could not possibly contain enough powder to do more than detonate one mine-like blast on the cliff. I pointed out to Jorgenson that he couldn't have much powder left after effecting such an eruption. I experienced some pangs of foolishness at conversing so reasonably with an evident maniac in front of my men. But his eyes held a glint of intelligence that was at odds with his almost-fevered, repeated insistence that he could be of help in the venture we were embarked on.

"Jorgenson's response to my observation was to suggest an exhibition of his abilities. 'I yoost show you, I show you,' was how he phrased it. 'Dis is not gunpowder but mooch better. You vill see.' Such a trial struck me as a happy idea, since a demonstration of his qualities as an explosives mechanic would confirm to my satisfaction whether he had or hadn't taken leave of his senses.

"The sergeant was wary. 'What are you going to let him try to explode, Lieutenant?' Mitchell wanted to know. I had been pondering that myself, and shared my conclusion. The sergeant and I had determined that we would try to eliminate the smaller trestle first. Our plan was to separate the upper deck from its connection with the ground on either end, before toppling the cribbing from below. 'Let's see if he can cut that trestle free on its furthest side,' I told the sergeant. 'If he can, I'll believe his story. If not, we've still got the mystery of what hit the cliff, but . . . '

"'But at least we'll know this man's a spy or a Berry Picker,' Mitchell finished what he took to be my thought. 'Or merely a charlatan, or a common lunatic, Sergeant,' I cautioned him.

"Either way, I had resolved that with the discovery of suspicious items among Jorgenson's gear we would have to keep him under watch until we returned to Morrisburg. I put my proposition regarding the second trestle to our prisoner and he responded enthusiastically. 'Good, good. I can do it, ya?'

"He and I stood up from the wooden boxes. He then asked that he be untied. 'I cannot do my verk trussed up like a goose,' he said, grinning. The confidence in his smile rather annoyed me. I felt that by agreeing to the man's request to verify his claims I had been talked into something I would later regret.

"'Mr. Jorgenson,' I stated, as formally as I could, 'you are henceforth to consider yourself a prisoner of the Army of the Republic, held on suspicion of spying for the Confederacy. The penalty for espionage in time of war is death.'

"I let the silence hang to underscore the seriousness of the matter I wished to communicate to him. 'We have discovered you armed, and not in the service of the Union. Furthermore, you claim to have detonated an explosion which could have grievously harmed if not killed a member of this detachment. If I see the slightest sign or activity on your part that I regard as a threat to the men under my command, or to the mission with which we have been entrusted, I shall shoot you myself.' I waved my revolver at him. 'Do you understand?'

"His face clouded. 'Ya,' he muttered. I ordered his hands to be untied.

"Once freed of his bonds, Jorgenson produced the keys to his padlocks from under his hat band, and opened the boxes. One container held coils of fusees as well as ordinary string, a couple of boxes of lucifers, a surveyor's measuring tape, and a waterproof packet containing several pages of writing in another language, including what looked to be recipes as well as sentences. Also in the packet were some lined pages, as though torn from a schoolboy's copybook, containing various arithmetical computations. Below these items, filling about half the box, were numerous paperboard cylinders measuring about ten inches in length by about two inches in diameter. They most closely resembled overly-large firecrackers, although missing a fusee attached to one end. The second box, which I had assumed would be full of powder, was about three-quarters filled with more of the cylinders.

"The troopers were delighted with these revelations. 'Lieutenant, your Berry Picker here is going to wreck your bridges with firecrackers,' was McKay's comment, accompanied by hoots of agreement from the other men. The response seemed to annoy Jorgenson. 'You vait, you vait,' he scolded, wagging a finger at his audience, who only jeered the louder at him. 'Vait and see; you vill see,' he replied doggedly. He extracted one of the cylinders from the pile and displayed the object at the end of an arm extended toward the troopers. 'Dis you haf not seen before,' he proclaimed. 'Dis vill show you someding you haf not known.'

"The men were not convinced. '*Medicine* show, medicine show,' one replied. 'That's the "show" you're going to give us.'

"'No, dese are special. Far more powerful than you haf ever seen . . . Boom!' Jorgenson's arms swept up and outward, miming an explosion, his right hand still holding the cylinder.

"Mitchell was as unimpressed as the men. 'McKay's right, for once. The Berry Picker sounds like a nostrum salesman.' The sergeant addressed me earnestly. 'I've seen shows where the faker plants his own people in the audience. They claim to be cured of their ailments after one sip from the miraculous bottle of extracts. We better be damn sure that what the Berry Picker blows up ain't already rigged with powder, like with the cliff.'

"I appreciated the sergeant's need for caution. I suggested to him, though, that while the prisoner might have guessed our troop would follow along the rail line past the cliff, he couldn't predict what we might ask him to demolish. The sergeant disagreed, pointing out that wrecking the trestles was the obvious next chore for us.

"I brought the argument to a close by recommending we thoroughly inspect the site we had chosen for a trial prior to giving Jorgenson access to it. With that concern laid to rest, I issued my orders. I was starting to be haunted by a conviction we were wasting time with this Jorgenson. Should he prove a fraud, I was anxious to destroy as much of the trestles as we could and return to Morrisburg before we discovered a far more threatening explanation for the blast on the cliff face than a mere lunatic.

"I decided only five of us were to proceed along the trestles: myself, the sergeant, Jorgenson, his guard, and a second private in case another hand was needed. The prisoner made a selection of about a half-dozen of the cylinders and a coil of fusee, plus he insisted on carrying with him the measuring tape, the copybook paper, and his pencil stub. From his saddlebag he selected two of the odd percussion caps.

"We traversed the first trestle, relieving the sentry at his outpost as we passed and sending him back to rejoin the others. I left the extra trooper on the rail bed between the two trestles, and four of us continued to the far end of the second structure.

"Here the sergeant and I made an examination of the locale as we had planned, to ensure it had not been earlier prepared for demolition by our madman. No evidence of powder kegs or loose powder or fusees were found. We then bid Jorgenson attend to his task.

"Like ourselves, he made a careful survey of the cribbing. He secured the surveyor's tape, paper, and pencil and began to measure and calculate with great attention and care. He then called for a rope and assistance to lower himself from the edge of the upper deck, because he said he had determined from his figures that the proper spots to place his cylinders were the first junctures where beams intersected several feet out from the bank. These were about eight feet below the level of the rails, but I could well understand his wish for a rope to secure himself. On one side the drop to the ground was only a further eight feet, but on the other at least twenty.

"The private I had left stationed between the trestles was sent to obtain a suitable rope from some we had in our wagons. When this was fetched, Jorgenson clambered down along the cribbing and lashed three of his cylinders on each side where the beams forked.

"Once the cylinders were in place, he inserted a percussion cap into the end of one of his devices in each group of three. The fusee coil was then affixed to this cap. He passed the coil up to us from either side to be cut, so that in a few minutes a length of fusee led separately from the deck down to each cluster of his firecrackers. Regaining the top of the trestle, he knotted together the ends of the fusee lengths attached to the cylinders, and also knotted one end of the fusee coil to this point. He payed out a couple of arm lengths of the coil, and then held the spot up to be severed.

"'How long?' Mitchell asked. Jorgenson calculated briefly. 'Three minutes.'

"We retreated back across the trestle to the furthest extent of the fusee now attached to the cylinders below the rails. I sent all but myself, the guard and Jorgenson to rejoin the rest of the troop, over the sergeant's objections. None of the three of us having thought to bring lucifers, I had to call back the extra trooper to provide us with some he had in his pockets for lighting his pipe. We lit the fusee, and then dashed to the cover of the square of logs that had been built to function as our observation post on the first trestle.

"Jorgenson had indicated that the balance of my men were in no danger where they stood, but I ordered them to take cover as a precaution. The three of us out on the trestle huddled down within the crude log structure. I had my pocket watch out and watched the second hand sweep around with its usual tardiness in times of anticipation.

"'Vat did you verk for your living, before de army?' Jorgenson suddenly asked me. Had he concluded my commission did not antedate the war? I tried to review what in my performance of my duties had led him to decide I was a volunteer and not a regular. I did admit to him, though, that I formerly was employed at my father's glass manufactory, a little distance outside Berlin, Michigan. 'Burnett & Son Glassworks,' I said, as though he were a potential customer. 'I'm the son.'

"His reply was drowned out by the second roar of explosives I had heard that day, this one much magnified in scale. I later realized Jorgenson had probably used rather more of his cylinders than were actually needed. If his intent was to impress me, he succeeded. After all, I had as much as threatened him with execution should his story not hold water. The blast he effected now unquestionably established in my mind his bona fides.

"The rails we partially lay upon within our shelter throbbed and strained at their spikes with the force of the eruption. Later I observed how the rails directly above the epicentre of the blast were twisted back into fantastic loops and curves resembling metal embroidery. But in our shelter on the trestle I clutched a tie for support as a heave of the air rolled underneath us, rocking the structure ferociously. Down the track, a billowing cloud arose, out of which hurtled beams and ties in all directions. A portion of support strut arced above us, landing on solid ground past the end of the trestle, between ourselves and the rest of the men. A huge beam was propelled with wonderful vigor aloft, looking like nothing so much as a gigantic signal rocket as it streaked skyward, hesitated in mid-flight, faltered, and dived end-over-end into the woods of the canyon below. A rain of wood splinters and other fine debris began to splatter down on us, and then the scene was silent for an instant. Crows broke the stillness with a harsh expression of their outrage at the disturbance, followed by the melodious trill of some woodland songbird, and then another. One by one the ordinary sounds of the forested hills resumed. I glanced over at Jorgenson, but he had already risen and was staring fixedly down the tracks at the column of smoke. I had the impulse to extend my hand to him by way of apology for doubting his word. Yet at the same time I was in awe of the evident power of the invention he possessed. How had a backwoods homesteader like himself stumbled upon such a harnessing of nature's destructive energies? I was aware, too, that the explosive substance contained in Jorgenson's devices had the potential to be both a fearsome weapon of war and a vital tool of peace.

"We clambered over the logs of the sentry post and headed out to inspect at close quarters the destruction the cylinders had caused. The top two tiers of cribwork had ceased to exist at the second trestle's far end, having either been reduced to smithereens, hurled smoking to the canyon floor, or collapsed into a tangle of shattered lumber precariously balanced atop a level of the cribwork sixteen or so feet below us. I complimented Jorgenson on his achievement. "Ya, ya," he muttered. Then grinned at me. "I tink I did it, ya?" He started to laugh — out of relief, I believe. His good humor, however, was infectious, and in a moment the other two of us were chuckling along with him.

"In that pleasant spirit, we rejoined the sergeant and the men. The troopers were somewhat abashed at realizing Jorgenson's claims had a basis of fact. I ordered the preparation of our midday meal, and during its consumption the men regained their ordinary composure. I resumed my questioning of Jorgenson, although with a lighter heart than earlier in the morning.

"His story, which I have no way of verifying other than the circumstantial, is that the substance within his cylinders has very recently been invented by a Swedish relative. This man, a cousin and thirty years of age, has been anxious to exhaustively test the uses for his invention, both out of a scientific habit of mind and in order to impress potential backers for a commercial production of the substance. Also, according to Jorgenson, the cousin is aware of military applications of such material. Jorgenson states that his cousin is of the opinion that such is the devastating power of the cylinders that they will be the means to effect an end to all wars from this time forward. No general or government, in the cousin's belief, would be willing to risk the annihilation promised by widespread detonations of the cylinders.

"This notion I am inclined to doubt, if I may interject. My own experiences under fire have led me to conclude that if witnessing the hellish power of some piece of weaponry were able to ensure eternal peace among the nations, the means of prosecuting war we already possess were more than sufficient for that happy outcome. My guess is that a darker goal impels the cousin, in that he rather is cognizant that the utilization of his explosive substance in war would be of especial interest to governments and investors alike.

"Whatever his motive, the cousin strongly desired to see his cylinders put to use under actual circumstances of combat, with a careful record kept of the results. The Crimean War ended four years before the Swede's invention was perfected, and another protracted European war does not seem imminent. But the cannonade striking our Fort Sumter last year appeared a God-sent opportunity, since Jorgenson's cousin was aware that the branch of his family settled in America had a son of both a practical and intelligent turn of mind. Naturally, Jorgenson did not describe his value to his relative in this fashion, but I deduce this by reading between the lines, as it were, of what Jorgenson did utter.

"To be brief, the cousin has shared the recipe for his invention with Jorgenson and charged him to find means to employ the substance under war conditions and keep accurate note of the particulars and outcome. My understanding is that in return for this perilous undertaking Jorgenson was advanced some monies and has been promised an additional portion of any future profits. Jorgenson is a few years younger than his Old Country cousin — that is, a few years older than myself — and evidently holds his relative in high regard. Yet neither Swede appears to have grasped the savagery displayed in the current war, and hence how much of a personal risk Jorgenson has volunteered for in attempting to intercede in the conflict in this way. On the other hand, to have the occasion to demonstrate such a device must be more exciting for our homesteader than to practice farming in a remote locale, with but meager hope of adequate reward for his considerable labors.

"In any case, Jorgenson requested of me that he be permitted to record the morning's work in his notebook kept for the purpose. This document was produced from his bedroll attached to his saddle. Once the noon-time meal was concluded, Jorgenson carefully sketched and inscribed, in what he affirmed was Swedish, the results of our activities.

"I was bursting with further questions, but also felt the pressure of time and so endeavored to relieve my curiosity in fits and starts during the afternoon. I had acquired a fear — rational or not — that the noise and smoke that accompanied our operations on the rail line might well attract more attention than a wandering demolitionist touting a new invention, that Confederate rangers or a cavalry patrol might come calling to investigate what the commotion was about. My goal was to apply Jorgenson's matériel to our ends, and then withdraw toward Morrisburg with dispatch.

"I divided the detachment into two parts. One, under the command of the sergeant, was to bring up the wagons and prepare the larger trestle for demolition in the conventional manner. With the likelihood of near-total destruction of at least one of the trestles due to the Swede's invention, I concluded we had little need to eradicate the railway bridges as we had planned en route back to Morrisburg. So I believed myself justified in applying all our remaining powder to the nearest trestle. The second part of the men, under my command, were to assist Jorgensen in placing his cylinders to bring down as much as possible of the further trestle. I maintained the pickets posted on our height of land, and in the woods to the east, due to my aforesaid sense that we were vulnerable to discovery — an apprehension I could not shake.

"The trestles were soon aswarm with troopers, while shouted orders and banter floated among and between those working on the tiers of cribbing just below the level of the rails and just over the canyon floor. A pair of hawks floated on the warm afternoon winds above the industrious scene.

"I managed to ascertain from Jorgenson additional information concerning the substance that filled his cylinders. His cousin Alfred, the inventor, has named the material Dynamic Powder, although its origin is rather different than gunpowder's. My comprehension must be weighed against Jorgenson's rudimentary English, and my lack of specialized knowledge of chemistry. I do have some understanding of the chemistry of glass from my profession, however. As I interpret Jorgenson's account, his cousin's Dynamic Powder derives from glycerol obtained from animal fats, which is combined with a mix of sulfuric and nitric acids. This product is then absorbed into pulped wood. A percussive force is required to detonate the resultant substance. Primer caps, adapted from the percussion caps in common use in firearms, were developed for this purpose. When ignited, the explosive substance within the cylinders expands in a manner his cousin has aptly called 'dynamic', although 'dramatic' would be an equally accurate term of description.

"The cousin, according to Jorgenson, is experimenting in Sweden with a purely liquid form of the material which promises even more spectacular results. But to date, Jorgenson reports, this fluid is too unstable for employment under field conditions.

"We blew the trestles late in the afternoon. Because of my concerns regarding our discovery by roving Confederate forces, I would have preferred to fire the charges early in the morning immediately before our departure. But the day clouding over gave some likelihood of rain before dawn. Rather than risk damp powder and a failure to successfully conclude our assigned duty, I gave orders to light the fusees.

"The noise was astounding. The cylinders of Dynamic Powder once again proved their mettle. My ears rang for up to fifteen minutes once the last of the falling debris had settled from the sky. For comparison's sake, I had arranged that the smaller trestle would be exploded first, and then a few minutes later the trestle the sergeant had prepared in the conventional way. Although the second blast consumed the entire quantity of powder we had left, both the sound and the results seemed puny compared to that of the first.

"The smaller of the trestles was left wrecked beyond thought of repair, a splintery mass of charred and torn wood heaped where the foundations for the cribbing had stood. The larger trestle was effectively ruined, but I estimate that two and half times the powder we had applied would have been required to create the same mayhem as wreaked on the other trestle by Cousin Alfred's invention.

"All my men were safe, and exhilarated by the scope of destruction we had achieved. Preparations for the evening meal were begun in an excellent humor. I spoke to the troop, congratulating them on their devotion to duty so far on this expedition, and about my resolution to commence our return to Morrisburg at first light. The latter statement generated further cause for celebratory feeling among the men. But I cautioned them that we would be maintaining pickets throughout the night, since our presence in the area the past few days was unlikely to have been overlooked by the enemy, should any of their number be about. This announcement failed to darken the men's spirits. I seemed alone in my anxiety. Nevertheless, we had loosed off a clamorous din that afternoon that I was sure was audible across the continent in both Washington and Richmond. And we had raised a flag of smoke that I was equally certain made our whereabouts glaringly obvious to every Rebel in Kirby Smith's army at Knoxville, leagues closer to us.

"After supper the men not on guard duty were lazing about by the cookfire, enjoying the late evening light of June. I was seated in front of my tent speaking with the sergeant concerning the watches of the night and some details about our route and deployment during the next day's travel. All at once, shouts and some frenzied motion originated where I had earlier observed Jorgenson diligently scribbling in his notebook. He had been corroborating some details of the destruction of the smaller trestle with a couple of troopers who had been his main assistants in placing his cylinders. The hubbub grew until it enveloped the entire camp.

"What best to do with Jorgenson had been much on my mind. His cousin's invention obviously was a weapon that should be kept from Confederate hands. The Ordnance

Bureau, if not the War Department itself, would undoubtedly want to examine this new explosive. Jorgenson assured me he had not brought his cousin's formula with him, and so I had insisted we not explode every cylinder he carried but retain a few for scientific examination by our side. I had no hint of the man's inclinations: Union or Rebel. We were operating, after all, in a border state that was home to vociferous sympathizers on both sides, and whose government had attempted to remain neutral during many months before finally declaring for the Union.

"My aim was to discuss with Jorgenson his return to Morrisburg with us. I apprised the sergeant that, should the Swede prove reluctant to accompany us with his samples of Dynamic Powder, I felt the exigencies of war must outweigh any of Jorgenson's rights under civil law. If we failed to obtain his consent, I planned to arrest him and convey him with us in chains, if necessary.

"My conversation with Mitchell on this topic was barely underway when the corporal marched the subject of our discussion toward us at gunpoint. Accompanying the pair was a trooper clutching Jorgenson's notebook, followed by the rest of the men. Once I silenced the volleys of accusations and threats being voiced by every throat, I sorted out the situation to be as follows.

"Jorgenson, having completed his recording of our day's successes, had left his notebook where he had been seated and gone into the woods to relieve himself. One of the troopers who had participated in Jorgenson's compilation of events had idly picked up the document and leafed through it. Although having no familiarity with Swedish, he had come upon what appeared to be an account of the use of Dynamic Powder to demolish the courthouse at Box Crossing. The private, who could read a little, identified words in English naming the structure, and knew well that the destruction of this building was the work of the Rebel force operating hereabouts in May. This evidence of Jorgenson's treachery was loudly proclaimed, and the men again seized on the conviction that the Swede was a Confederate spy or guerilla.

"I emphatically reminded all present of the man's help to the Union cause this day in assisting us to reduce the railway trestles to firewood. I dismissed everyone but the main parties to the discovery. On questioning Jorgenson more privately, he freely acknowledged his participation in the ruin of the building in question. His motive, he claimed, was not to aid either side in a war in which he regarded himself to be a complete outsider. His purpose was simply scientific and commercial. He said fate and chance were the main determinants as to whether he had the opportunity to detonate his cylinders on behalf of the Rebellion or the Union.

"I admit to being taken aback by such a complete absence of moral sense. But the man stubbornly insisted he had done nothing wrong, since he believed himself entirely impartial as to the outcome of the war. He was convinced that his contribution to the aims of each side should stand him in the good graces of both warring parties. He repeated that his allegiance was to his cousin in whose employ he had enrolled himself, and to the testing of the cylinders which constituted the reason for his employment. Why, he repeatedly asked, if he was a Confederate agent would he offer to assist a Union detachment in nullifying a transport route potentially useful to the Rebels? Nothing I said could convince him he was in mortal error with regard to his stance.

"Finally I informed him that the recent revelation of his part in the enemy's raid on Box Crossing had compromised him in my eyes. Still, in view of his significant help at the trestles, I would accept his parole attesting to his willingness to accompany us back to Morrisburg. There, the merit of his arguments could be resolved by higher authorities. If he failed to accede to my demand, I would be compelled to arrest him forthwith. After a few seconds' thought, he gave me his word, on condition that his notebook be returned to him. This I could not agree to, whereupon he made a curious counter-offer. He asked for permission to copy the day's report in the form of a letter to his cousin, which I would swear to post on our arrival. The contents of the rest of the notebook he had already sent to his employer, he said. His proposal, according to him, would thus fulfill both our needs: his for giving fair and due service to his cousin, and mine for retaining evidence of his "neutral" — as he described his role — assistance to both combatants.

"These terms being acceptable to me, we shook hands on the bargain. I told him his decision to freely travel with us might well mitigate any adverse opinion of his former activities. The sergeant and corporal both expressed the sentiment that I was foolish to trust Jorgenson. But having found him a man open and honest in his responses to every query put to him — despite whether his answer might fly in the face of common opinion or even preservation of his own safety or liberty — I saw no reason to doubt his parole.

"Jorgenson completed his letter by dusk, and presented me with the sealed envelope addressed to his cousin. Our detachment was underway by about six in the morning, although considerably delayed at the start by the necessity of levering the wagons over the pile of rubble Jorgenson's initial blast had caused. The Swede offered to use his remaining cylinders to open an easier path for us. But because I was convinced Ordnance would wish samples of the Dynamic Powder, I wanted these last cylinders conserved.

"The obstacle of the rockfall overcome, we made good time toward Morrisburg, and paused for the night on the near bank of Still Woman Creek. As a precaution, I set pickets to watch while we slept. But in the morning, Jorgenson and one of the horses had vanished, and the guards had heard nothing. The Swede's pack horse remained, but he had carefully removed the remaining samples of Dynamic Powder.

"Despite a sweep of the area, we found no tracks or other indications of the route Jorgenson followed in making good his escape. Upon reaching the Morrisburg encampment late that afternoon, I reported to Colonel Whitney. I suggested that a patrol under my leadership immediately attempt to overtake Jorgenson, and to locate and search his homestead in the Rutland Lake region, if indeed such a farm exists as he claimed. A patrol, which includes the corporal and a couple of troopers from my detachment who could identify Jorgenson, was dispatched but has not yet returned.

"His letter does provide the name and address of his cousin in Sweden — a maternal cousin, obviously, since the last name is different. Unless Jorgenson lied about the identity of this individual, my suggestion was to have our representative to the Swedish government pursue contact with the cousin. I believe that, despite Jorgenson having dishonored himself with regard to his promise to withdraw with us to Morrisburg, he spoke the truth about his cousin. I realize Jorgenson himself may be the inventor of Dynamic Powder, and the tale about the cousin merely flimflam. But an approach to the cousin in Sweden should settle the matter.

"I certainly acknowledge I erred in trusting Jorgenson's word, and so may be wrong about my conclusions here.

Regardless, Captain, I remain willing to assist you and your department to my utmost with your investigation into the events at the Bright Canyon trestles.

"Was I unclear about any matter? Do you have any questions?"

THE DEAN OF THE DISTILLERY

THE SHADOWS OF GRAIN WAGONS ROLLED INTO a yard dappled with sunlight filtered through birch leaves. Barn swallows flickered among the branches, or swooped over the horses and drivers. Each time a hoof descended, a puff of summer dust rose from the earth. Axles and springs creaked as the mounded loads of barley passed. Waiting between the shafts of emptied wagons parked helter-skelter alongside the granary, other horses nickered and neighed; harnesses clinked as the animals tossed or shook their heads, and snorted. Shouts from the men within the large buildings were audible above the constant low thunder of machinery.

Floating over every structure, every cart, each person or beast of burden was the sweet heavy odor of malt. From some areas of the compound drifted varying scents: close to the stables, for instance, the malt was overlaid with hay and manure. Within the granary walls, odors from piles of hops, or wheat, or rye predominated. A cesspool for mash slurry beside the largest building emitted a stench of vegetative decay. But pervading the entire site and our clothes was that pungency of wetted, germinated grain, thick enough almost to taste, to chew.

Peasants I had never seen before, hauling their crop to sell to us for the first time, seemed to know who I was. They would lift a huge hand from the reins and wave when they noticed me by the courtyard well watching them arrive. They would cry out the syllables I knew were their name for me. Or when I played around my father's desk, their lined faces were suddenly grinning in the office doorway, teeth blackened or worn to stubs or missing. Caps in hand, they addressed me in proper words as *the dean*. *Good morning, dean*, they would say, laughing. Or sometimes *Tovarish Dean*. Or *little dean*. For my owlish look, a child not yet six wearing glasses? I never saw another child my age with spectacles. My father's friends from synagogue, drinking tea from the office samovar, or strangers in grubby caftans that smelled of herring and cigarettes, men with goods to offer my father or looking for work, would sometimes refer to me as *the melamed*, teacher. But to anyone part of our everyday, I was the dean.

I had the run of the place, although could my parents really have permitted this? There was the high-roofed shed containing the enormous, gleaming fermentation stills, with their fires underneath, and lattices of piping. Outside was the wood yard, our source of fuel when coal became scarce or too expensive. Mikhail Alexandrovich, the largest man employed by my father, oversaw the acquisition and sawing to size, and splitting of the wood. He had an enormous beard and said he had a son my age. Under Mikhail Alexandrovich's authority, I was allowed to be a wild Indian or fierce pirate among the stacked piles of logs. When he had a free moment, he would pull string from a pocket of his leather apron. His thick fingers could weave complicated figures faster than my eye was able to follow. I begged him to teach me the secret, but he just winked and trumpeted out his laugh.

Sheltered by a lean-to built against the wagon barn was a mountain of coal sacks, when they were available. Another shed held glass carboys filled with mysterious fluids. The decanters and bottlers, who worked in a different building, were mostly Jews, unlike the majority of the men. One of the teamsters, Mikhail Alexandrovich's youngest brother, Vlad, would let me ride with him when he took sealed barrels and boxes of bottles from our warehouse to the railway station or the merchant's in Khobesk. Both were exciting places, with swarms of people milling about, their talk a babble. Vlad was a teenager my father declared was very bright; he already spoke a little Jewish, which many at the place never bothered to learn. I was especially in awe when Mikhail Alexandrovich told me Vlad was waiting to go into the Army. I admired, too, his confident manner of command with the horse and wagon, and in negotiations with railway officials or the merchant's employees.

At lunch, my father and I would stroll across the yard to the house for a meal that began first with the intoning of the *broche*, and then invariably a bowl of borsht — cold in summer, hot in winter. I didn't care for the white dollops of *smeteneh* everybody else seemed to relish stirring into their soup. My father would report to my mother on the events of the morning, and my mother would occasionally comment or offer her advice. My father never failed to mention to his cronies when they visited the office that my mother was the favourite daughter of the famous Rabbi of Mglin, so her words were worth listening to. She, and on weekends, my sister Miriam, four years older than me, passed the days in sewing, cooking, gardening and weathering mysterious household crises that were announced at lunch or supper, or, if severe, would involve pulling my father away from the office or some other distillery business to resolve.

Weekdays, my sister attended the village school, a half-hour walk across the fields. She taught me a special song her class was to present at a recital, about how children everywhere love Comrade Stalin, because he brings happiness to all people. I was impressed by her acquisition of learning at the secular institution, and grateful for her willingness to share her knowledge with me, even if she was bossy in the process of instructing me in the tune and words. I had no idea — nor did she, really — what the song was about. Miriam did once identify for me the picture of Comrade Stalin that my father, as manager, had hanging in his office. I never heard my father refer to him in any way.

Such matters as who ruled in Moscow seemed infinitely remote from Khobesk. In any case, this information, like the household worries that at intervals preoccupied my mother, was beyond my comprehension or concern. They wafted past as did clouds which briefly darkened a spring morning. I was conscious of less vague threats to the round of my days, but I had no reason to believe my father was not protection against any trouble. My parents, my relatives who lived nearby, and my father and his friends sometimes mumbled in low voices about attacks on Jews and Jewish homes and businesses over in Bialystok, or in some settlement between ours and Minsk, or away south near Lvov. Things were also very bad with Jews in some further country called Germany. Once when I was in town with Vlad on the wagon, a man walking by where we were halted waiting to unload yelled angrily at us. Vlad shouted back, and the man shook his fist and spat on the street. I asked Vlad what the man had said. "He thinks you should not have so much money," Vlad explained. I thought of my tin box at home, where I kept my Chanukah gelt and other coins my uncles and aunts had given me.

"I have saved twenty-six kopeks in a tin box I got from my zayde," I informed Vlad, puzzled. "Does that man think I have too many?"

Vlad's laugh boomed out, nearly as loudly as his brother's. "No, no. He means your father has too much money. I'm sure he doesn't care about your kopeks."

"Does my father have a lot of money?"

Vlad spat over the side of the wagon. "Forget the man. He is an idiot."

Three times, a dozen or so men from Khobesk appeared at the yard, shouting. They weaved about and bumped into each other, but their red faces were fierce when they yelled. After the first time, one fall afternoon, I asked Mikhail Alexandrovich what they had wanted.

"They were saying, "Give us vodka, Jews," Mikhail Alexandrovich explained. "Except they used another word for 'Jews'. Not a good one."

My father had sent me for his foreman, Yuri Petrovich, when the men appeared. Then he had stepped into the yard to face them. Yuri Petrovich told me to inform Misha, which I knew meant Mikhail Alexandrovich, and then to hide indoors. Several others near where Yuri Petrovich was working grabbed sticks and shovels and hurried out to form a half-circle behind my father. When I found Mikhail Alexandrovich, he hoisted an axe to his shoulder and uttered something sharply to a gang of men unloading logs from a wagon. They, too, picked up axes, and also poles with sharpened metal tips they had been using to maneuver the timber. Mikhail Alexandrovich and his crew joined my father and the others in the yard. I stared out through the office window.

The visitors screeched at my father's men. The foreman shouted a reply in a firm voice, and then my father spoke. Yuri Petrovich's and my father's words led to much howling and shaking of fists and spitting on the ground by the newcomers. But after a time they stumbled off down the lane, turning every few steps to yell at my father and his men. Everyone around my father remained in place until nobody was visible on the road.

Another time, one of the angry visitors from Khobesk picked up a stone and threw it toward the line of my father's employees. The rock hit one of Mikhail Alexandrovich's crew on the side of the head. The stricken man dropped his pole and knelt on the ground with his hands against his hair. His hands were slickly red across the palms when he lifted them for a second. At the sight, Mikhail Alexandrovich released a roar and charged toward the man who had thrown the rock. The giant's abrupt advance, axe in hand, startled the visitors, who retreated several paces. The stone-thrower tripped as he tried to withdraw. Mikhail Alexandrovich was on him in a second, and raised his axe. "Misha!" several voices from among my father's employees yelled, urgent with a warning. Mikhail Alexandrovich dropped the axe and began punching and kicking the man who had thrown the stone, like Goliath pummeling David. A cacophony of yelling from both sides erupted, and then my father's men charged, waving their sticks and axes. The men from Khobesk fled, abandoning their companion to his fate, a beating.

After that, the intruders only came at night. First someone cut through the wire fence surrounding the compound. They broke into the warehouse, and stole some boxes from a shipment ready to be dispatched. One winter evening I was lying in my upstairs room under my quilt, and heard shouts and pounding on the large wooden gate into the yard that was now closed and barred at night. My father had hired two watchmen by this time. One knocked on our front door and spoke excitedly with my father. From my bedroom window, I could see lights moving beyond the fence, in the lane. The watchman was sent by my father to rouse some of the employees, who lived in cottages clustered not far from our house. When the little force was marshaled, I waited to learn what would happen. But except for a few stones hurled over the fence, and several fruitless attacks from the lane that shook the gate, the assault dwindled away. My father and his men remained on patrol for an hour or so afterwards in case the townsmen returned.

Because of my faith in my father's ability to effectively shield my life, our lives, these incidents were no more to me than a heavy snowstorm, or when one March weeks of rain washed out the roads around us, leaving us marooned on an island ringed by submerged fields. Once the excitement of such events dissipated, I did not imagine, let alone worry about, these episodes recurring. Each ordinary day the familiar mysteries of my father's enterprise beckoned me, welcomed me. I threaded between the bustling rhythms of men and horses and machinery, tasks and meals. The personalities, the contents and conditions of buildings, and the open spaces between the structures I encountered were mine to explore, marvel at, try to understand. I was the prince of this kingdom, the acknowledged dean of this world.

When my sister and I were sent away, I was apprehensive as any child is at a completely new venture, and a little bewildered by my parents' decision. But I never doubted that under my father's guidance all would be well for me, be for the best. For some reason we entrained at Baranovichi, where a number of rail lines converged. I think this was because leaving from there meant one less change of trains for my sister and me than if we had departed from Khobesk. Vlad drove my father and us the half-day to Baranovichi, so our farewells to our mother were said at the courtyard gate. A number of my father's men stood near my mother and one of my aunts to wave us on our way. Since my father was to accompany us on the first part of our journey, I was surprised by my mother's overwrought state, her tearful demeanor and desperate hugs. I assured her repeatedly, in answer to her admonitions, that I would be brave and obey my sister.

The confusion of the train station at Baranovichi, somewhat larger than that of Khobesk, made an impression on me. But our subsequent swims through the crowds jamming the huge, noisily echoing station at Warsaw, and at Ostrava at the Czechoslovakian border, dwarfed the tumult of Baranovichi. More vivid in my mind is the enormous locomotive chugging by me where I wait on a platform holding my sister's hand. Great clouds of steam billow out from under the metal wheels and the oscillating shafts of the engine as it flows past us, overwhelming with its sound no less than the fog generated by its might.

My sister must have successfully negotiated with Polish officials, as well as getting us across two other borders. But what remains with me is the brown, varnished, wooden window ledge of a train compartment somewhere on the voyage. The width of the ledge was perfect for playing with a miniature wagon and some carved cows, favourite toys I had been allowed to bring to while away the hours. Also I have never lost the vision of a river observed through, and then obscured by, trees in green leaf as the rail line sped along a river valley. Perhaps this was the Morava as we approached the Austrian border, but perhaps not.

We were met in Wien by my father's sister Tante Freyde, and her husband Fetter Nathan. He said we were to call him *Onkel* Nathan. The ride from the station to their house was my first in an automobile, with my newly met onkel at the wheel. At their house were thick rugs, and paintings on the walls, and more devices I experienced for the first time, including a flushing water closet. Their telephone was the only one I had ever seen in a private home. The distillery office had one, but its use was strictly limited to official functions, and I was astounded when that first afternoon my Tante Freyde had me speak over the apparatus to Onkel Nathan's brother.

I was to share a room with my tante and onkel's son Shmuel, a year older than I. His room was filled with books, and shelves of toys, and he had a crystal set radio he had built himself, over whose earphones he could listen to broadcasts. Next to the bed assigned to me was an empty dresser, where my tante put the clothes I had brought. And soon more. Thus began my life with the Zukermanns.

A myriad of things were strange: the size and glitter of the bathroom, with its thick towels and sweet-swelling soaps. The rich, creamy foods served in the household, which seemed heavy in my stomach until I got used to them. The wondrous pastries served with almost every meal — here, not a delicacy or special treat as at home, but as basic as borscht had been. The presence of servants — a cook and a maid. The crowded city streets, carriages and automobiles and trucks and the streetcars, and sidewalks filled with strollers and people in a hurry. The German spoken by the Zukermanns even at home and by everyone else everywhere else. Enough

German is found in Jewish that I often grasped what people were saying, or at least got more of the gist than I did among strangers at home. I rapidly acquired a level of comfort with the language.

I missed my parents, though Tante Freyde was warm and welcoming. She could produce a Shabbes kugel pudding that tasted almost the same as my mother's — perhaps the noodle dish was concocted from the same recipe. Onkel Nathan was far more distant than my father was toward me, his face stern and worried-looking. Yet he was punctilious about asking me each evening how my day had gone. And he could bend surprisingly at times: he brought home marvelous toy sailboats unexpectedly for me and Shmuel just before the family was to leave for a June holiday at the Atter See, a couple of months after Miriam and I were sent to them.

Shmuel must have resented my sudden presence in the family circle, and in his bedroom. He was cool to me for a long time in matters to do with our room — his toys were *verboten* to me, he declared the first evening. And he demanded his father's attention first when my onkel returned home from the store each evening, not that this was something I had any inclination to challenge. Yet Shmuel was more like a brother than a cousin to me when we were away from the house. I was sent with him to attend a Jewish school almost as soon as my sister and I arrived in Wien. From him I learned of the perils of the streets, and that the school was new to him, too, and that he would stand up for me among the boys who studied there.

Shmuel led me along one route through the avenues and business districts to school, and a lengthier route home. He pointed out a Catholic school we walked by mornings, in front of which a rock-throwing battle had erupted between its students and passing Jewish children the month before. Both sets of scholars were in a hurry to get to class each morning, so we were in no danger walking quickly by the Catholic academy at that time of day, Shmuel claimed. But once classes were dismissed, the potential for trouble was large. Numerous smaller harassments had occurred before the explosion of the previous month, which I gathered had been precipitated one afternoon by a group from Shmuel's school determined to confront the situation.

On our second day travelling to school together, we were proceeding past a row of shops when Shmuel roughly grabbed my arm and yanked me toward the entrance to one of them, a milliner's. Unable to fathom what we could want with women's hats, and taking his gesture as an unprovoked assault, I pushed back at him. Not relinquishing his grip on my coat, he hissed words at me I did not understand, and nodded his head mysteriously in the direction of further up the sidewalk. But the frightened expression on his face convinced me I was in danger. I trailed him into the shop.

A woman behind the counter moved to intercept us, and Shmuel spoke to her at length. She produced a couple of straw hats for his inspection, and he lingered a long time examining each. He and the saleswoman talked further, and Shmuel stepped to the window display to peer at the hats there. As he lifted one off its stand, I watched him glance both ways along the street. He paraded the selected hat to the counter, and additional words followed. Then he gave a half-bow and we were back outside.

I looked at him questioningly. "*Heimwehr*," he pronounced, as though the syllables alone were an explanation. Sensing my bafflement after a moment, he pointed to the far end of the block where I caught a glimpse of the backs of two crisply-uniformed men, apparently police or soldiers. I shrugged, to indicate I was still in the dark as to what had just happened. Shmuel said more to me that I could not fully grasp, before he gave up and we resumed our route to school.

But I did comprehend that these particular uniforms were a source of great fear to Shmuel. Bit by bit as the days and weeks sped by, I learned from him and others at school why face-to-face encounters with members of the *Heimwehr* were to be avoided at any cost. In February there had been a war in Wien between the *Heimwehr*, who hated Jews and would hurt you on sight, and the *Schutzbund*, who were the volunteer soldiers of the city government, and whose ranks not only included Jews but would defend Jews and Jewish gatherings from attack. In the winter war, I was told, our protectors had been defeated by artillery fire and the icy temperature, with thousands of them killed, thousands more arrested, and many executed afterwards. Ever since, Jews were in extra danger; this was when Shmuel was sent to the Jewish school. I bragged to my classmates that where I came from, my father and his men easily vanquished those who would harm us Jews. Even in telling my story, I for the first time conceived of a connection between those confrontations I had witnessed at the distillery and a threat to me in the greater sphere of life. I wondered if my Onkel Nathan shared my father's unbounded power to shield my sister and me.

The tale of my father's success where the *Schutzbund* had failed increased my status among my classmates. Initially, I had been subject to the suspicion and isolation accorded all new arrivals at any school. Shmuel had from the outset worked to break down these barriers, natural to children as a lingering instinct of tribalism: the fear and hence hatred of strangers. My first days at the Khobesk *cheder*, where

I originally was taught my Hebrew, had been no different essentially than what I encountered in my early weeks at the school in Wien. Except, at Wien my cousin introduced me to his *chavarim* as worthy of their attention. Since his pals were, like him, in a higher grade than me, they and he could and did intervene to successfully blunt the worst of the hazing and scorn that was my lot for a time at the hands of certain of my classmates. My status of semi-outcast at the school bothered me much more than having to abruptly dodge down side streets to avoid approaching uniforms, or than participating in a hit-and-run stoning of a gang of Catholic children the afternoon following another blood-drawing fusillade directed at a homeward bound Jewish group a couple of blocks from my school. One particular tormentor among my Wien class-mates, a sullen-faced youth much larger than myself named Dovid, demanded under threat of a beating that I surrender each day the sweet pastry invariably included in the lunch provided me by Tante Freyde's cook. I had already suffered being unaccountably pushed to the floor by Dovid, painfully skinning open my knee, in physical culture class. I offered no protest to the newest outrage. But during one walk home with Shmuel, I confessed to being the victim of Dovid's extortion, to my shame. The next day my cousin put a stop to Dovid's thefts, and his covert bullying of me subsequently trickled to an end.

While we lived at the Zukermanns', Miriam and the daughters of other well-to-do families were driven to and from classes, held at a different school than the one I and Shmuel attended. Because of my sister's age and gender, her life once we arrived in Wien was as distant from mine as it had been at home. We both, though, pored over letters from our parents posted jointly to us faithfully every week. Miriam was better than I about replying with news of our own. Often my communications were a few sentences tacked on to her beautifully scribed pages.

I presume she must have been even more lonely at the Zukermanns' than I, since I at least had Shmuel's constant company. Onkel Nathan's brother had a daughter a little younger than Miriam, Adele, who, with her circle of friends, sometimes included my sister in outings. But Miriam never became, as far as I could tell, close to any of these girls. I regret I never asked Miriam if she felt as sad as I often did at being separated from our former life, from our mother and father. But I was deep in that fog called childhood, self-obsessively attempting to chart a course through threats, mysteries and pleasures of whose dimensions and implications I perceived only a portion. Nor, even in Wien, had I lost the sense of my father as omnipotent pilot, who would safely steer me across any waters, any storm. I cheered myself during daily intervals of longing to be home with thoughts of his beneficence, his wise guardianship of my life. I did not doubt he would speedily bring my and my sister's sojourn with the Zukermanns to a happy end, and I would be restored to how my hours were before.

One July afternoon, however, Onkel Nathan returned to the house unexpectedly and forbade any of us to go outside, even to play on the lawns. Friends of his, with grim faces, rang the bell and were ushered into his study. Shmuel's and my confinement to the house, which in practice meant primarily our bedroom, extended to the next day, as well. Miriam told us that the leader of Austria, Herr Dollfuss, had been killed in an attempted revolt. I had heard his name mentioned with loathing at the Zukermanns', as the man responsible for the slaughter of the *Schutzbund*. But his assassins were not people like ourselves, Miriam said, but men as bad as him. With Italy's aid they had been suppressed, and Herr Dollfuss' deputy, Herr von Schuschnigg, was the leader of Austria now. At dinner, Onkel Nathan said what occurred was a falling-out among murderers, and none of this would help the Jews.

Several days after, on a Sunday morning, the household was again disrupted by the arrival of two of my onkel's friends with disturbing information. This time, when Onkel Nathan emerged from his study after receiving his visitors, his expression was as strained as I had ever seen it. "Where's your tante?" he asked me. "Freydele?" he called. "Freyde?"

She emerged from the kitchen. "Ja?"

"Please come with me into the study. Herr Heinke has been arrested."

My tante took a step back, then lifted a hand to cover her mouth. "*Gottenyu*," she whispered. She followed my onkel into the study; the door again closed.

Once more we were forbidden to leave the house. All day strange men appeared and left the Zukermanns'. The phone rang frequently. I asked Shmuel who Herr Heinke was, but he didn't know. Dinner was eaten in nearly complete silence, and the visitors and phone calls continued into the evening. Shmuel and I were sent to bed early.

We were told to stay indoors the following morning, also. My onkel left after breakfast, but was back by noon. After lunch, he called Miriam and me into his study.

Onkel Nathan told us certain events had happened that meant we would all be leaving Wien the next day. He and Shmuel and I were going by train to Italy, and then by ship to London. He had telegraphed a business acquaintance in England, who would arrange a place for us to stay.

Tante Freyde, meanwhile, would travel with Miriam back to our home. Our tante wanted to visit our zayde and bubbe, her parents. And of course see her brothers and sisters, including our tateh and mama.

I felt a swirl of emotion at this news. Excitement, apprehension at another uprooting, but mostly a powerful desire to be reunited with my parents. I interrupted my onkel, an act I had never dared to attempt, and asked why I couldn't accompany Miriam and my tante, rather than go with him and Shmuel.

"The arrangements already have been made, Meir," Onkel Nathan declared.

Tears filled my eyes, despite my determination not to cry.

"You will see your parents very soon," my onkel added, observing my distress. "In London."

I gaped at him.

The plan had always been, my onkel explained, for my parents to obtain documents that would permit them to join Miriam and me in Wien. His tone implied he was reviewing information my sister and I already knew, but I, at least, had never been told this. My parents intended to journey further, to America, my onkel continued. They knew that the situation for Jews in Wien was not much better than in Russia, but the threat to my and Miriam's well-being was not as immediate here as they had judged it to be in Khobesk. When my family reached America, my father's skills would enable him to find employment such that he could save passage money to send to Russia to enable the rest of Miriam's and my relatives to leave.

Now, however, recent problems required that all of us in Wien must depart without delay. Associates of my onkel would continue to operate his business, he informed us, until it could be sold. I had only visited my onkel's shop once, a hushed and elegant fur clothing salon on a main street. Miriam and my tante would entrain from Khobesk with my parents for Warsaw, Berlin, Amsterdam, and meet us in London. From there my family would leave for the New World, and perhaps the Zukermanns would follow after a while.

My head reeled with the intricacies of the plan. I still did not grasp why I would be accompanying my onkel, rather than Tante Freyde. But the thought an itinerary had been established that would result in me soon being with my parents again filled me with joy.

"What will happen to this house, Onkel Nathan?" my sister asked.

I stared at her. I had not considered such a question.

My onkel appeared uncomfortable for the first time. He briskly said that the disposition of the house would depend on many factors, ones he did not choose to enumerate to us at present. For the moment, his brother in Wien would keep an eye on it. The servants would continue to be employed for the near future. And now, he said, dismissing us, we must see to our packing.

Since Shmuel and I and my onkel were to leave before Miriam and my tante, I said goodbye to my sister in the Zukermanns' front hall. When we reached Livorno, in Italy, I stayed for the first time in a hotel, while we waited for our ship. Both on the train through the mountains, and at the hotel in Livorno, I found the cessation of any significant daily interaction with females an odd experience. As I never had before, I related only to my onkel and Shmuel, and not also to mother, or sister, or tante.

Shipboard, however, offered a wonderful series of activities. Shmuel and I tirelessly roamed from deck to deck, befriending a crewman who showed us areas of the ship off-limits to passengers. We got to peek down into the broiling din of the engine room, and to be present when another crewman fed and exercised passengers' dogs, which had to endure the voyage in kennels in the baggage hold. My cousin and I observed others playing shuffleboard on the upper decks, and eventually were allowed to try the game ourselves.

I enjoyed the cramped luxuriousness of our stateroom, where I had a small wooden ladder to climb each night up to my bunk. The steady thrum and vibration of the ship's engines soothed me to sleep. One morning I awoke to find the ship still and silent: in the darkness, we had docked at Barcelona. A new motion affected the vessel once we had steamed beyond the Strait of Gibraltar and encountered the swells of the open Atlantic. The rolling of the hull bothered a number of adults, including Onkel Nathan. Shmuel and I, however, found the change exhilarating. Now we really felt like sailors braving a storm, although the weather remained fine across the Bay of Biscay and up the English Channel.

We waited for the others at London in vain. We stayed first in the home of a furrier my onkel had dealt with over the years. Then Onkel Nathan rented an apartment. In September, Shmuel and I were enrolled in a school. At first our facility with English was too meager to let us engage with our classes in any meaningful way. But little by little I understood more of what was said to me.

My onkel doggedly attempted to elicit information via telegram and letter as to what had happened to his wife, my sister, and my parents. At the time I knew there were delays, difficulties, obstacles. Later I was aware that trumped-up charges had been brought against my father, either because he had attempted to obtain exit papers for himself and my mother, or because of a jealous superior or envious employee, or because he was a Jew. He was arrested. My mother and sister did not want to desert him, naturally, and so remained in Khobesk trying to muster what help for him they could, with the assistance of his friends and our relatives. Tante Freyde resolved to return to Wien and follow us to London. But she was detained by the authorities, accused of being an accomplice in my father's crimes, the foreign recipient of funds my father was alleged to have misappropriated, or some such. Since my tante was technically an Austrian citizen at this point, my onkel tried through his brother to have the Austrian embassy request her release. This they declined to do, on the grounds that her husband, my onkel, was a fugitive from the police. Besides, she was born a Russian Jew, and her fate was for the Russian government to decide.

I believe money at some juncture changed hands, and Tante Freyde was freed after several months. But on her return to Wien, she was forbidden to leave the country. In effect, she was a hostage for Onkel Nathan's flight to England. I came to understand, years later, that he had used his international connections as a furrier as a cover to help obtain arms for the *Schutzbund*. Hence in the eyes of the government he was closely associated with the doomed attempt to defend Wien from the armed attack by the *Heimwehr*, who had been assisted by elements of the police and army. Onkel Nathan's contribution to the *Schutzbund*, brought to light by the arrest of a man who had worked with him in the arms-smuggling scheme, carried with it the likelihood of imprisonment or even execution.

I had found it difficult to share Shmuel's and my onkel's euphoria when news came that Tante Freyde was to be permitted to travel back to Wien, since my own family remained stuck in Khobesk. Subsequent events quickly dampened the elation of any of us in London. By spring, too, we had worn out our welcome as far as official Britain was concerned.

Through the good agency of Onkel Nathan's contacts in London, we sailed in August of 1935 to Montreal. Within a year, my onkel had become a partner in a Spadina Avenue clothing company in Toronto.

He and my aunt continued to stay in as close communication as possible through intermediaries, developing many schemes to accomplish her escape. Even after the Anschluss in 1938, the government continued to claim it favoured Jewish emigration from Austria. Tante Freyde, apparently, was an exception. Of my own family we heard less and less.

And then nothing, as the war rolled through Russia. My parents and sister and relatives went into the Great Silence. We did not know the place or hour of their leaving. Shmuel was eager to join up and fight, especially since with his German accent he had to make clear repeatedly to his high school classmates that he was a refugee from the Nazis, and not a member of the master race. In 1944, at seventeen, he managed to enlist in the Royal Canadian Navy, but in the end never heard a shot fired in anger.

In 1943, the Red Cross informed my onkel that Tante Freyde had been shipped from Wien to the Theresienstadt ghetto the previous year. Since this Czechoslovakian location was considered a "model" relocation camp, Onkel Nathan was hopeful for a reunion at the war's end. But in late 1945, he learned she had been included on a transport to another camp the year before, and no further record of her exists.

Thus men and women who saw us as receptacles for spit and for rocks, lashed us into agony, into shards and charred sand. The wind through the birch leaves swept us away. In

1968 I rode the rail line southwest from Minsk to Baranovichi, accompanied by an Intourist guide. But no one in the towns along the right of way had heard of Khobesk. Nor of my family. Nor even of the distillery. At the little museum in Baranovichi, which I visited to learn if there were historic maps of the district, my government minder disappeared into the bathroom. The elderly clerk, badly stooped, suddenly inquired in Jewish if I were a Jew. Startled, I admitted I was. He identified himself as a co-religionist, and asked me, in an insistent voice, if I could help him emigrate to Israel. I took his name and particulars, and promised to pass the information along to those Canadian organizations devoted to assisting in such matters. He expressed his gratitude, although with enough resignation in his words that I could tell he knew nothing would come of his request. "How goes it for a Jew, here?" I asked. He glanced around the room, then down at the counter where he had spread such maps he had, maps that showed no trace of the village in which I was born. "Hard," he whispered, as though anyone present could understand us. "Very hard."

Yet sometimes when I carry a burden against my chest — a heavy bag of groceries, for instance, or an armload of fireplace logs brought in from outside — I hear through my mouth the strained inhaling and exhaling of my father's breathing as he bore me in his arms between the granary and the decanting shed or across the courtyard toward our home, in that place where I was dean, that place no one on the earth but myself remembers, myself and the birch trees and the light.

THE MURDER

MY FAMILY WAS HAUNTED BY THE MURDER, even in the New World. I can't remember when I first was told the tale, since I'm unable to recall a time I wasn't aware my great-grandparents and a great-aunt died at the hands of an assailant in Amlin. This was the shtetl in Byelorussia where my father's people came from, a little distance northeast up the Dvina from Vitebsk.

Perhaps I heard about the crime originally from my Aunt Zifra, my father's twin sister, or from my uncles on my father's side, or maybe from Reb Lucharsky. He was a melamed who came from Velizh, a town in the neighbourhood of Amlin, and so he was classified as a landsman and welcomed as such in our house. "A terrible, terrible thing," was the invariable comment that followed yet another retelling of how my zayde's father and mother and younger sister perished one dark night. Every reference, however peripheral, to the tragedy provoked the same phrase. And a mention of the crime could occur in a conversation about almost any topic aired around the table or the front room — the women with their sugar cubes and tea, the men occasionally also enjoying a *Lomir machn a schnaps.*

The customary response to even an allusion to the murder was identical to that uttered automatically at news of any serious setback suffered by a family member, by an inhabitant of our street, by a fellow employee, by individuals or organizations involved with the socialist movement, or by Jews anywhere in the world. Other such predictable, never-omitted verbal tags sprinkled the texture of conversation. Anyone who had died was thereafter perpetually rewarded with the honorific *alav ha-shalom*, as in "my former boss, that crook Meyer Ablowitz, *alav ha-shalom*," or in the case of a female, "You look just like your Aunt Bessie, *aleha ha-shalom*." Similarly, discussions of *potential* troubles were sprinkled with an incantatory word guaranteed to ward off the *tsouris*' realization: "In times like these, surely the landlord *cholilleh* won't raise the rent" or "If Moishe *cholilleh* became a poor melamed like Lucharsky . . . "

The never-omitted pronouncement — "a terrible, terrible thing" — regarding *tsouris* that had actually occurred meant that as a child I failed to grasp the awfulness of events described. The familiar phrase rendered homey any mention by an adult of a bank collapse, a fatal streetcar or train accident, European pogroms, the refusal of Eaton's department store downtown to hire Jews, factory closures, or the furriers' strike that could affect Uncle Avrom's livelihood. Whispers about our neighbours the Maloffs' divorce, or my mother's friend Mrs. Gronsky's abandonment by her husband, or the appearance of a truck and men with handcarts to repossess the Halperin's furniture a few doors down equally were transmuted. Adorned with the ritual tag, any threat to my world implied by such occurrences was softened into safety: the expected words created a small island of normality, a haven in the midst of a storm-tossed ocean of adult catastrophe.

Of course, growing up on Major Street off Harbord in Toronto provided a lot of scope for the awarding of the appellation "terrible, terrible thing". This was the Depression, but in its first years we didn't call it that. Shortages of jobs, shortages of money were routine to our neighbourhood and our family before and after October 1929. If life was a little worse this year, every newspaper insisted that better days were just around the corner. *Nu*, isn't that why we *takkeh* were in America? All right, all right: Canada.

So even the murder was sanitized for me for a long time, the accounts of it mixed in with news equally remote from my world of public school, Hebrew *cheder*, evening card games with my relatives, Shabbes solemnity, snowball fights against the kids who lived a couple of streets over on Borden, playing marbles in the spring mud, or watching men unload coal down a chute through our basement window or the ice deliveryman bearing on his shoulder huge tongs that gripped a sawdust-streaked block for our refrigerator. "That Mussolini fellow is a real *gozlin*, like whoever murdered our grandfather, *alav ha-shalom*," my Aunt Zifra might sigh, looking up from reading a Jewish-language newspaper that Reb Lucharsky had brought to the house the day before. At ten years old, I could already make out many sentences in this paper, *The Advance*. "He and that Hitler are such *paskudnyaks*," agreed her husband Uncle Leo, seated beside my father on our sagging chesterfield. "How is it men like that can even exist?" And my father would duly chime in, as required, "It's a terrible thing."

Curiously, I don't remember my father often referring to the Amlin tragedy. But Aunt Zifra and her other brothers — my Uncle Chaim and Uncle Lemuel — more than made up for my father's reticence on the subject. Nor do I recollect my zayde mentioning the loss of his parents, but then my memories of my zayde are dim. I recall being taken on visits to a dank-smelling front parlor, where through a door a radio in the kitchen was deafeningly loud. My father was a little abrupt with me during and after these excursions, not like his usual easy-going self. We sat facing a bearded old man in a stained black suit-coat and skullcap, peering nearsightedly at me occasionally. But he never asked me about my victory in the Grade Four spelling bee at school or whether I ever had been taken by ferry to the beach on the Toronto Islands or if I delivered papers or had some other after-school job — the way most guests or people we visited would inquire. He and my father conversed in low tones, with long periods of silence. If I was referred to at all, it was as my father's *Kaddish*. "Your *Kaddish* would like tea?" Zayde might mumble.

He was an infrequent visitor to our home. When he was settled in the best chair, he appeared bewildered amidst the comings and goings of his sons and their wives (except for Uncle Chaim, who was single), his daughter Aunt Zifra and her husband, and a proliferating host of grandchildren. At Pesach once during the reading of the Haggadah he suddenly shouted, "When do we eat?" Everyone at the Seder was shocked, but I was secretly delighted: this was a thought I had each year, yet I wouldn't have dared speak it. My father, who was in the early stages of reciting the Ten Plagues, faltered until Zifra came to his rescue by suggesting an abrupt abridgment of the list and of the balance of the service.

Eventually came murmurs of doctors, examinations, tuberculosis, and Zayde's complete absence from the family circle. Then there were trips by streetcar to where he was institutionalized — which meant for my brother and me a Sunday picnic on the park-like grounds with my mother while my

father went inside the grim-looking structure. I remember the
sad excitement of sitting shivah with my family, towels over
the hall and bathroom mirrors, and receiving an apparently
ceaseless stream of visitors paying condolences and bringing
us food: hard-boiled eggs and odd-tasting ganef, kreplach,
latkes, borsht and even a roasted chicken. My cousins and my
friends from up and down the street in their Shabbes clothes,
more subdued and well-behaved than usual. I remember, too,
each year thereafter the Yortzeit candle my father tended,
set on a white cloth placed on the chest that served as a low
table in our front room.

So I never heard from my zayde a first-hand, almost-
eyewitness, account of his parents' death. But the Velizhir
rebbie, Lucharsky, and even some relatives from my mother's
side such as my Aunt Tillie and Uncle Avrom, could be relied
on to keep the memory of the event before us.

My relatives were killed with a hammer. As the story
goes, my great-grandfather used to keep his money under
the mattress in his hut. One day, he happened to notice
the paper rubles had become moldy. He took the bills out,
washed them off as best he could, and spread them on a table
to dry. Someone passing by on the street must have glanced
in through the window and seen the money.

That night, someone broke into the house. Because
the doors and windows were locked, they came in through
the thatch of the roof. My great-grandfather probably was
awakened by the intruder searching for the rubles. In any
case, the burglar grabbed my great-grandfather's hammer
which had been left on a bench he was repairing, and after
a struggle my great-grandfather was struck a mortal blow to
the head. Perhaps his wife was already awake and terrified,
or awoke now. In any case she, too, was killed the same way.

Their youngest child, six years of age, who slept by the stove in the room, was found dead beside my great-grandmother, behind whom perhaps she was cowering in the face of this nightmare of adults grappling and shoving in the dark, shouts and curses, hammer blows, blood. My *zayde* and his two brothers slept in a loft above the main room. When at last they crept out to view the scene of horror, the murderer was gone.

Though the crime was investigated, the identity of the culprit was never determined. A regiment had been stationed in the area at the time, and suspicion fell on the soldiers. But nothing was proved. The boys ultimately were sent to live with a relative who had emigrated to Bracebridge, Ontario, in the Muskoka district north of Toronto.

Their upbringing in Bracebridge was not a happy one: their foster-father — an uncle on their mother's side — scraped an existence as a peddler going from farm to farm. The boys left home at the earliest opportunity. This is why we had relatives in Cleveland we seldom saw, although they did show up for Zayde's funeral. The New York branch of the family was closer to us, with plenty of letters and occasional visits back and forth. My earliest memory is sitting on my mother's lap on a bench at the Brooklyn Zoo, staring up at an impossibly tall giraffe. I remember the wooden buttons on her grey-and-white striped dress.

Indeed, my father and mother first met in New York. My father had gone down to stay with his Uncle Nathan for a week, and was taken to a Jewish play. At intermission in the lobby, he happened to strike up a conversation with a young woman who turned out also to be from Toronto, temporarily living with relatives in the Bronx while she looked for work.

Six months and a good deal of letter writing and train travel later, they were married.

The home my parents eventually created on Major Street was close to the garment district along Spadina Avenue. My grandfather had worked most of his life in the needle trades, and my father for many years ran a cutting machine for Tip Top Tailors — a large enterprise that boasted a chain of retail outlets as well as factories. I believe it was my father's happy disposition and relaxed charm that made our house the customary gathering place for most of his siblings and their spouses and children, not to mention my mother's sister Aunt Tillie and her husband Uncle Avrom. And not to forget the numerous friends of my parents, or the Velizhir rebbie, Lucharsky. I realized as an adult that Lucharsky was the family *nuchslepper*, the hanger-on who won't let go, a sort of permanent version of the needy person one is obliged as an act of charity and fellowship to invite home for Shabbes, to be *on oyrech auf Shabbes* for the household. In Reb Lucharsky's case, his role as he saw it extended to the rest of the days of the week, too.

Yet it was to my father's house that Reb Lucharsky came, not to that of any other family member to whom he could put the same claim as landsman. People gravitated to my father. Sometimes this was to my mother's despair, in her attempts to feed and entertain on very little money a veritable horde crammed into what I became aware in later life was a tiny parlor. Among my mother's papers after she died was a legal document giving the dimensions of the house: it measured eleven feet wide. Naturally, the place was vast to me as a child. In any case, the agreeable talk and tea and blintzes and sour cream or equally delectable treats that were usually available at my father's and mother's home acted as a magnet to their relatives and friends.

I believe, however, my father's cheerful outlook was the biggest draw. Despite his guests' frequent insistence on detailing the latest examples of the world's *tsouris*, my father — while truly sympathetic — never lapsed into gloom. He got enormous pleasure from the life he had built and that formed around him. His feet might drag up the front stoop at the end of a long day on the job. Yet he had an ear-to-ear grin when he saw us assembled in the hall to offer him a welcome home. He would be still beaming half an hour later as he greeted the guests at that evening's meal and pronounced the appropriate *broche* before we dug into our fish and a *tsimmes* of carrots, onions, prunes and potatoes.

His spirit stood him in good stead at work, too. The summer before my zayde died my father was laid off due to shortage of work. When the news reached Major Street a great *tummel* of anguish, worry, advice, admonitions, and appeals to the Creator broke out among those who customarily frequented our household. But my father, seemingly unfazed by both losing his job and being the cause of such uproar at home, simply strolled a block over to talk to a friend, one of his *chaverim* from the Arbeiter Ring. This man, often a guest with his wife at my parents', had recently been promoted to a foreman's position at Salutin's, another Spadina Avenue clothing manufacturer. My father started there the next Monday, although on shortened hours. Three weeks later his former supervisor at Tip Top Tailors, Mr. Applebaum, was sitting drinking tea with my mother when my father returned from work. After the preliminaries were out of the way, Mr. Applebaum grandly announced, "Yaakov, I'm authorized to give you your old job back. We still don't have much work, but I'll *takkeh* find enough to keep you busy. The place is all long faces and endless *kvetching* and *krechtzing* without you around." My mother glanced over at my father expectantly. He only nodded. You could tell he was pleased, but then he perpetually looked delighted to be home among us.

His unfailing good nature extended to family grievances, too. One enduring complaint among my mother's *mishpocheh* was that their grandmother Fruma, *aleha ha-shalom*, had for a time owned property near Bay and Dundas Streets but had foolishly sold it for a song. Fruma was in fact the business head in her marriage. While her husband was in Montreal attempting to earn passage for her and the children to come to Canada, back in Poland she established a thriving trade in goose fat, selling into Warsaw. Her husband's ineptness at money matters was legendary, so Fruma was the one who amassed the necessary funds to permit her and the children to travel to Quebec. Family legend had it that she thought long and hard about whether she wanted to resume her marriage to such a *nebbech*. Fruma was offered grudging respect by her descendants for her overall financial abilities: when the family moved to Toronto, from operating a tiny store off Brunswick near Bloor she ended the landlady of three houses. When her name was invoked, however, she was routinely castigated for having missed the opportunity of a lifetime to hang onto a valuable piece of downtown real estate.

Even my Uncle Chaim, my father's oldest brother, would weigh in when Fruma's inexplicable failure to cash in on Toronto's future was dissected. Ordinarily he had little to say on any subject, yet his participation in a ritual denunciation that properly belonged to my mother's side matched Aunt Tillie's and Uncle Avrom's willingness to contribute to yet another reconsideration of the murder of my relatives in

Amlin. My father, just as he rarely joined in talk about that subject, abstained from pillorying the short-sightedness of his grandmother-in-law. "Don't we all do the best we can?" he would inquire. "*Nu*, who would like more of Raizel's excellent knishes?" Though my mother also appeared uncomfortable when Fruma's sole failing was focused on, there definitely were moments when my father's eternal level-headedness and even temperament exasperated her. Stressful domestic emergencies like a flooded toilet, a bird that had become trapped in the house, or news that her younger sister Rivke in Hamilton was engaged to a *shaygets* were never crises to him: he declined to engage in dramatizing a problem, but instead aimed at effecting a solution. My mother found this attitude of his maddening. But she seemed grateful when my father refused to be drawn into one more speculation of the current value of Fruma's former property.

My Uncle Chaim differed from my father in more than a willingness to reflect on Fruma's unforgivable business error. In physical appearance the brothers scarcely resembled each other. My father was slight in build, with a mildly stooped posture, thin arms and tapered fingers. Uncle Chaim was squat and stocky, as though his body had thickened from his years at heavy manual labor. He had quit school as soon as he could and worked for CN Rail in the Toronto yards unloading freight. Then he was in and out of jobs, employed intermittently as a construction laborer and in a small foundry out Queen Street West. His fingers were swollen-looking and square-ended and even his face appeared a rough-hewn version of my father's.

Uncle Chaim, too, had far less connection to the Jewish community than my parents. I knew from occasions when I had met his friends on the street, as my uncle was taking me for pop or on a shopping errand for my mother, that he lived and worked mainly in a non-Jewish environment. If we encountered workmates of his, their repartee with my uncle suggested they regarded him as an equal. Yet their nickname for him was "The Schnoz". Even as a child I found this reference to a prominent feature of my uncle's face disparaging. My uncle didn't seem to mind. When we stopped to chat with these men, his talk was equally aggressive, peppered with words he later always cautioned me not to repeat in front of my mother. From the conversations he had with his pals in my presence, I understood that he spent considerable time in a pub they frequented along College Street, and also that on sunny days when they were unemployed they often met at certain park benches at the Christie Pits. I was impressed by my uncle's ability to move with ease in a non-Jewish world. Although there were Gentile children in my school, I had little to do with them.

Uncle Chaim's bachelorhood my mother took as a personal challenge. She would suggest he might like to meet various unmarried female friends of hers, or friends of friends, but my uncle waved off such ideas with one massive hand. "It's *takkeh* your duty as a Jew to marry and have children," my mother insisted. "Ahhch," my uncle dismissed the notion. Once she even offered to contact a *shadchen* on his behalf, to see if a match couldn't be found for him via a more organized approach. That idea, too, was speedily rejected. My uncle lived in a boardinghouse a few blocks over, but I remember a period of several weeks one winter when he moved out to live elsewhere. Though my father retained his habitual equanimity, I deduced from urgent whispers my mother directed at him — in which Chaim's name was hissed — that my uncle had somehow become a transgressor. During those months he never ate supper with us, he came by once on a Sunday for tea, accompanied by a woman I'd never met previously. My father tried to enliven the gathering by telling jokes, but the episode was strained on all sides. I couldn't remember such a lengthy stretch when Uncle Chaim had so little interaction with our family. One supper he was back at his accustomed place at the table, and life went on as before, except my mother was noticeably cold toward him for several additional weeks.

Also unlike my father, Uncle Chaim was not religious. He did not go to shul, and despite being the eldest son, he absolutely refused to preside at Pesach. Thus this role devolved to my father. Following one Shabbes meal, my uncle and I happened to be sitting side-by-side on the couch. In addition to drinking a glass of wine with supper, he had since downed two or three schnaps. And when he had arrived at the house late in the day, he had made a point of informing my mother he had come from the pub, not shul. He had been laid off again that afternoon, but he said he had a few ideas where he might search for work on Monday. His breath, when he suddenly leaned toward me on the couch, was redolent of alcohol. "Moishe, if I find after I die that there *is* a God, I'm going to punch him right in the face for the shitty mess he's made of this world." I was thrilled and terrified to hear an adult utter such monumental blasphemy.

My uncle's threat was pronounced on a hot, humid July evening. Later that night, as I lay sweating atop the sheets on my bed, one of Toronto's summer thunderstorms drifted noisily across the city northward from Lake Ontario. Wide awake, I nervously counted the space between each flash and the accompanying overwhelming roll of unearthly sound. The storm drew nearer and louder, then passed overhead.

I wondered if Uncle Chaim, a few blocks away, was about to suffer divine retribution for his audacious statement. But nothing happened.

Except for this lapse, my uncle kept his antipathy to religion to himself, other than also steadfastly refusing to attend shul or partake in any of the prayers when he was at our house for a holiday feast. My uncle even displayed a tolerance for Reb Lucharsky, greeting the bearded melamed as dispassionately as he acknowledged anyone he encountered at my parents'. Uncle Chaim might have had little use for religion, but he obviously had traveled through strange worlds in Toronto inhabited by strange people. I had the impression he had learned not to judge too quickly or overtly the good and evil in those he met. In this regard he possessed a variation of the laissez-faire attitude of my father, although without my father's innate happiness. Uncle Chaim recognized the Velizhir rebbie as a fellow-satellite in orbit around my parents' hearth, and treated him accordingly.

My father's other brother, Lemuel, had his own family and thus was less frequently seen at our home. My mother often remarked that Lemuel had married into his wife's family, rather than Beryl having married into ours. In a manner of speaking, Uncle Chaim occupied the place in our lives that might have been filled by both paternal uncles. I once heard him offer money to my mother to help defray the cost of his many meals at her table. She indignantly refused, saying *here* he was *mishpocheh* and no boarder.

Thus Uncle Chaim was present the evening a new dimension to our relatives' murder was revealed. I could tell something was amiss as I opened the front door about five p.m. one April day after *cheder*. I had run into Reb Lucharsky at the corner. He was not *my* melamed; he conducted his own after-school *cheder* in a neighbourhood further east, almost to Ossington Avenue. But as he habitually did, he was making a beeline to my parents' house when instruction was over, the same as me.

As Reb Lucharsky and I entered the small vestibule, I heard a voice wailing horribly in the kitchen. I froze, my body tense. What disaster could have happened to provoke such anguish? In the midst of hanging up our coats, I looked over at Reb Lucharsky. He seemed as disturbed as I was. After a few seconds I recognized the voice as my Aunt Zifra's. I had listened to such grief from her only once before, when my zayde died. My mother spoke: she sounded nearly as upset. Had something happened to Uncle Leo? My father? My brother?

Reb Lucharsky tended to defer to me a bit once we were under my parents' roof, although on the street he was capable of grilling me regarding what I had or hadn't learned in a rival *cheder*. I realized now he was waiting for me to act first, to lead us both from the comparative safety of the hall toward a closer proximity to such sorrow.

I gathered my courage and stepped into the kitchen. Both women glanced up with stricken faces as I, shadowed by the melamed, approached the table where they sat. My aunt's cries ceased, and she wiped tears from her face with a handkerchief. My mother embraced me tightly.

Reb Lucharsky hung back, hands clasped near his chest, his fingers pulling at and wringing each other. "What's wrong? Something is wrong?" he blurted.

"Tea, Reb Lucharsky?" my mother sighed, climbing to her feet. "We've had some terrible news."

I noticed a torn-open envelope and some papers and a photograph resting on the tablecloth.

"Thank you, I would like tea," Reb Lucharsky said, his agitated hand gestures slowing a little. "I hope nothing *cholilleh* has happened to . . . " His voice trailed off.

My mother busied herself at the stove. "No, but the news is upsetting. From Russia," she added, bringing the teapot over to the table.

The melamed moved forward and sat down. "And the news is . . . ?" He helped himself to sugar cubes.

"From the past. But I think we'll wait until Yaakov gets home. He'll know what best to do."

A strained silence fell, broken only by Reb Lucharsky slurping his tea. I heard the door from the street open. My mother and my aunt raised their heads expectantly. Then as one they rose, and hurried toward the vestibule. I heard my father's cheerful words, and then a hubbub of feminine cries and exclamations.

My father entered the kitchen with an arm around the waists of both my mother and my aunt. Fresh tears were evident on my aunt's cheeks. My father exchanged greetings with the Velizhir rebbie and tousled my hair. Once he was seated opposite my aunt, my mother brought him tea.

My father looked around at us. "From the beginning," he said.

My aunt took a breath. Her lips moved, but then as if her earlier expression of strong emotion had stripped her voice of power she whispered, "He's come back."

"Who has come back?" my father asked.

"The . . . the *murderer*." My aunt's speech regained force in the midst of uttering the phrase.

"Who?"

"The one who killed our zayde and bubbe and poor Aunt Chana."

"Aha. How do you know this?"

My aunt pushed the pile of papers on the table toward my father. "Look, read."

My father spent several minutes examining the handwritten letter. I edged over to stand beside him as he studied the pages. I could see that the photograph on the table had been taken in a cemetery, with a particular tombstone front and centre. I picked up the picture and began to try to make out the Hebrew inscriptions on the grave marker. My father finished with the letter and gently took the photo from me. He put his hand on my shoulder as he stared intently at the image.

He lowered it to the table and leaned back in his chair. "Why do you say the murderer has returned?"

"Isn't it obvious?" shrilled Aunt Zifra.

"No, not to me," my father said.

"He's taken his hammer again and bashed away at the inscription that says our grandparents and little Chana were murdered."

"Anybody can deface a cemetery."

"But read, read what the relatives say. No other tombstone was touched. It has to be the murderer, come back after so many years. Perhaps he has been locked up in jail for some other terrible act. Now he's angry that his crime has been remembered and is determined to seek revenge." Her face was twisted.

"How could it be the murderer who did it, Zifra?" my father said. "Our zayde died forty years ago."

"A person *epis* — " Aunt Zifra gulped air " — does not live forty years? What if he *cholilleh* tracks us down? What if he *cholilleh* does to us here what he did to the stone there?"

"Zifra, that's not going to happen."

"Why not? A crime like that: to kill a harmless couple and their little child? Such a person would be capable of — "

"Why should anyone want to murder us? Some *meshuggener* took offense at the inscription, perhaps. That's all. Or maybe it was an accident."

"Oy! An accident!"

"Kids, kids looking for something to do. Perhaps they happened upon this marker and struck it."

My mother stood up. "Or a *shaygets?*"

"He would not be able to read the inscription," my father observed. My mother withdrew toward the stove and began to bustle about with preparations for dinner.

"Only the inscription was damaged?" Reb Lucharsky broke in.

"Just the word 'murdered'," my father said. He slid the photo in the melamed's direction.

Reb Lucharsky raised the photo close to his eyes, then lowered it. He stroked his beard. "I think . . . I think this is perhaps the work of a dybbuk."

"Dybbuk!" Aunt Zifra shrieked.

My father turned toward him. "Lucharsky . . . ," he cautioned.

"If the murderer is maybe dead, his evil spirit has inhabited another poor soul. Under the control of the dybbuk, this person — "

"*Feh!*" my father said decisively. "Save such tales for children. This is the Twentieth Century."

"What does evil know of time?" my aunt asked.

"A dybbuk was driven out of a woman in Velizh when I was a boy," Reb Lucharsky insisted. "Less than twenty years ago. Maybe in this case — "

"No more, Lucharsky."

Reb Lucharsky, subsiding, gestured toward the letter. "*Nu*, what do the relatives say?"

"When they wrote, whoever committed this act was unknown," my father replied. "By now the mischief-maker has probably been caught. They ask for money, of course, to help repair the stone."

"Mischief this is not, Yaakov," my aunt said. "A *gozlin* is loose in the world. He attacks our family's heart once more."

"We only know what we know," my father declared. "Let's not make two problems where there is one. I think — "

At the sound of the outer door opening, Zifra was on her feet. "Leo? Leo? Is that you?"

Her husband's voice called from the vestibule. "I came quick as I could." Uncle Leo strode into the room, trailed by Uncle Chaim. "I got home and read your note," Uncle Leo said, crossing toward his wife. "Are you all right, Zifra-*léb*?" He embraced my aunt, who began again to sob.

"Sit down, Chaim," my father invited while my aunt was being comforted. "Tea?"

"I met Leo on the streetcar," Chaim said. "He told me something bad happened from Russia?"

Once Uncle Leo persuaded my aunt to resume her chair, the recent event in Amlin was revealed to the newcomers. Uncle Leo rejected Reb Lucharsky's idea of an infernal origin of the desecration of the monument, but sided with his wife that the blows delivered to the stone were the work of the murderer somehow manifest again in the village. His concern was how to advise the relatives to properly deal with the outrage.

My father attempted to nudge the conversation toward the more practical matter of sending money for the repair or replacement of the stone. "I'll telephone Lemuel tomorrow.

His shop is doing well, he says. He should be able to spare some money sooner than Chaim or I."

Aunt Zifra had calmed down now enough to assist my mother in readying the ingredients for a *tsimmis*. My mother, flustered that the crisis had delayed her cooking, was desperately singeing the skin of a chicken with a candle to eliminate the remnants of quills. "We'll be eating very late," she apologized to the group around the table. "Moishe, find your brother and tell him." No one took much notice of her announcement, and I stayed where I was.

Ideas about the cause, significance and appropriate reaction to the assault on the tombstone swirled about the room. As meal preparation duties permitted, my aunt and my mother contributed their opinions. Only Uncle Chaim did not participate. My father swiveled to face him. "If Lemuel sends money immediately, you and I can repay him our share when we can."

Uncle Chaim lowered his teacup. His large hands lay on the tablecloth, one on either side of the cup and saucer, blunt fingers curled slightly inwards. His fingernails were long, and, as ever when he was employed, black under the tips.

"It wasn't the murderer who damaged that stone," he said.

No one spoke for a second. Then Leo burst out: "Who else would it be?"

"What makes you so sure?" Zifra added over top of her husband's exclamation.

"I know who the murderer is," my uncle continued.

"Do you mean — ?" All the adults talked at once. "You can't." "How is it possible that you — ?" "Did our tateh tell you something he didn't us?" "Chaim, how could you imagine such a — ?"

My uncle wasn't through. "I have *takkeh* seen him."

"*Gottenyu!*" "Where?" "How can you possibly recognize — ?" "You can't know — " "*Where* have you seen him?"

"He is here. In Toronto," Uncle Chaim finished.

"Sha, sha," my father tried to quiet the uproar that followed my uncle's words. "This *tummel* isn't getting us anywhere." The excited voices of the others eventually faded to mutters, and my father began a quietly persistent questioning of his brother.

"You've seen the murderer, here in Toronto?"

"Yes."

"How, after forty years, can this be?"

"I'm not free to tell you."

"You can't tell us? What do you mean?"

"I'm not at liberty to explain. But he is here. It could not be him who damaged — "

"How can you know the murderer?" Reb Lucharsky interrupted. "You weren't born when your relatives were killed."

"I know who he is. I've seen him here. That is all I can say."

"I don't believe you," Zifra declared.

Uncle Chaim shrugged.

"I don't understand," my mother ventured. "Chaim, why are you so sure you've seen the guilty one?"

"He's just talking," Leo pronounced. "Unless one of his *goyisher* friends — "

"This has nothing to do with my friends."

"Chaim, then how — ?" my father began, but he was interrupted by his sister. Wave upon wave of doubt, of rejection of his declarations, surged toward my uncle. But he was a rock buffeted by the combers of a gale. The dispute raged all through supper, once my mother at last disengaged from the controversy long enough to finish organizing the meal and my brother was found. Everyone quieted momentarily for my father's recitation of the *broche*. Then the argument flared again. I say "argument", but no one was able to pry a single additional explanation or particle of information from my uncle. I say "all through supper," but the response to my uncle's statements has never lessened since.

Henceforward, whenever the murder was spoken of, whether my uncle was in the room or not, the ensuing discussion soon considered his stubborn refusal to account for his convictions about the murderer's identity and presence in Canada. Each possible interpretation concerning these mysteries was either rejected by Chaim or disallowed by some reasonable objection suggested by another family member. Did my grandfather and his brothers commit the deed? Unthinkable. Also, the boys were too young, and too pious. As well, they could have stolen the money any day when their parents were absent from the house rather than attempt the crime in the middle of the night when everyone was home.

Was Chaim simply bidding for attention, striving to regain his rightful place as head of the family, being the eldest? Unlikely: at gatherings Chaim shunned the spotlight, and he usually preferred to spend time with his Gentile friends than with his relatives. Or did a missing piece of the story suddenly occur to Chaim, a vital clue to the tragedy that everybody else had overlooked? He firmly denied it.

The mystery of the murder thus became entangled with another enigma that not even the subsequent horrific news from Europe could distract the family from pondering and disputing. For my own peace of mind, I developed a sequence of events that might make sense of Chaim's assertions. What if my zayde had in fact witnessed the killings in Amlin? Then, decades later, he encounters the perpetrator. Completely traumatized by the chance sighting, Zayde informs only Chaim — possibly because Chaim functioned in the *goyish* world of which the murderer was part. My zayde swears my uncle to secrecy: maybe due to fear of vengeance if the man is identified, or an unwillingness to risk notice by, and hence trouble with, the authorities by alerting them. After Zayde's death, Chaim starts to betray that vow just once, at my parents' house.

I never tested my scenario by seeking to verify it with my uncle. I was afraid he would scoff, and I would be left again solely with questions. Also, I lacked confidence in my explanation why Zayde would acquaint Chaim with his discovery. Chaim rarely visited the old man, and even as a boy seemed to have virtually no rapport with his father. Why would Zayde entrust such momentous knowledge to this one of his four children?

Chaim must have been aware of the effect his words would have. Yet in all the years afterwards, he doggedly repeated only that he knew who the murderer was and had seen him in the streets of Toronto. On any elaboration of these claims, my uncle, *alav ha-shalom*, remained as silent as the grave.

The Photographer

MR. SPONGEBY COULD NOT UNDERSTAND WHY HIS wife imagined a professional photograph of himself was a suitable gift to mark his fiftieth birthday.

"A person's fiftieth is an event, one of life's passages," Priscilla insisted. "You've never been to a commercial photographer. What better reason to have a professional portrait taken than to celebrate half a century of living, of achievement?"

He had listlessly reopened the argument at dinner the evening before his appointment with the photographer. Mr. Spongeby's birthday was still three weeks away. But Priscilla, who was two years younger than her husband, had been in touch with the photographer to learn when to start the process to ensure a properly-framed portrait of Mr. Spongeby would be produced by April 13th, the big day.

"Really, dear," Mr. Spongeby said, "I have that picture of myself your brother Ivan took a few years ago: the one I use on my business cards. It's very nice." He went back to chewing on the allegedly-mint-flavored liver and onions that he felt was overcooked to near tastelessness. Priscilla claimed the dish was excellent nutritionally, and in any case was a favourite recipes of her mother's, whose cooking Priscilla frequently extolled.

"We're not going to go over this again, Hugh. That was an acceptable snap my brother took of you, and looks fine for your advertising. But it's ten years old, and you've never had a professional portrait. Your appointment is at eleven o'clock tomorrow, you've known about it for over a month, and that's all there is to that."

Mr. Spongeby sighed.

"You needn't pout, either," his wife said. "I asked what you wanted for your birthday, and you repeatedly told me that you didn't want any fuss about this being your fiftieth. 'Let's just go out for a quiet dinner someplace,' was your suggestion."

"Exactly," Mr. Spongeby said.

"We do that every year," Priscilla continued. "We're becoming quite the fuddy-duddies. Even if you have no intention of marking the occasion, I'm going to. Unless, that is, you've changed your mind and finally thought of something for your birthday that you'd especially like. Something that's always been . . . your secret passion or frivolous desire." She waved her fork in an elaborate flourish.

"Which suit do you think I should wear tomorrow?"

At ten-thirty the next morning Mr. Spongeby told his personal secretary he was going out and left the office. His business, besides offering the usual range of life, household and vehicular insurance, specialized in policies for desperate cases — children born with severe disabilities, or adults handicapped or worse due to an auto accident or sports mishap. The nature of his special clients, the growth of his business, and a long marriage to Priscilla had taught him that sometimes you have to face what you'd rather not. You tuck down and tackle it. No whining. Get on with it. There is no other way.

The neighbourhood in which Mr. Spongeby had set up shop twenty-five years ago had drastically altered over time — slowly at first, and then at an accelerating rate. Upscale apartment blocks had erupted amid streets of modest, well-maintained homes with window boxes, low shrubs lining walkways that curved up to front steps, and sharply-trimmed hedges of laurel, privet or cotoneaster that announced the lot boundaries between neighbours. Mr. Spongeby had bought one of these houses himself long ago, once he was confident the enterprise he had launched would not founder. Priscilla had pronounced the district a good one in which to raise children, but the children (at least, their children) had not appeared. Lately, annual increases in property tax had driven many of their old neighbourhood acquaintances to sell. Each summer now the avenues echoed to the percussive sounds of demolition crews, the roars and beeping of cement mixers and flatbeds of lumber being delivered, and the shouts and metallic stitching noise of carpenters with their nailguns.

The changes to the area meant a lot of walk-in trade for Mr. Spongeby from people seeking the more customary types of insurance. Mr. Spongeby found he had to expand his front counter staff, and then a few years later expand again. He remembered his anxieties around buying the building his company presently operated from, a block down Cambie Street from where he began. There was a morning when he walked from his own office into the front and realized he only knew half the twenty or so employees bustling around or meeting with clients in partitioned cubicles.

And the trauma of the shift to computers remained with him, bound up in his mind with Douglas, a bright MBA that Serge, his office manager, had hired right after Douglas' graduation from the university. Douglas was Chinese by descent. Before long Mr. Spongeby was surprised to see Chinese signs in his windows, and first one and then two new Chinese clerks serving a clientele arriving in the city in ever-larger numbers from Hong Kong. Douglas was hard not to like: cheerful, extremely competent, thoughtful. He was curious about the business in his conversations with Mr. Spongeby, almost to the point of impudence. He would knock and enter Mr. Spongeby's office late in the day, and stand waiting to be recognized. When Mr. Spongeby looked up from the document he was perusing, Douglas' eyes stared at his employer with a startling mix of what seemed to Mr. Spongeby awe and hunger. Douglas' inquiries were vast in scope, and abruptly proposed.

"Yes, Douglas?"

"Sir, do you think we have fully tapped the prospective market for us of the businesses up and down 12th Avenue near here?"

The move to computers was mainly Douglas' idea, although Mr. Spongeby was amazed to discover Serge was allied with Douglas in advocating the concept. Eventually Mr. Spongeby had succumbed, although he preferred now not to think of the weeks and months of frustration and chaos triggered by the implementation of the system. His own halting attempts to learn how to use the devices was another memory best forgotten. Douglas had worked tirelessly throughout the phasing in of the computers. Nevertheless, Mr. Spongeby had experienced moments of pure rage at Douglas over the disruption of decades-old routines caused by the new machines. Then there were the horrors of lost files and accounts that resulted from botch-ups by resentful office staff only half-trained in the mysteries of expensive computer programs — programs containing glitches that were, apparently, the fault of no person who could be deemed accountable. Yet as the months passed, and the office settled down again into procedures that became increasingly efficient and familiar, Mr. Spongeby was aware of how much he owed Douglas for prodding them all into modernity. He realized he anticipated with pleasure his daily interactions with Douglas' sharp mind around the office. Something close to affection grew in Mr. Spongeby toward his employee, a sensation he guessed was similar to that a father might hold toward a superbly gifted son.

Mr. Spongeby had never before felt emotionally drawn toward anyone who worked for him, except Lisa Simpson many years previously. He was much younger and she was only ten or so years his junior. She was a student taking time out in the midst of a master's program, and Serge had hired her as a summer replacement secretary. Lisa had some of the same bouncy energy that Douglas radiated, but there was a sexual tension between Mr. Spongeby and Lisa, too. Against every principle forbidding office romances that Mr. Spongeby knew to be true, he and Lisa had drifted into an affair. He had been willing to continue his involvement with her after she left his employ in September, but she gave him a deadline for leaving Priscilla.

Mr. Spongeby had agonized over the choice Lisa had gently but firmly presented to him. He admired Lisa — how she applied her brilliant restlessness not only to her studies but also to social causes like environmental degradation: she had insisted his office institute a recycling program, and had fully researched what was required to launch it. As well, when Lisa and he began to be intimate she had been enrolled in an art school extension course in weaving, and went on to take a further one in colour theory. Mr. Spongeby marveled at how she could be completely intrigued by the different issues or ideas or skills she pursued. And he yearned to experience much more of the exciting abandonment she displayed in bed. Yet as Mr. Spongeby considered how he should proceed, a stubborn sense of loyalty toward Priscilla surfaced. While he sat at his desk, his office door closed, attempting to list and sort his feelings, images of Lisa's fiercely tender gestures toward him jostled with memories of his wife's hard hours of work as secretary and counter salesperson in their first few years together. Though Priscilla had stepped aside from an active role in the company about the time they bought the house, he still discussed with her the details of each daily problem or success related to the business.

Mr. Spongeby could not shake the sense that everything he had achieved had been built shoulder-to-shoulder with Priscilla, even if most of her energy for years now had gone into preparing the house for the children who never were born, and then into various charitable works connected with their church. Priscilla regularly attended — more regularly than he — St. Mary's Anglican in Kerrisdale, a wealthy area of the city some distance from where they lived. She had been a member of that congregation since the district was less prestigious, and she was a little girl.

Mr. Spongeby began to conceptualize leaving Priscilla as an act of base ingratitude. In her own way, directly and then indirectly through her listening ear and steady counsel, she was integral to his accomplishments. Lisa was a dazzling opportunity he could only accept at the cost of a selfish denial of how his wife had helped him. And yet he felt so youthful and, yes, manly around Lisa's sweetly-evident love for him.

He recognized he was tormented to the point of paralysis by his conflicting emotions regarding her and Priscilla. He was grateful that Lisa tried to offer enticements for a continuation of their relationship, rather than pressure him to choose in her favour. Her deadline had to do with her needs, he understood, rather than being a ploy. She couldn't float forever in the limbo of his indecision.

And he *was* enticed. Strolling arm-in-arm in the anonymity of the Stanley Park seawall one afternoon, they had stopped to admire twin babies asleep in a carriage halted by a bench on which the mother was resting.

"Wouldn't it be nice if we had a kid?" Lisa had said as they resumed the walk.

"I'm too old for that, I'm afraid," he answered, flattered and excited by her idea.

"You're not too old," she smiled. "Plenty of men your age start another family."

He said nothing. A seagull hovered over the inlet just offshore, keeping pace with them. She remarked quietly after a while: "I'm not too old, anyway." Seeing a stricken look cross his face, she kissed him.

When he failed to make the break with his wife, Lisa had brought their affair to an end. Mr. Spongeby still corresponded with her one or two times a year; she currently lived in Toronto. Her letters were sent to the office. She had married a good man, and seemed content with her life and two children.

With Douglas, Mr. Spongeby eventually had determined on a significant promotion and raise, along with a tacit understanding throughout the company that he was the heir apparent. But on being presented with this reward in Mr. Spongeby's office, Douglas also had news. His father was bankrolling him to start an insurance agency in Richmond, where many of the newest immigrants from China were establishing themselves. Mr. Spongeby, to his surprise, felt personally rebuffed by Douglas' announcement, as though he or his business lacked some desirable quality Douglas believed he could obtain elsewhere.

"Get a grip," he lectured himself after Douglas had excused himself, pleading an appointment with a client. "You're acting like a rejected suitor. A business of his own is a big advance for Douglas. Don't you want the best for him?"

Yet for some weeks afterwards Mr. Spongeby was irritable with people around the office, and even short with Priscilla. He began to walk down to the seawall by False Creek at lunchhour, and wouldn't return to the office until 2 or 2:30 p.m. He noticed he had scant enthusiasm for chores which had previously brought him little waves of pleasure, such as reviewing the month-end statements with his chief accountant. Hearing certain rock and roll ballads from his youth over the car radio — he kept it tuned to an oldies station — resulted in a tangible pang in his chest, and occasionally his eyes watered. After such incidents he spoke sharply to himself on the need for self-discipline, on not succumbing to useless self-pity.

His life resumed a more predictable course. Douglas phoned frequently for advice, and Mr. Spongeby was always pleased. The two would speak animatedly together. But when Mr. Spongeby hung up, he experienced an energy sag, a feeling close to melancholy, that overcame him for fifteen or twenty minutes.

More than a year elapsed before such post-phone-call reactions to hearing Douglas' voice disappeared. One day, after chatting with Douglas about the nominees for the provincial executive of their professional association, Mr. Spongeby was struck by how his new freedom from any particular response to Douglas' calls was identical to how he no longer felt flushed and unnerved when he saw Lisa's handwriting on an envelope placed on his desk after the delivery of the morning mail.

Now, with a decade and a half of computer-assisted growth of the company behind him, and five decades of his life nearly attained, Mr. Spongeby strode alongside the busy traffic on Cambie to keep his appointment with the photographer. Priscilla had given her husband the man's address, which she stressed was only a few blocks from the office and so hardly represented much of a disruption in Mr. Spongeby's working day. She had selected this photographer after his work had been praised in a newspaper review of the city's premiere portraitists; the reporter quoted critics as saying the photographer "combined a perceptive apprehension of character with technical mastery of his medium." A sample of the photographer's work was reproduced in the paper: a woman with half her face in shadow gazed off to the right of the picture, while her folded hands clutched in her lap what looked like a small mixing bowl. To Mr. Spongeby this portrait seemed indistinguishable from the other five samples from the other five photographers featured in the article. But since he had capitulated to Priscilla's wishes on the overall question of the portrait, he wasn't about to argue the detail of exactly who was going to do the deed.

The address Priscilla had handed him led to a doorway he had never noticed before between two stores, although he had walked past this spot on hundreds of occasions. The door proclaimed only the number of its location. Inside, a flight of stairs led upwards. Off the top landing a frosted glass door offered: *Willowhaven Photographers. Please enter.*

"I have an appointment at eleven."

The young woman behind the desk gaped at him. Mr. Spongeby's first thought was that the receptionist must be retarded, the beneficiary of the same work-placement program his own company took part in from time to time. She seemed unable to close her mouth and her eyes were fixed with unnatural concentration on his face.

"P-p-please sit down and make yourself comfortable. I'll . . . I'll tell Mr. Willowhaven you're here." The young woman gestured to some expensive-looking padded chairs arranged in a semicircle around a low table crusted with magazines.

Mr. Spongeby removed his coat and settled himself in one of the chairs. He chose a current *Time* to leaf through, then glanced up. The young woman had remained in her place, gawking at him. "W-would you like a . . . coffee or anything?"

"No, thank you," Mr. Spongeby said.

He experienced a rush of unease. Inappropriate behaviour like this was why he at first told Serge he was reluctant to hire the mentally handicapped. The compromise was to keep participants in these programs well out of the path of clients.

Or, Mr. Spongeby wondered, did he have something on his face, or his tie? Was his fly open? He risked a quick passage of his hand across his mouth, and a brief glance downwards to check his clothes, even though he had inspected himself in the mirror of his office bathroom before leaving work.

He addressed the still-immobilized young woman. "Is something wrong?"

"No, no," the young woman blurted. "It's . . . really *weird*, that's all." Her eyes were still focused on Mr. Spongeby with an expression he couldn't decipher. Disbelief? Shock? What about him appeared so hideous as to provoke such a gaze?

"Weird?"

"You look *exactly* like Mr. Willowhaven," the young woman uttered. "I mean, you're a *perfect* copy. You're not his twin brother or something, are you? God, you're like *clones*." Her body seemed frozen, staring at him. Then she abruptly melted into motion and stood. "Excuse me. Sorry. I'll go find Mr. Willowhaven."

"As far as I know, we're not twins," Mr. Spongeby said to her back, as she opened a door to an inner office. A few seconds later she reemerged, trailed by an older man.

Despite Mr. Spongeby being forewarned by the receptionist's reaction to him, he was astounded at the sight of the newcomer. Mr. Spongeby had the impression he was confronting a virtual replica of himself. Same shortish pepper-and-salt hair, same strongly-featured face, same thickening body, same slightly-hunched posture. The man advanced with hand outstretched. Only his clothes were definitely not to Mr. Spongeby's taste: some sort of stylish pants with pockets sewn on thighs and calves where pockets ought not to be, and an open-necked shirt of expensive cloth but oversized, almost smock-like, as was the fashion of the moment.

"Mr. Spongeby? Good to meet you."

His hand clasped Mr. Spongeby's, and withdrew. "My daughter says we look alike. Can't say she's wrong."

"No. Yes. Quite a resemblance, Mr. Willowhaven."

"Indeed."

"Maybe . . . maybe we're just a type." Mr. Spongeby heard his voice betray the agitation he felt. He attempted to adopt a different tone, the reassuring, any-of-us-are-just-human mode he utilized when his special clients haltingly revealed some tragic aspect of a child's or other relative's life history. "I'm sure you know what I mean, Mr. Willowhaven. In my business I meet a lot of people, as you must. It's amazing how often I'll swear I've met someone before when in fact I haven't. For all intents and purposes, they look identical."

"Call me Doug. No, I like to imagine we're each unique." He observed Mr. Spongeby closely. "But this is uncanny."

Mr. Spongeby heard only the name. His insides swirled. "Your name is . . . is Doug?"

"Yes. Don't tell me you have a *twin* named Doug?"

"No, I — "

"I heard on CBC radio about this book on twins. The author had scary stories about how much alike twins can be. Their habits and preferences match down to models of cars they drive or favourite colours. Even when the two grow up in different foster families thousands of miles apart."

"No, no twin. I don't know why . . . that is, you . . . you don't look like a . . . Douglas." Mr. Spongeby inwardly winced at his confused response.

"I've been a Doug as long as I can remember," the photographer said heartily. "But more important right now for me is learning who *you* are, who . . . what's your first name, Mr. Spongeby?"

"Hugh."

"Who Hugh Spongeby is. That's how I work: I can't create a portrait if I don't know something about the person. Otherwise I'm just taking a snapshot, which anybody could do for you."

"I don't know what there is to tell." Mr. Spongeby felt suddenly emptied, like a balloon whose air had leaked away.

"Come on into the studio while I set up for the session, and we'll talk. I won't go so far as to say I have an intuitive sense of people. But together we'll get a notion of who you might be."

Mr. Spongeby's reluctance to undertake the whole project flooded through him. The photographer was leading him toward the door behind the young woman's desk. Mr. Spongeby recognized an overwhelming sense of dread at the thought of passing through that threshold.

He recalled steeling himself once in seventh grade to walk through the school's main office door. He had been ordered to report to the principal for whispering to his best friend during English class. There also was the door to an insurance brokerage Mr. Spongeby had to open to first apply for a job when he had graduated high school. The nurse at his doctor's the year before had said, "You can go in now, Mr. Spongeby." Dr. Wallace had gotten information back from the tests after Mr. Spongeby had started to pass blood. That malady was diagnosed as only an intestinal ulcer, treated by antibiotics. No worse than an infection, now, and not the cancer he feared. But to have to turn the handle and walk into Dr. Wallace's examining room, maybe into the last days of his life, took all Mr. Spongeby's resolve. He stopped beside the desk of the photographer's receptionist, and glanced desperately around.

"That's an interesting picture." His eyes had registered a matted rectangular photo, about a foot tall by a foot-and-a-half wide, displayed on an easel to the right of the door.

"It's a prize-winner," Willowhaven's daughter declared. She had watched the two men move past her desk toward the open doorway. "Best of its class at the BC juried competition. We're going to be shipping it back East in a few days to the nationals."

The black-and-white photo showed the rear of a row of large highway transport trailers. The rods and levers to operate the doors of each were similar in design, yet each trailer had aspects that distinguished it, even if only to a small degree, from the others adjoining it: different signage with respect to warnings to motorists of wide turns, or phone numbers to report unsafe driving. A few of the trailers were slightly taller than the majority, but all were the same width. The backs of the trailers showed varying amounts of the grime of travel. Below the mudflaps on each, however, the two sets of dual tires were identical.

"Like it?" The photographer had returned to stand beside where Mr. Spongeby had stalled. They looked at the photo together.

"This isn't a portrait." Mr. Spongeby hoped his voice communicated a jocular tone.

"I meant it to be," the photographer said. "Historical."

"Historical?"

"I call it 'The Twelve Caesars.' Do you know Roman history, Mr. Spongeby?"

Mr. Spongeby bent closer to the photo. "There *are* twelve trailers."

"Yes. I wanted to capture what those men were like. Power. Efficiency. And of course my aim is to invoke our modern Caesars."

"Not very human. Not really human at all. But they deliver the goods." Mr. Spongeby wasn't sure where his comment arose from. The statement was out of his mouth before he was aware of his words.

"That's it. Precisely." The photographer sounded impressed.

"I didn't think of *that*," the young woman broke in. "I like the composition, the blocks and squares. But I had no idea why my father gave it that name. Isn't there a restaurant downtown called 'The Twelve Caesars'?"

"You obviously have an artistic side, Mr. Spongeby," the photographer said. "Maybe you paint? Take photographs yourself?"

Mr. Spongeby shook his head.

"You express yourself artistically in some other manner? Do you write? Throw pots?"

"No." Despite himself, he glanced at his watch.

"Now, you come with me, Mr. Spongeby," the photographer said.

$\sim$

"Are these some sort of joke?" Priscilla had the fan of photos spread out before her on the cloth of the dining room table. She regarded the proofs with an incredulous expression. "We paid for this? We paid good money for this?"

"They weren't what I was expecting, either," Mr. Spongeby admitted.

"He's going to have to take them again," Priscilla stated. "What do you mean, they weren't what you were expecting? Isn't that you in the pictures?"

"I guess."

"You guess. Is it you? Or not?"

"It's me."

"You told me how much this Mr. Willowhaven looks like you. These aren't photos of *him*, are they? You *do* remember posing for these particular pictures."

"It isn't that simple. I was there over a week ago."

"You can't remember what you did last week? Should we make an appointment for you at the Alzheimer's clinic?"

"No."

"I'm just trying to be sure I understand, Hugh, before I speak to this Mr. Willowhaven. You agreed to these . . . these settings?"

"It wasn't quite like that."

"What do you mean, it wasn't quite like that?"

"It wasn't exactly a matter of me . . . agreeing."

"It wasn't."

"No."

"Then maybe you can tell me exactly what it was like."

"It's hard to explain. We went into the studio, and he had me sit down. He began to fuss with the lights, and a pull-down backdrop. All the time, we talked."

"Talked."

"Yes.

Priscilla bunched a fold in the tablecloth with her fingers, and smoothed it flat. "And what did you talk about?"

"About me, him, we spoke about business. About art."

"You know what I think? I think you didn't want to have your portrait taken in the first place. I think this is just your way of getting back at me for insisting. This is hurtful. I only wanted to commemorate your birthday, because it's a real milestone. Instead you — "

"I assure you, Priscilla, that was not my intention." He resisted an impulse to touch her arm to soothe her. "By the time I went to the photographer's I was quite willing. I agree with you that the idea of a portrait for my fiftieth is a good idea."

"You do."

"Yes. These pictures are just what happened. I'm not sure I can explain. But if they're not satisfactory, we'll get some other photos taken. Believe me, it was not my intention to undermine your idea."

"I'm glad to hear that."

"I know you meant the portrait to be a loving gift. And I appreciate it."

"You appreciate it."

"Certainly. Of course. I'll make the appointment and we'll have another set made."

"Good. Because these are ridiculous. Ridiculous!"

Mr. Spongeby said nothing.

"Maybe we should switch to a different photographer," his wife added. "This man could be deranged."

"He comes highly recommended, as you know, dear. And he didn't seem deranged to me. Besides, I paid him an advance. And it's stamped right on the invoice that if the portraits don't meet with the customer's satisfaction they will be reshot."

"I should hope so." Her forefinger tapped the sheaf of prints. "These simply will not do."

When his wife left for the kitchen, Mr. Spongeby examined the photos an additional time. In one, Mr. Spongeby was seated in his suit smiling as he held up toward the camera a large salmon, his fingers hooked in its gills. They were not real fish that Mr. Willowhaven . . . Doug . . . had brought into the studio, but movie-quality props. The photographer had fetched from some other room a cardboard box of the fish replicas soon after the photo shoot had begun.

Another photo depicted Mr. Spongeby seated with his hands resting on the arms of a chair, staring at the camera with an earnest expression. Four or five fish were piled in his lap. Other species as well as salmon were arranged there: trout and a flounder and what looked like a rockfish or other groundfish.

Mr. Spongeby studied the photos. He didn't even like fish. Seafood had never been a favourite of his. And he hadn't been fishing since his father had last taken him as a child, almost forty years previously. He was repelled by how fish when caught would be dumped into the bottom of the boat, to gasp for breath and periodically flip wildly around. They would even suddenly thrash back into frenzied life long after you were sure they had died and were still.

Yet here was a photo of him sitting with his tie askew, his jacket off, his shirtsleeves pushed back, and even his pant legs rolled up exposing his socks and bare calf. Fish dripped like icicles from both hands: his elbows were tight against his sides, his palms were turned upwards and his fingers curved into the gills of the various props. Hoisting the photographer's fish was unlike Mr. Spongeby's memory of touching real fish — with their slime and the resilient firmness of fish-flesh and an acrid odor like bathroom cleanser. Instead, the props resembled nothing so much as a pillow: inside these gills his fingers met the blandness of fabric, despite how realistic the images of the fish were in the proofs.

The closest to a conventional portrait was a head-and-shoulders shot of Mr. Spongeby. But an inch or so over his left shoulder, pointed squarely at the camera, was the face of a salmon. Mr. Willowhaven's daughter had been pressed into service for that one — she had crouched out of the frame of the picture to lift the salmon replica into position with a stick. Somewhere in the developing of the photo the stick had been made to vanish. The salmon floated in midair above Mr. Spongeby's shoulder.

Why had he consented to the inclusion of these creatures in the portraits, Mr. Spongeby wondered. He recalled an atmosphere of deep seriousness: suggestions were made by Mr. Willowhaven . . . Doug . . . and he had concurred. He remembered contributing a couple of ideas of his own. Had he gone temporarily insane? Posing with these props had not felt odd at the time, or silly, or even zany. Yet did he actually believe Priscilla would look with favour on a portrait of him that showed him interacting with fish?

~

"Fruit? Now it's fruit? And vegetables?" Priscilla's voice broke with indignation. She stared at the glossy rectangles laid flat in a line on the tablecloth, the brown envelope they had emerged from half-hidden under the first photo. "What sort of game do you and this Willowhaven think you are playing?"

Mr. Spongeby's birthday had come and gone. He and his wife had enjoyed a mildly festive dinner at the Pavilion Restaurant in Stanley Park — an establishment with some of the stiff-white-linen-tablecloths-and-heavy-silver-cutlery ambiance they both remembered from elegant hotel dining rooms, and the dining cars of cross-country trains, many years before. When Mr. Spongeby had arrived for his second appointment with the photographer, he carried with him strict instructions as to what was wanted in a portrait. Priscilla had also telephoned the photographer herself, and found him, she confessed to Mr. Spongeby, quite obliging. He understood perfectly what was required and he apologized sincerely for any distress the earlier set of proofs had caused. However, the photographer did not explain what was in his mind with all those idiotic fish. She had asked him; oh, she had asked him. But he had somehow moved the conversation onto another subject, and after she rang off she remembered he had never specifically answered her. "No matter," Priscilla had told Mr. Spongeby, "I'm sure he now knows better than to trifle with me."

Yet in these proofs Mr. Spongeby held armfuls of lettuce, bananas, oranges, potatoes. Other shots showed a mound of tomatoes, onions, spinach, cucumbers and melons in Mr. Spongeby's lap, or broccoli, carrots and celery bulging from his shirt pocket or the breast pocket of his suit jacket. In a composite photo Mr. Spongeby appeared to be juggling apples, clumps of radishes and heads of cauliflower.

"The man is quite mad," Priscilla raged. "You're either as mad as he is or else incapable of standing up for yourself. I suppose you don't know how this happened, either?"

Mr. Spongeby wasn't certain. Doug . . . Mr. Willowhaven . . . had begun the session by shooting a series of what Mr. Spongeby regarded as standard portrait poses.

"No props?" his wife inquired.

Not that Mr. Spongeby could recall. Then while he and Doug had been talking, the idea of vegetables and fruits had been introduced, and some of the prop foodstuffs had been brought out. As in the first session, the matter had been discussed gravely and much thought and care had gone into the poses, with the photographer listening carefully to Mr. Spongeby's suggestions and proceeding to —

"You made suggestions? You *encouraged* him?"

It wasn't a question of encouragement, as much as a back-and-forth concerning what might be most effective in —

"Effective? Effective to do *what*? What game were you two about?"

Of that Mr. Spongeby wasn't sure. Ideas were being generated that he could —

"*Ideas*? What ideas are there in a bunch of *vegetables*? I don't want any ideas. I wanted a proper portrait of you for your birthday. This is *my* gift. *Mine*. Nobody asked me for *my* ideas. I'm paying this man to produce a simple portrait of you because I thought that would be . . . oh, never mind." Priscilla seemed angered beyond speech. She lifted each photo in turn and replaced it on the table.

A long silence ensued. Mr. Spongeby castigated himself. Why hadn't he been more forceful in ensuring that only the conventional photos of himself had been printed up for consideration by his wife? Had he or the photographer imagined Priscilla could accept cabbages when she rejected cod? What did these choices of props indicate about Doug? Or was the man merely a nut-case? Was Doug trifling with him? Mocking him? Trying to show him something? Show him what? If Willowhaven was mad, what about himself? Why had he gone along with this craziness? Had these unusual props made any sort of sense? Or was he under some spell, like those he had read about cast by the leaders of cults?

"Here is what is going to happen," Priscilla announced. "First thing tomorrow I am going to stop by your office, and you and I are going to pay a visit to your Mr. Willowhaven. I am going to explain to him in no uncertain terms that I consider his actions unprofessional in the extreme. And that I intend to report him to whatever official regulatory body exists for photographers, if any. Failing that, to the Better Business Bureau. Or both, come to think of it. Then we are going to get our money back — every cent. Finally, I am going to make an appointment with a decent photographer, an appointment to which I will accompany you. I trust I am making myself clear?"

At ten o'clock the next morning Mr. Spongeby climbed the stairs to the photographer's for the third time. His wife's face projected a tense severity he had observed only after her mother passed away. Priscilla had been designated by a meeting of her siblings to speak to their father. She had to inform him that due to his infirmities he could no longer continue in the house alone, that his house would have to be sold and other arrangements made for him.

But when Mr. Spongeby opened the door at the top of the stairs for his wife to precede him, the photographer's reception room was completely altered. Where the desk had been were a row of six easels, each bearing a blown-up head-and-shoulders portrait of a man in a business suit. As Mr. Spongeby stepped nearer, he saw that the man was himself. He leaned closer, aware that Priscilla, too, had been drawn to inspect the photos. He observed from the tie he was wearing in the pictures that the shots originated from both of his sessions with Doug. Each picture displayed differences in lighting that subtly emphasized varying features of Mr. Spongeby's face, and created a range of backlighting effects. But the subject of each photo radiated a calm self-awareness, a certitude about life, that was compelling and attractive. "Here I am," the pictures said to Mr. Spongeby. "This is me after my years alive. This is who — whether you approve of me or not — I have become." Mr. Spongeby scarcely recognized himself in the portraits, but he could tell these were excellent photos.

"May I help you?"

Mr. Spongeby turned toward the sound of a male voice. Against the right-hand wall was the desk that formerly had stood where the line of easels now did. Seated behind the desk, staring expectantly at them, was a young man in a shirt and tie. Mr. Spongeby flushed, aware that he had been so absorbed in the photos he hadn't observed anyone else was in the room but his wife and himself.

"Uh, I'm Mr. Spongeby and — "

"We wish to speak with Willowhaven," Priscilla cut him off.

"Mr. Spongeby, yes," the young man said, standing up. "My name is Jeremy and I'm Mr. Willowhaven's assistant. He left this package of proofs for you to make a selection from." He lifted a brown envelope from the desk and held it out.

"What'll it be this time, *trees?*" Priscilla exploded. "Birds? Ladders? Or maybe naked ladies?"

"I beg your pardon," the young man said.

"We've had some other proofs from Mr. Willowhaven — " Mr. Spongeby began.

"And they are totally unacceptable. In fact, *garbage,*" his wife finished for him.

"I don't understand," the young man said. "Garbage? You've viewed six of the eight in here already." He gestured at the easels. "I don't quite see in what way . . . In my view, these portraits are remarkable. Mr. Spongeby appears very . . . commanding in them. I think these are some of Mr. Willowhaven's best work. That's why he had them blown up, to display for prospective clients."

"I want to talk to your Mr. Willowhaven," Priscilla demanded.

"Is there something wrong with these?" The young man gestured with the envelope at the easels. "I'm sorry if earlier versions were not satisfactory. But I can't imagine any portrait photographer doing a better job than these. At the moment, Mr. Willowhaven is away in Toronto at the nationals, the National Photography Exposition. He instructed me that you'd be coming by to pick up these latest proofs."

"And his daughter?" Mr. Spongeby inquired.

"Daughter?" Priscilla asked sharply.

"His receptionist. She's the one who is ordinarily in this room," Mr. Spongeby said.

"Went with him. She usually accompanies him to the shows."

Priscilla had swiveled back to examine the row of portraits once more.

"What do you think, dear?" Mr. Spongeby asked after a few seconds. "They seem fine to me. Flattering, even."

Priscilla spun around. "Why couldn't he have given us something like this the first time?"

"I don't know, dear. Does that mean you find them adequate?"

"If he'd done what I'd asked, I'd have had your portrait all framed to give you on your birthday. The man *is* mad. He can take pictures like this but first made us look at you festooned with produce, or those stupid fish."

Mr. Spongeby reached out and took the envelope from the young man. "My wife and I will make a choice from these and we'll be in touch by phone."

"That's fine, sir. I'm not certain when Mr. Willowhaven will return, but I can develop the prints you want to whatever size and numbers you require. Did you get our brochure with your options?"

Mr. Spongeby followed his wife down the stairs and onto the sidewalk. As they set off amid the noise of traffic, he passed the package of photos to his wife, who seized hold of it. Mr. Spongeby did not immediately relinquish the packet, however. For some moments they walked together toward his office, the brown envelope borne between them, like a child.

Amnesia Café

I HAVE ARRANGED TO MEET MY FRIEND Ian for an early breakfast one May morning before he leaves for work. Ian is employed to torture the young at a suburban high school; his subject is Math. I labor at the coal face instructing English composition at Vancouver Community College. Thus, unlike Ian, I have already begun my summer. I drive over to Ian's duplex and am just getting out of my Explorer when he briskly descends his porch stairs with his briefcase.

He stashes his coat and briefcase in his sporty Honda. "Where do you want to eat, Dennis?" he asks.

"Any place you like. You're more familiar with this neighbourhood than I am."

"There's a café not far from here on Nanaimo Street," he suggests. "I think we've been there together."

I shrug. I have rendezvoused with Ian for breakfast several times previously but nowhere we ate made any particular impression. "Let's go," I say. "It's hard for any restaurant to ruin breakfast."

We decide to take the Explorer. We talk about real estate as we roll south along Nanaimo. He is planning to buy a condo later this summer with his girlfriend Margaret, so we chat about what a step it is to actually move in with somebody after a divorce. I josh him about giving up his revitalized bachelor status and about how I intend to hang onto mine. Margaret has no kids, but was married for years to a guy who is an elementary principal in Maple Ridge.

Ian and I drift into exchanging views about the latest peak in Vancouver's housing market, the areas of the city that remain affordable, and what district might be best as a compromise between where he and Margaret each work.

"There's the restaurant," Ian declares. He points to an awning in the next block. The awning must display the name of the café on the side toward the street; all I can read on the edge of the awning facing us is *Family Dining Licensed Premises*.

Before we reach the restaurant, an empty parking spot appears. I pull over and in moments we are at the café. I open the glass door, but Ian hangs back. He looks around, acting puzzled.

"What is it?"

"I'm not certain this is the restaurant I meant," he says.

I let the door close. On the glass is only a sticker announcing membership in the Better Business Bureau, a couple of years out of date, and a decal from last year testifying to participation in the city's Chamber of Commerce. "Are we going in?"

"This is probably the place," Ian decides, a little hesitantly. He follows me inside. "Even if I'm wrong, chances are this one is okay."

Please seat yourself requests a sign on a stand. Ian and I slip into a booth and sit across from each other. The restaurant is almost empty. A couple of men in ball caps hunch over plates of food at one of the tables in front of large windows that look out onto Nanaimo Street. We are in a row of booths located further within the interior. The rest of the seating is more tables: in the dim light, a cop, his portable radio in front of him, is seated at one alone; at another, a man and a woman study menus.

Nothing about the place seems in any aspect memorable. At our booth, the arborite table supports the usual bowl of neatly-stacked small plastic cream containers. A rectangular open box is stuffed with packets of white sugar, brown sugar, and sugar substitute. A standard shiny chrome dispenser holds tissue-thin serviettes. Two groups of knife, fork and spoon are aligned along each side of the table facing the booth's seats. And an overturned coffee cup rests on a saucer beside each assemblage of cutlery.

A young guy walks in and sits at a window table near us. His back is to me. He takes off his jacket and drapes it over his chair, unfolds a newspaper and starts to read. A waitress approaches us.

"You boys want coffees? Menus?" She is tall and post-forty; her face is gaunt. Whenever she responds to our infrequent attempts at pleasantries, an artificial smile creases the area between her nose and chin for an instant. Then her visage resumes its expression of boredom.

"You bet," I announce enthusiastically. "I *need* a coffee."

"Decaf for me," Ian says.

"And we'd like menus," I add.

"Sure," the waitress replies, efficiently gathering up the surplus utensils from our table. She gazes in the direction of what I assume is the kitchen. "I'll have to make a fresh pot of decaf. Won't take long."

"Thanks," I respond.

"No trouble." I observe her stop, hands full, to speak to the newcomer reading the paper.

Ian and I turn our coffee cups right side up. A silence follows. After a minute, Ian asks me how I resolved a recent disagreement with my department chairman about course assignments for next year. While I am chattering away, I notice the waitress approaching from the back of the room, a coffee pot in hand.

She fills the cup of the man with the newspaper, then moves to stand by our booth. She pours the lightly-steaming coffee into my cup first, then swings the pot toward Ian. He quickly puts his hand out over his cup to protect it.

"I wanted decaf," Ian reminds her.

"That's right," the waitress agrees. "Sorry. Just be a minute."

"And we wanted to see menus?" I say, lifting my voice as though the utterance is a question, in order to minimize her oversight.

"Oh, yeah," she replies. "I'll be right back."

I open one of the cream containers and empty it into my coffee and swirl the liquid around with a spoon. I lift the cup to my mouth. The hot fluid flows down my throat, and I experience a rush of well-being sweep outward through my chest and down my arms and legs.

"I'm probably addicted," I announce. "But I sure like coffee."

Ian is staring fixedly after the waitress. He rotates to face me. "Dennis, I can't believe they wouldn't have a pot of decaf already brewed." A tone of urgency is in his voice. "Maybe this place is too cheap to get the decaf going first thing. They wait until somebody like me comes along and asks for it."

"More likely they realize you decaf drinkers are particular," I soothe. "They want that decaf to be fresh for you." I've known Ian since university; as a consumer, he can get pretty cranky if crossed. Last winter his bank, for a second month in a row, took his mortgage payment out of his current account instead of his savings account, and then sent him a statement that there were insufficient funds available. As Ian tells the story, he had telephoned the bank. "Let me speak to somebody there with a *brain*!" he shrieked into the receiver.

At the moment, there is no sign of either his decaf or our menus. I try to conceive of something to divert him. I like Ian, but his temper unnerves me at times. Driving with him through city or freeway traffic reveals a reservoir of barely suppressed fury. People who drive too slow or too fast, or who cut us off changing lanes, all are potential targets of a denunciation. He told me once about driving to work and having another sports car abruptly pull out in front of him, forcing him to stand on the brakes to avoid an accident. Ian followed the transgressor in a violent rage for block after block, blaring his horn and continually flipping the driver the finger through the front windshield. Eventually Ian lost his position directly behind the guy when a stoplight changed and the other vehicle gunned through the amber. But Ian kept tabs on the errant sports car ahead of him the entire distance to school. Ian was stunned when the other car steered into the teachers' parking lot. The driver turned out to be a colleague, new that September, who Ian had not recognized. Ian said he felt shamefaced, although the other teacher did not seem to bear a grudge. "I guess I went a bit overboard, eh?" Ian had laughed in an embarrassed manner when he related the incident to me.

I decide to ask Ian a large open-ended question, a technique I picked up long ago when I had a summer job as a reporter on a local newspaper while I was at university. "What would you say was the highlight of this term so far for you?" I propose. Yet even as Ian begins to recount an episode involving his intricate revenge on an especially undisciplined student, I observe he is fidgeting with his watch and glancing around the room in an attempt to spot the waitress.

Once Ian reaches the climax of his story, and then finishes it, silence settles between us again. I am relieved to see the waitress proceeding toward us with a couple of menus in one hand and a coffee pot in the other. She pauses at the table of the newspaper reader to top up his coffee, then places the menus on our table while refilling my cup.

"You didn't want coffee, right?" she confirms to Ian. Before Ian can answer, I intercede to prevent any trouble. "My friend asked for decaf. You said you were going to brew it."

"That's right," the waitress acknowledges. "Jeez. Slipped my mind. I'll go do it right now." She swivels and vanishes.

"What's *wrong* with this place?" Ian complains vehemently. "We've been here fifteen minutes already and I haven't even got a cup of coffee. This is the last time we ever come here."

"Look at the menu," I urge him, passing him one and opening mine. "That way we can order as soon as she brings your coffee. She's the only waitress; maybe she's run off her feet."

"There's hardly anybody *in* here besides us," Ian explodes. "She's just dumb."

"Let's decide what we want," I try to pacify him. "We don't know what goes on in the kitchen. Maybe she's under a lot of pressure. They've given her extra responsibilities or something." I scan the breakfast offerings, select one, and close the menu.

"I'm going to order the mushroom omelet," I proclaim. "How about you?"

"I'm going to have the special: sausages and eggs," Ian mutters, folding his menu. "This is the last time I eat in this dump."

"At least the service can't get any worse," I attempt to joke with him. "Was it like this when you were here before?"

Ian looks blank. "The truth is," he says after a pause, "I can't remember. It *must* have been okay, though, or I'd have stricken the place off my list. If this *was* the place. Didn't you eat here with me once? Don't *you* remember if the service was this awful?"

I have no recollection of ever having been in this café, and tell Ian so. He protests, insisting that we have eaten here together. But he doesn't push his point.

Knowing that Ian enjoys both eating and cooking good food, I nudge the conversation towards hearing about any interesting restaurants he and Margaret might have discovered lately. While he describes a new Italian bistro they found on Fourth Avenue, the waitress emerges from behind the kitchen doors with a plate of food and a bottle of ketchup. She places these in front of the man nearest us, who folds his newspaper and arranges it to one side of his meal. She leans over our table.

"Your decaf is about ready," she reports. "I'll be back in a sec' with it, and to take your orders."

Ian does not respond. "Great," I say to her. As she retreats across the room, I try to mollify Ian a little. "Things are improving."

"Hey," Ian snaps, "we got here before that guy — " he gestures to the newspaper reader " — and she not only already took his order, he's already got his food." Ian is practically hissing with indignation.

"Could be he's a regular," I answer, anxious to stop him from accumulating too much resentment about the waitress. "If they know you, you probably get priority."

The man we're discussing suddenly stands. From his position above his plate of food, he bends down to lift his coffee cup and take another sip before returning the cup to its saucer. Then he walks by us and out the door. I watch him leave, and after a brief interval see him pass the restaurant's windows and halt at a phone booth near the curb.

"Either his food is terrible, or he just realized he promised to call somebody," I say to Ian, who appears to be brooding.

"What?"

I nod toward where the man had been sitting and repeat my observation.

Ian shakes his head. "I wasn't paying attention."

The waitress is crossing the room again. I am pleased to see she has a coffee pot in each hand. She tops up the cup of the absent diner near us, then mine, then from the other pot fills Ian's cup.

"Sorry it took so long," she says to Ian. He utters something inaudible. After lowering both pots onto the table, she extracts a pen and a small pad of order forms from the pocket of her apron. "What'll youse have?"

"How's your coffee?" I ask Ian when she has departed.

He shrugs. "At least it's here." He checks his watch again. "I hope the food doesn't take as long to arrive. I need to be at school a half-hour early. I have an appointment with the vice-principal before classes start."

Ian's mention of time reminds me about the man with the newspaper. I glance at his still-empty spot, where wisps of steam hang over his barely touched food and refilled coffee cup. I peer out the window to where I'd seen him last.

"That's odd," I remark to Ian.

"Huh?"

"The guy who was here and who went out to make the phone call? He never came back. And now he isn't in the phone booth either."

"Probably skipped out without paying."

"I doubt it." I point to the chair. "His jacket is still here. And he hardly began eating."

"It's nothing," Ian insists. "He went up the street to get some smokes or something."

"There's a cigarette machine by the door."

"Maybe he came back when you weren't looking, and is taking a leak."

"I'd have seen him. He'd have to walk right by here."

"Okay. Okay. He's been captured by space aliens."

"I admit there's probably an explanation. But the whole thing is weird."

"Couldn't his phone call have been so interesting or so upsetting he forgot to come back?"

I shrug. From a corner of my eye I glimpse the waitress with a coffee pot in each hand beginning to make her rounds of the sparsely scattered customers. "Thanks," Ian murmurs, when she pours him a refill. I decline any more of the regular, since I already am conscious of a buzz after so much coffee and no food.

A well-dressed man and woman enter the café, and move past us to sit at the far end of the row of booths. "You're probably right about the guy who disappeared," I muse to

Ian. "I consider the whole thing mysterious, but I guess he'll rematerialize before long."

"Our food better materialize in the next few minutes," Ian says. "I have to leave soon."

"It *can't* take much longer," I reassure him. "What we ordered isn't hard to cook, and it isn't as though there are lots of customers."

The waitress is back, pouring coffee for the well-dressed couple. She deposits the pots on our table, then produces her pen and pad. "Have you two decided?"

"Uh, you already took our orders," I reply hastily, as Ian's face starts to redden.

"I did?" Her tone is more matter-of-fact than surprised or apologetic.

"We wanted," Ian emphatically states, "a mushroom omelet for him and the sausages-and-eggs special for me."

"Got it," the waitress says, jotting the information down. "And I'll check with the cook, to make sure you don't each get *two* breakfasts." The horizontal crease appears for a split second across her lower face. "More coffees?"

"No, thanks," I answer.

"We're . . . in . . . kind . . . of a hurry," Ian exaggeratedly articulates each word, as people do to indicate annoyance.

The waitress makes no response, but withdraws toward the kitchen. "Amazing," Ian says, shaking his head. "How do you suppose a place like this stays in business with such dreadful service?"

"Has the place been open very long?" I ask.

Ian's face takes on a perplexed expression, then clears. "I'm not even sure this *is* the restaurant I intended us to eat at. Perhaps the owners recently changed. God knows, it isn't a change that's an improvement."

I manage to deflect the conversation to a current scandal involving the federal cabinet. Ian and I run through a ritual accounting of projects that the various levels of government are wasting money on while they claim no further funds are available for education. While this catechism is dying away, the waitress returns to circulating from customer to customer with her two pots of coffee. No sign of our food.

"What could *possibly* be taking so long with our breakfasts?" Ian snarls.

"I can't imagine," I soothe. "But here's the waitress with more coffee for you."

"I'm *never* coming back to this place," Ian declares, more aggressive than ever.

"Perhaps the food here is exquisite." I jokingly attempt to blunt Ian's wrath, although I am a little bothered myself. "Delectably gourmet. Worth the wait."

"Dennis, I can't wait much longer. I have to get to school."

"That's right," I confirm. "You mentioned you have an appointment."

"An appointment?" Ian asks.

"You have to meet with the vice-principal before class."

"Who?"

"No? Maybe I got it wrong."

"I don't recall any appointment with Roger," Ian says slowly. "I'm sure I'd remember if I'd planned to see him today."

I don't reply.

"My appointment notebook is out in my car," Ian announces after a moment. "I really told you I had a meeting with him?"

I nod.

"I'd better double-check." Ian begins to shift his body sideways, preparing to leave the booth.

"Hold it," I remonstrate. "Where are you going?"

"To the parking lot, of course. My appointment book is in my briefcase." Ian, now standing, gestures toward the door. "Why?"

I stare at him. "Ian," I say, "we drove over here in *my* vehicle. Which we parked on the street, not in a parking lot. Your car is still in front of your house."

Ian sinks back into the seat. "This is disturbing. I was certain I drove over here."

"Don't worry," I reassure him. "Near the end of term, everybody has too much on their mind." I crane my neck to learn what happened with the waitress.

She has vanished. I commence babbling to Ian about how restorative I have found my first few days off work for the summer. My hope is that my spiel will distract him from our situation.

All at once the waitress reemerges from the kitchen carrying two plates of food. I cease talking and indicate her approach to Ian. "In the nick of time," I say happily. "I'm starved." I unfold a serviette and tuck it in.

But the waitress proceeds to the booth where the well-dressed couple had recently seated themselves.

"They're getting served before us!" Ian howls.

Something is wrong at the other booth, though. After an animated discussion the waitress picks up the plates again.

"She got the table wrong," I observe. "I'm sure those are our orders. What a scatterbrain."

Yet instead of heading our way, the waitress carries the plates back into the kitchen. Ian groans in disgust.

"They *can't* be much longer with our breakfasts," I aver.

The waitress is out again and walking purposefully toward us, but empty-handed.

"Your breakfasts will be up in a jiffy," she announces. "I just want to double-check your orders. You're having pancakes" — her forefinger aims at Ian — "and you're bacon and French toast" — the lacquered fingernail swivels toward me.

"No, no!" I blurt. "He had sausages and . . . "

"It's too late," Ian proclaims. "We can't wait any more. We've been here nearly three-quarters of an hour. All we've managed to get served is a couple of coffees. I have to go to work." He slides out of the booth and stands.

"Sorry," the waitress says. "There's been kind of a mix-up in the kitchen."

"In the kitchen, eh?" Ian mocks.

I put some money on the table and slide out to join Ian in the aisle. "Do you *believe* that restaurant?" Ian hoots once we're outside. "They couldn't get *anything* right. Now I have to go to school without eating."

"I was sort of looking forward to breakfast, too," I agree. "Can you get some take-out on your way to work?"

"There's an okay bakery across the road from the school."

We return along the sidewalk toward my Explorer. "You really can pick 'em, Ian," I needle him just a little.

Ian stops walking; his demeanor is serious. "I really thought I had eaten at that café before."

"Uh-huh."

"I'm certain I've had breakfast in this block." Ian sounds confused. "In fact, I'm sure *we* ate around here. That restaurant looked like it was the one."

"I've never been there," I remind him. "If *you* had, and the service was that lousy, I'm positive you'd remember."

"Nothing about the restaurant was different from what I recall," muses Ian. "But I didn't particularly recognize anything inside, either."

"Not even our wonderful waitress?" I taunt.

"Especially our waitress," Ian laughs. His good humor subsides. "Of course, staff turnover in these places can be high."

We reach the vehicle. "Yeah," I confirm as we climb in. "The staff have to put up with people making unreasonable demands like wanting to actually eat breakfast."

"At least we got to have coffee together," Ian says. I twist the key to start the engine. "What frivolities are you up to this morning while I'm toiling at work?" he asks.

I hear Ian. But my mind suddenly fumbles as it does when I meet a person I know and strive to recall his or her name. Or like when I wake in the morning and a dream lingers briefly at the very edge of my mind. I have the approximate shape of what I just dreamed, the overall mood or emotion, maybe even a detail or two — something about a funeral or being in the cabin of an airplane that never rises far above the ground. Yet the harder I attempt to solidify the memory, the quicker it recedes. I'm left only with the awareness that knowledge I once possessed is not available to me now.

I remember I planned a series of activities for today; breakfast with Ian was the first of these. I am conscious that at least one of my plans is important for some reason — that recollection even comes tinged with a slight dread, a little mist of uneasiness hovering around it. But the concrete agenda for my day is gone.

"I've got a whole bunch of chores to do," I mumble, my mind desperate to penetrate this vagueness. I check the outside mirror, and glance over my shoulder in preparation for steering into the street. I feel an urgent need to reacquaint myself with my itinerary for the day, to refer to my desk calendar at home on which I list my projects and obligations. "I keep busy," I hear myself tell Ian.

The traffic thins. I could accelerate into a gap that has opened in front of a slowly oncoming bus. But I don't. My left foot continues to depress the clutch. I am struggling to remember any route that will take us back to Ian's house.

ZEN MOTEL

I'M BEHIND THE WHEEL OF MY TRUSTY Toyota in the lane where Don said to wait, engine off, no lights. I can hear the hum of traffic on Interstate Five through the open window — I'm that close. I'm dying for a cig but Don made me promise: no illumination of any kind till he's broken out and we're on our way. Then he cracks up laughing at the word "illumination." Don, Donny, Donald. What a goof.

Naturally, he's late. Time drags butt when you're hanging around someplace and just want to be gone, out of there, history. I can see the black shapes of the buildings I'm parked behind, plus a yard lamp through some trees down the road. Or maybe that glow is from the cluster of on-ramp lights at the freeway. I look at my wristwatch, but it's too dim in the car to read the numbers. I feel with my fingers for the right button, push, and a tiny gleam sprays over the dial. Two-fifteen in the morning. Dead quiet, except for the steady chirping of frogs, clicking of crickets and the rumble from the highway. A sudden thought makes me giggle. I put a hand over my mouth to stifle the noise. I got a flash of that sing-song intro to the old Johnny Carson TV talk show, "And now, heeeeere's Johnny!" When Don finally sneaks out to the car, probably

249

looking dead serious as he does in the middle of his scams, I should yell real loud: "And now, heeeerrrreee's Donny!" He'd be major pissed. Serve him right, though. Why do I keep getting talked into his schemes?

Before I knew Don, he was friends with The Axe, one of the guys on a gyproc crew I was part of about ten years ago. I don't know how The Axe met him, probably in a bar or at some party smoking and toking. We awarded The Axe his nickname because of the jagged edges he cuts in sheetrock. "Aw, the tapers will cover the edges," The Axe would say when we'd be on his case for doing such a crappy job. Every time, his knife would wander away from the chalkline; there'd be plaster crumbling, rips in the paper, ugh. "Why do you guys care, anyway, how I cut these stupid boards?" The Axe would argue. "You suckholes trying to make foreman?" The Axe is one of those people who's always right, and you're always wrong.

Our foreman at that time occasionally referred to The Axe as The Hacker because, on top of The Axe's skills at cutting gyproc and his charming personality, he has an incredible cigarette cough. He's younger than me — must have been twenty-one or twenty-two in those days — but he's been smoking since he was in diapers. He'll start to cough and the gagging and heaving goes on for longer than you'd think anybody could gasp for air and still live. Then he'll recover, hawk a greenie, and fire up another smoke.

I was on the scaffolding the day I met Don. We were working reno in a seedy part of downtown Vancouver, redoing this store so it would have a loft over the back half of the floor area — sort of like a mezzanine — and the front part of the store would be two stories high. I'm up on the scaffold about twenty feet off the deck, and I don't want to be there. For me, twenty feet up feels like sixty feet.

I don't like heights, okay? I sometimes have to work 'em, but I don't have to like 'em. The very first day of my very first construction job the boss says: "All right, Gordie, up onto those beams and saw them off as marked." This was house construction. The beams he was pointing to were sticking out past a porch, and the porch was built over a gully. If I slipped, I'd fall seventy or eighty feet to my death. I climbed a ladder onto one beam, then carefully shifted my ass inch by inch toward the end. I'm freaked out of my skull. I try not to look down, or drop the Skil saw, or get tangled in the extension cord I'm dragging. Finally the boss notices I'm more or less paralyzed up there and useless for trimming the ends. He lets me come down and pile lumber. Great impression to make as a new-hire, eh?

The afternoon I first encountered Donny we were installing drywall for the ceiling of the front part of the store. The gyproc was five-eighths-inch thick for fire retardant, instead of half-inch or quarter-inch, and the boards were extra long: four feet by twelve feet instead of four by eight. So they were major heavy and awkward as hell to maneuver. Plus, since it was a ceiling, we had to lift them and nail them in place over our heads.

I'm at the top of the metal scaffolding with another guy, Bruno, and I'm being ultra cautious because, like I say, I'm no good at heights. Some guys will work the scaffold standing on a single plank or maybe two. Not me. I make sure I've got at least three two-by-sixes laid down across the frame for a platform. I'll spend the additional few minutes to maneuver up another plank. Or two planks. Call me a wimp if you want. My motto is, "Safety first, second and third." Why shouldn't

I be as comfortable as possible when I work? And I'm not getting paid to be killed on the job.

As each sheet of gyproc is passed up to Bruno and me, we press it tight against the ceiling joists. Then we attempt to hold the sheet aloft in the right spot while one of us tacks it temporarily in place. Then we both nail it properly. All this time we've got our arms over our heads. Try that for a few hours, if you've never done it. Your muscles become like a rubber band stretched out of shape. If you push your arms past their limit, after a while they go weird. You start to feel that all that's dangling from your shoulder is a limp rope.

Bruno and I hoist this one sheet into place at the far edge of where we can reach from the scaffold. Bruno, who's got more guts than IQ points, decides to climb onto the very top of the scaffolding above the platform. He wants to use his shoulder and back to hold his end of the gyproc; I guess his arms have about had the bun. So he scrambles up onto the scaffold's highest metal bars. He wedges his shoulder and the upper half of his back against the gyproc, while he pushes with his legs on the scaffold frame to brace himself. What is keeping him from plunging to certain death is only the tension he's applying upwards, and the five-eighths inch of gyproc where this sheet is butted against the edge of the one we've just finished nailing. If the edge slips, or the sheet slides sideways, both Bruno and the gyproc are going to crash all the way to the floor. I point out to him this move of his is dumb and major dangerous and we should shift the scaffold instead. But who listens to me? I'm working as fast as I can to pound in six or eight nails to hold the damn thing up so Bruno can climb back down onto the platform.

I've only got two nails in when the scaffold suddenly starts to sway like we're in an earthquake. I grab onto a metal scaffold bar, terrified, and nearly drop my hammer. Bruno manages to keep his balance, teetering out over the floor and then somehow back.

Up the scaffolding and onto the platform bounces Donald. "Let me give you guys a hand," he announces. "I've worked lots with drywall." Remember, I've never seen this idiot before in my life. Worse, without asking us or anything, he suddenly lunges past me along the platform and jams his hands up against one end of the gyproc sheet we're hanging. The sheet has sagged down because after Don's attack on our scaffold Bruno is concentrating on not falling to his death or to living the rest of his life as a cripple.

Don's heave pushes the sheet back into position but shakes the scaffold frame in new directions. I have to clutch again for a bar to save my worthless life. Meanwhile, Don's lurch upward also successfully dislodges Bruno from his spot on the rail. Bruno drops off the scaffold sideways. He just manages to snag a metal strut with one hand as he falls. He scrabbles desperately to catch another bar with his feet, and then hauls himself back onto the platform beside me.

Both Bruno and I are spooked. Bruno, who always claims heights don't bother him, is looking decidedly white. Don by this time is starting to buckle under the weight of the sheetrock over his head. His arms and those couple of nails I had managed to tack in are the only things supporting the sheet. "Hurry up, you bozos," Don yells. "I can't do *all* the work myself."

I can see Bruno wants to pound Don into shit right then and there. Bruno is steamed. He doesn't get riled easily, but at the moment he's got his hands gripped into fists while smoke pours out both ears. And I'm standing between him and Don on this narrow platform miles up over the floor. Two thoughts go through my head, mixed in with the adrenaline from all the rocking and rolling the scaffold is still doing, like aftershocks from a slip along the San Andreas. The first idea I have is that this fool who just appeared — remember, I've never even seen Don before — must be a government-certified, A-1 goof. And I also think, "This is not a good place for Bruno and some guy to start punching each other."

I don't mind if people fight. It's usually good entertainment. But if they get to clobbering one another, I prefer not to be located between them balancing on a board a hundred feet up in the air. I'm just a little guy with glasses, okay? And I doubt the foreman will be overjoyed when an expensive twelve-foot sheet of five-eighths gyproc sails down from the ceiling like some rectangular flying saucer and smashes itself all over the new hardwood.

So I suggest as forcefully as I can that we nail the gyproc up first and afterwards the two of them can climb down and smack each other to their heart's content. Bruno and Don spend about ten minutes glaring at each other and calling each other names while they help me secure the sheet. By then nobody felt like fighting.

I later find out that Don had stopped by the site to see if The Axe wanted to head out for a brew at quitting time. The Axe was busy hacking sheets to size, and since nobody was going anywhere until we finished hanging the ceiling, Don decided he should assist us in order to speed up the process. That's the kind of guy Don is. Doesn't always think things through.

Don wasn't working construction then, but driving a forklift and cutting junk at a scrap metal place. He's not much taller than me, maybe an inch, but he's stocky, with bigger muscles. As if he lifts weights, except he doesn't. He was married in those days, too. Later he got a job pulling parts in a warehouse. We sort of became friends after he found out I like to read science fiction. He and I would yak about *Stranger in a Strange Land* or *Dune* or some other book we had both read, if I ran into him in the pub. On that reno job there was a hotel beer parlor right across the street from the building. The crew would go over for a brewski or twoski when we got off work most days.

I never became as good friends with Don as he was with The Axe, but now and then Don stopped by my apartment on a weekend. My girlfriend, Katie, didn't like him; she thought he was loud and crass and too unpredictable. She would agree Don often meant well. I advised her to think of him as a big eager puppy. But since Katie and I weren't exactly living together — that was before she gave up her place and moved into mine — Donny and I hoisted some beers down the street at Morgan's Pub a few times on a Saturday afternoon when Katie wasn't around. Once in a while he and I took a walk along Kits Beach. Despite both of us being involved with somebody, we still enjoyed checking out the talent in bikinis. "I may be married, but I'm not dead," was Don's explanation for our activity, although Katie didn't think that was too funny when I told her.

Hardly anybody in my life was interested in talking about science fiction, except him. He also went for sword-and-sorcery novels: dungeons and dragons, magic and mayhem stuff. I don't particularly like that kind of book. But Donny eventually got curious about the Oriental-type mysticism they drag into those stories. That's how he discovered Zen.

And Zen is how I end up parked in a lane after midnight one June morning in Castle Rock, Washington, USA. I'm starting to feel cold. The day had been warm, but the town is in the Cascade Mountains, after all, and the temperature had dropped below my comfort zone. I want a smoke bad, and even more I want to open the trunk to retrieve my jacket. Donny had warned me, though: keep it stone quiet and no lights. I start rubbing my arms to increase circulation. The idea crosses my mind that maybe something has gone very wrong with Don's plan and he isn't going to show. I'll feel like a loser if I shiver here in the car all night while he's happily asleep in his nice warm cell.

I've been suckered by Don before. One time I was laid off and not doing much when he phones and asks if I want a week's work. I'm suspicious, because how would Don have work to give away? Sure enough, there's a catch. Some pal of his has a gas station out on the Lougheed Highway. Don says this friend is tired of the job after a couple of years and intends to break the lease with Chevron or whoever and split for Europe. Don tells me his buddy hasn't been making much money in return for slaving sixteen hours a day. But the guy knows the oil company has about a hundred lawyers and he can't just walk away from the contract he signed.

The scam is that Don and I will pump gas each day until the station's tanks are empty. Then we notify the oil company. By that time, Don's friend will have disappeared in Europe. We of course won't know a thing about where the guy has gone. Don insists it's a cinch: we'll just pump gas for a week, maybe more, and pay ourselves cash out of the till so UI won't know about it either.

Sound like a sweet arrangement? I show up at six-thirty the first day, and Don is already there loading new tires from the station into the back of his pickup. He's going to sell a chunk of the station's inventory through some fence he knows. He figures the oil company won't be able to determine what stock is missing, or at worst will blame Don's buddy. Don tells me cheerfully that his pal will already be in so much shit for breaking the lease that tires or batteries or other unaccounted-for inventory will be the least of his worries.

Don shows me how to control the pumps from inside the station, and I find a pair of coveralls to wear that say "Fred" on them. Then the station gets busy as the morning rush hour starts, and I'm pumping gas at the full-serve island and resetting the pumps for the self-serve, and operating the register, and checking customers' oil and tire pressures, and answering stupid questions, and generally just flying. I'm doing the work of two guys, while Don is off peddling — I have to admit — stolen merchandise. Every so often I wonder how the cops would regard this situation, and about eight a.m. I nearly pass out when a cruiser pulls onto the lot. But the cop only wants to use the can, and aside from asking me where Don's friend is — I forget the guy's name — he doesn't see anything amiss. I'm major sweating, though.

When Don finally gets back he asks if I'd like a cut from the tire sales. I tell him, "No way. I just work here." I'd been practicing my speech in court since the cop car left: "I was hired to pump gas. I didn't know nothing else was going on." When I insist I don't want any of his profits from crime, Donny tells me, "In that case, we deserve a raise." He had already paid us both a day's wages out of the float in the register before we started; now he raids the till again.

Don's pal had assured him we wouldn't run out of gas for at least a week. But the tanks went dry about eleven the first morning. Don was plenty upset. He starts yelling that we'd been double-crossed. He's ranting that he'll hunt his friend down in Europe and hammer him senseless, except he genuinely doesn't know how to find him. Don had been looking forward, I guess, to a leisurely looting of the place during the week and instead he has to phone the oil company and tell them his friend had split. I don't understand why he couldn't have just put up a "Closed" sign when we ran out of gas, and stolen the place blind. But maybe the oil company has inspectors who drive around and notice if any of their gas stations aren't operating? Or perhaps not selling their gas for a few hours is considered a more serious crime than breaking the lease?

Anyhow, by noon there were a couple of suits and ties sitting in the office while Donny had to do lots and lots of talking. The suits asked Don and me to stay until six, which was fine by me because everything slowed down once the morning rush hour was over, and because we couldn't pump any gas until they got a tanker to us about one-thirty.

Don was super choked at what his buddy had put him through. He goes ape. A geological survey company was storing three or four of their trucks, crummies really, on the station lot, around behind. A deal Don's friend had arranged for extra income. Don finds some rebar lying out by the dumpster, and heaves a piece through each truck's windshield. The bar slides through the glass real quiet, pop, doesn't shatter the windshield or anything. Wrecks it, of course, and you can see the bar lying on the front seat. "Fuck 'em," says Don. "They got insurance." Then Don slashes a bunch of tires on each truck, too. After that, Don announces, "Fuck the oil company; we're going to shut the station down." We were out of there by four. He'd given them a phony name for himself. If they thought about me, which I doubt, they probably figured I was somebody called Fred.

There's that side to Donald: ugly temper once in a while, as well as being dumb. Great guy for a friend, eh? But you have to admit he's more interesting than a lot of people I know. Another time he needed me to drive him over to North Van on some emergency errand. "*Have* to be over there right now," he tells me. This was after he and Adrienne were divorced; his pickup was in the shop or maybe somebody borrowed it. While we're en route, from the hints Don drops I'm pretty sure that this trip is some drug deal. We arrive at a house near the top of Lonsdale, and Don declares he'll be inside ten minutes, max.

I sit in my car pulling my pud for close to an hour. Eventually Don emerges. I guess the purpose of our little expedition didn't go his way. The front door slams, and he stomps down the steps. I can tell he's in a feisty mood. But I'm feeling major pissed myself. I have better things to do with my life than be a chauffeur for a pot dealer who probably would have made tons of money if his scam had been successful. Of course my share of the profits would be zip.

We got into a screaming argument on the ride home. He's on my case about how I'm driving or what route I'm taking. No way I'm going to be his target just because he got double-crossed or something. I'm thinking, "Yeah, this is the thanks I get for helping you, asshole." Under any other circumstances I would have decked him, I was that cranked. But I was driving, okay? When at last we arrived back at my place, we both had calmed down a little.

Neither of us mentioned the trip to North Van again. Actually, I didn't see much of Don after that. I got hired at Williams Wire Rope, which was union, and a year or so later I was elected to the safety committee. Junk and oil spills were all over our shop floor. Half the time there weren't safety glasses at the cutter. And I bitched to the shop steward once too often about the inadequate rating of the overhead crane we were supposed to use. Next I know, I'm on the damn committee.

One day I was downtown on Seymour Street and two guys with shaved heads are walking toward me. They seemed like Hari Krishna types, but off duty, wearing regular clothes. They weren't skinheads, either; no leather jackets or boots. Just a couple of ordinary-looking dudes with shaved domes. One of them stops me, and it's Donny.

Turns out while we weren't in touch he got religion and now is studying to be a Zen monk. If you can believe it. Somebody he knew talked him into going to hear a lecture on Zen. The lecture was in the theatre at the planetarium. Donny thought that meant there would be some connection with space travel or science fiction. The guy who spoke was from a house in Kits that is a branch of this Zen monastery in Washington State. Donny started dropping over to the house, and eventually enrolls at the monastery in Castle Rock, between Tacoma and Portland. He has to spend some time in Vancouver each year to keep up his BC medical coverage. Because health costs in the States are so expensive, the monastery makes any Canadians who join hang onto their provincial medical plans.

Donny was about to head south again when I ran into him, and we exchanged addresses. I write maybe two letters a year. But I get a letter from him not long after, and then another. I can tell he hasn't totally changed. In one letter he announces he's been put in charge of the monastery's herd of goats. He claims he's named two of them Asimov and Heinlein, because he's still convinced there's some connection between science fiction and Zen. And in honour of drugs, which he says he doesn't do anymore, he's christened another couple of goats Leary and Alpert. He asks me to send news of what's cooking in Vancouver and what The Axe and other guys we know are up to. I had a meeting at the union office one Saturday last fall, and there was a mailout of the local's newsletter going on. I scribbled a few lines on one copy and sent him that. I get a letter back saying that he appreciated the mail but the abbot took away the newsletter and informed him that monks are not allowed to receive literature from competing sects.

George at the union office had a good laugh over that. "Yeah, sure, we'll organize the damn monastery," George says. "We demand better gruel, an end to the dress code, shorter hours tending the flocks. Down with the Pope." I explain to George that this is a Zen monastery, and he says he didn't know Zens had monasteries. Next letter Donny tells me he's named two baby goats Marx and Lenin just for me, because unions are pinko anyway.

I don't hear from Don for maybe six months. Then he phones. Collect, of course. He's fed up with the monastery and wants to leave, but needs my help to do it. The monks apparently have this whole elaborate procedure if you want to bail: weeks of meditation and prayers and counseling. If you know Donny, once he decides to do something, that's it. But the catch is, if he pulls a midnight flit instead of following the regular routine, he leaves with no money, no civilian clothes, nothing. Don goes into this big spiel about how he's calling me from a pay phone in downtown Castle Rock while on official monastery business so he can't talk long. But he wants me to drive down to Castle Rock with some clothes, pick him up, and be the getaway car.

I was laid off at Wire Rope by this time, and was going a little wiggy sitting around the apartment. Katie and I weren't getting along too good at that point, either. She kept hinting we should either get married or break up and start seeing other people. She even bought me one of those buttons to wear that says: "Why do I have to get married? I didn't do anything wrong." To me that wasn't very funny, but to Katie and her girlfriends it's hilarious.

So I was up for a little action when Don phoned. I admit there was a little voice inside me that kept asking: "Why pull Don's nuts out of the fire once again?" I told Don I'd have to think it over about rescuing him. He phones a few days later. Don talks and talks, and after a while I decide, okay, what have I got to lose? The place is only a few hours south of Seattle, and I've never seen a monastery. It's something to do.

Don had told me in one letter the reason for the monastery being at Castle Rock. In Oriental beliefs, volcanoes are holy. That's why various religious cults have been based for years at Mt. Shasta in northern California. Castle Rock is at the junction of Interstate Five and a highway that goes east to a national park created for viewing the Mt. St. Helens volcano. Better yet, according to Don, the highway from Castle Rock to the Mt. St. Helens vista goes past, get ready, let's have the theme music from *The Twilight Zone*, please: Spirit Lake. Is that amazing or what, Don says: a monastery at the start of the road to Spirit Lake?

I asked Don how to find his monkery once I got there. He said the town of Castle Rock is actually a half-mile west of the freeway, but the monastery is right at the Castle Rock exit. I imagined the monastery would look like a European church, with spires and turrets and towers. Or like one of those religious buildings on hillsides in Tibet. Don informs me, no, this monastery used to be a motel. The motel went broke when people's interest in visiting Mt. St. Helens faded, and the place stayed for sale for more than a year. The price kept dropping, which is how the monks could afford it.

I tried to get Donny to let me know the former name of the motel, so I could picture the sign outside: Starlite Motel & Monastery? Or how about: Volcano-Vu Motel with "Motel" crossed out and "Monastery" painted over? I couldn't pry the motel's earlier name out of him, though. He did assure me I'd find the place easy enough, which turned out to be true. It even still looks like a motel, although they've built a wooden fence about five feet high between I-5 and the buildings. There's a signboard with the place's name: Oooga-Booga Monastery and Retreat Centre, or something like that.

Once I'd agreed to pick up Don, he'd phoned one more time with these elaborate arrangements for springing him from the Zen Motel. To confirm my arrival, I was supposed to call when I first got to town and pretend to be this photo-finishing store and ask them to tell Don his photos were ready. I guess they are allowed to have cameras at the monkery. Then I was to be in the lane behind the monastery at one-thirty a.m., when Don would flee his cell, and we'd hit the road. He could change clothes in the car, and we'd be eating breakfast in Bellingham by six a.m. He estimated we'd be safe across the border and home and dry in Vancouver by eight.

As always with Don, there was a slight complication. He let me know that, after slipping out of his cell, he has to kind of enter into the main building and get some personal effects. I didn't like the sound of that. "Hey, if you're going to rob the place, count me out," I told him. "I've heard about what happens to little guys like me in American prisons." Don insisted he was only going to reclaim some personal effects. He kept using that term, which made me more suspicious.

"What do you mean by 'personal effects'?" I ask him.

"Some things of mine," Don answers helpfully.

"You mean like you donated money when you signed up and now you're going to undonate it back?" I could imagine myself trying that story out on a judge: "Your Honour, my friend informed me he only reclaimed his own money. I had no idea he stole everything in the till." "Yeah, sure. Accessory After The Fact: ten years in jail, no parole. Next case!"

My girlfriend Katie is always after me to stand up to people — people other than her is what she really means. So I stuck to my guns with Donald. "If you're going to try anything illegal, find somebody else to drive," I said. "And that's final, okay?" Don insisted he would just be repossessing a few items the monastery had stored for him when he signed up. He swore he wasn't going to remove money or anything else that didn't strictly belong to him.

I didn't trust him, of course. "If you double-cross me," I warned him, "I'm going to head for the first State Police station I can find. You can convince *them* everything is legit."

"No, no," Don assures me. "This is on the level. I leave my room, head into the main office, out again and into your car, and we're history. I know where all the alarms are in the office, no sweat."

"Alarms!" I couldn't believe this guy.

"Of course they've got alarms; it's America, dummy," he tells me. "I've worked in the office; I know how to set 'em, and how to turn 'em off. It's like flicking a light switch. Standard practice in America. Don't be such a pussy. I'm out, in, out and we're away. I shouldn't even have mentioned the office but I'm trying to shoot straight with you."

"Gee, thanks, Don," I say, hoping he'll get that I'm being sarcastic. "But I won't go to jail for you. I'm doing *you* a favour." Katie would have been proud of me.

"Out, in, out, and away," he repeats.

"All right," I agree finally. "But I'm warning you: don't fuck me over." I let a pause hang in the air to emphasize that I'm serious. That's something Katie always does when she announces some new ultimatum. I find it impressive. Works on me, eh? Then I tried to lighten the mood with Don, because we've been friends for years. "You can collect your personal effects. But don't try bringing any of your damn goats." I should have known.

I rolled into Castle Rock about seven in the evening, which meant I had to kill about six hours before rescuing Don. Talk about getting to work early. The town is nothing special, a strip with the usual lineup of fast food places — Wendy's, DQ, KFC, McDonald's, Taco Bell, Carl Jr.'s, A&W, plus car lots, gas stations, a mall or two. I made my phone call to alert Don I was standing by. I scarfed down some rat food at Burger King. I intended to get some sleep, since the night was probably going to be a long one. I drove out to the edge of town for some peace and quiet, and shut down the car along a side road. But I couldn't sleep. Too nervous. Finally I went back to a mall and caught the second show at a movie theatre. Some film about knights in armor. My mind wasn't on it. I tried to imagine everything that could possibly go wrong, but with Don the range of screw-ups is infinite. By a quarter past one, I was inching down the back lane behind the motel with my lights off.

One thirty a.m. is the middle of the night for the Zen monks, according to Don. They're in bed by nine and up at five for yoga and the day's activities. Tending their goats. Or duking them, who knows? Did I mention that the monks are supposed to be celibate? I couldn't picture Donny as celibate, so when he told me this I asked him if he was joking. He gave me this evasive answer. Emile, who I worked with at General Paint, knew a priest in St. Catherine's, Ontario, where he's from. The priest was always getting involved with women, but claimed his vows were for chastity, not abstinence. I asked Don if that's how he saw his vows, but he insisted the monks are celibate. Emile said the priest was found frozen to death one winter morning in the backyard of a house. The cops discovered he was having an affair with some woman in the neighbourhood and must have passed out from exhaustion or whatever while he was taking a shortcut home from her place.

I'm figuring I might freeze to death myself in that lane as the minutes crawl past and I keep getting colder. Finally I resolve that, noise or no noise, Don or no Don, I'm going to open the trunk and locate my jacket.

I crack the car door as quietly as I can. Instantly the Toyota's interior light comes on. The useless thing almost never works, but this time it functions fine. I kill the light and hold my breath for a couple of seconds.

No sign of trouble. I gingerly swing my legs out, and stand, my pins a little stiff from sitting. I pad around to the trunk. As I turn the key in the lock, the sound of the latch seems incredibly loud. I realize too late that there's no way to close the trunk quietly; you have to give it a mighty slam or the lock won't catch. I decide to leave the trunk lid up; I can shut it once we're away from here. I scoop my jacket and start to pull it on.

A hand out of nowhere clutches my upper arm. I jump about four feet straight up. When I land, and twist around to see who grabbed me, a dim figure in a robe with a shaved head is grinning at me. "Amigo," the robe says in a loud whisper. "Glad to see ya."

"Jesus, Donny!" I whisper back, still weak in the joints from my fright. "You scared the shit out of me."

"You're generally so full of it, you've got lots to spare," Donny hisses. "Now let's make like a goalie and get the puck out of here." He reaches over to place a large green garbage bag full of something into the well of my trunk. The car sinks a little as though whatever Don has been carrying is heavy. I don't ask.

Then I notice another robed figure standing in the shadows just behind Donny. I freeze.

Donny follows the direction of my stare. "Oh, yeah," he whispers. "This is Amanda. She's coming with us."

"Hi," the figure whispers, in a decidedly female voice.

"What?" I say to Donny. The figure behind him also sports a shaved head, and the robe hides anything that would indicate this is a woman. "You didn't mention bringing anybody else."

"Shhhhh!" Don cautions. "Get in and fucking drive. We'll talk once we're out of here." He gives me a friendly shove toward the front of the car. "Move it."

My brain is reeling as I slide into the driver's seat. I didn't know the monastery had monkettes as well as monks. I take a deep breath, turn the engine on, and peel out towards the freeway. I suddenly get this flash that the night's activities are more like an elopement than a jailbreak. Cracks me up for a second. As we approach the lighted interchange, I check out this Amanda in the rearview mirror. She doesn't seem like Don's type. With her shaved head and pale, pasty face, she looks like a finalist in an ugly contest. I'm giggling to myself that, on the other hand, she probably looks better to Don than his goats.

I hit the binders when we're almost at the on-ramp and jump out to shut the trunk. I light up a cig at last. As soon as I'm back behind the wheel, Don bums a smoke off me and then orders: "Take the southbound ramp."

"We go north to Vancouver, dummy," I point out.

"We're not going to Vancouver," Don announces. "We're headed for Eugene. Take the southbound ramp. And boot it. We've scooped some honey from the hive and the bees will be along any second. They aren't going to be too pleased."

"No way," I tell him. "I drove down to pick you up and take you back to Vancouver, okay? You want to split for Eugene? This ain't Gordie's Taxi Service."

"Just settle down," Don says. We're gonna — "

"*You* settle down," I insist. "I'm driving north. If you want to go south you two can hitchhike."

"It's the middle of the night and we'll be sitting ducks standing by the side of the road with our fucking thumbs out," Don replies. "They'll be along any minute gunning for us."

"Not my problem," I observe.

"Listen, Gordie, don't be stupid," Don says. "We appreciate your help. But there's been a slight change of plan, that's all. Quit bitching. Put that pedal to the metal and let's take off before we get company none of us want."

Against my better judgment, I steer up the southbound ramp, and fume inside myself while we rocket toward

Portland. I try to remember how far past the Oregon border Eugene is and calculate it's a couple of hours, maybe more. I had promised Katie I'd be back by midmorning, and I can see I'm not going to make it. In fact, as I add up the miles and hours, I realize I probably won't even be back by the time she's home from work that afternoon. That will mean major hassle for me. Katie already told me she thought this trip was a ridiculous idea. "Donald plays you for a sucker every time," were her exact words, and in spite of my defense of him when she said that, I'm beginning to think she's right. My high-beams hit a sign for a rest area and I signal to exit.

"Why are we stopping?" Don asks, as I slow to take the off-ramp. "This is as far as I go," I tell him, "until I know what you're up to."

We coast to a halt at the washroom building and Amanda departs to use the can. "Well, buddy," Don says as soon as she's walking toward the building, "I guess you do rate an explanation."

Turns out there were only a few monkettes, or nuns as Don called them, at the Zen Motel. Amanda was a fairly recent convert; she had shown up six or seven months ago. She had been assigned to help tend the goat herd. One thing led to another out among the flock, and after a certain number of violations of Don and Amanda's vows of celibacy they concluded this was true love. Since there wasn't much future for togetherness herding goats, they resolved to go over the wall. Don claims he knew that I'd scoff if he asked me to help the two of them escape, so he kept quiet about Amanda. "Hey, man, I believe in love," I protest. Don just laughs.

He and Amanda are aiming for Eugene because Amanda's folks live there. Her parents were so overjoyed when she wrote them about giving up being a Zen nun that they offered to set her and Don up in business. Her dad owns a string of car washes, and promised to let her and Don manage one.

Don informs me he wants to call his operation the Koan Carwash. A koan is a tricky Zen question, according to Don. "Can you dig it, Gordie? Our slogan up in lights: 'What is the sound of one car washing?'"

"I don't get it," I say.

"Exactly," Don replies, beaming. "That way the slogan will stick in your mind."

I don't know about that, but I make it clear to Don I absolutely positively have to be back in Vancouver before Katie returns from work. If not, I'll be reamed out for being inconsiderate and thoughtless and untrustworthy and a few more of Katie's favourite words. I offer to drop the happy couple at the Portland Greyhound terminal. I'm determined that Portland is as far as I'm going to take them.

But Don seems pretty twitchy to beat feet directly to Eugene. He promises to phone Katie at work later in the morning and take the rap for my delayed arrival home. He allows that Amanda's folks had told her on the phone that they are preparing a blowout fiesta for the return of the prodigal daughter. "They'll cover your gas costs and then some, Gordie, I'm sure of it," Don says. "Her mom and dad are loaded. They'll be so glad to see us you'll be swamped with good eats and all the booze you can drink. In the evening, Amanda's friends will supply us with the killer weed. And, who knows, you might get next to one of her girlfriends and forget about sweet, understanding Katie. Maybe you'll stay in Eugene. I'll even let you work for me. For us, I mean," he corrects himself, as Amanda is opening the car door.

So I agree to drive them to Eugene, fool that I am. About the only thing that is true in what Don predicts is that

Amanda's parents are pleased to see her, although her Mom bursts into tears at the sight of her and who could blame her Mom for that? Amanda's parents, who live in a pretty nice house, take one look at Don and me and the air turns chilly. Don has changed into the civilian clothes I'd brought. But I hadn't exactly outfitted Don in my best shirt and jeans. With my old gear on, and with his negative hairdo, Donny resembles a cross between a punk rocker and a wino. I'm not at the peak of perfection myself, since I've been up all night either waiting to spring Donny or driving driving driving.

After an hour or two seated in Amanda's folks' front room politely drinking coffee and talking, I can tell there isn't going to be any party, let alone a cent for my gas. I decide to cut my losses and split. I remind Don of his promise to phone Katie to explain why I'm going to be late. Then as I'm about to peel away from the curb, I think for a second Donny is going to jump in my old rice-burner and blast back north with me. That would have been the smartest move he ever made. But as you can tell by everything I've said, brains aren't his best feature.

Somewhere south of Seattle I review the events of the past twenty-four hours and conclude Don is batting about zero at keeping his promises to me. So I stop and phone Katie at work myself. Sure enough, Don hasn't called. He actually does phone the next day. He maintains that he felt pretty wasted after his escape from the monastery and crashed. He didn't wake up until after he knew I'd already be in Vancouver, he says. Uh-huh, I tell him.

Thanks to Donald, Katie and I get to have one of our "talks" the night I pull in, where yup, yup, yup, I have to admit that I am gullible as far as Donald is concerned and uncaring and selfish as far as she is concerned. I'm totally zonked from not having any sleep the past thirty-six hours, plus all that driving, so I probably don't hold up my end very well. Fuck Donald and Katie both, is what I'm thinking.

I figure Donald will last a month tops with Miss Monkette and her folks. But about three months later I'm sent a photo of Don and her getting married. I have to say she is a hell of lot better-looking with her hair starting to grow out. You could tell she had put on weight, and so had Don. I conclude the car wash business must be doing okay. A few months after the wedding, I get a picture of their new kid, Don Jr., and a letter from Donny where he raves on about how major great it is to be a father.

That's the last I ever hear from him. By now he's probably a car wash tycoon, as well as an ex-Zen-monk and a dad. But to me, he's still a goof.